Striker's Waltz

The Seattle Sound Series
Book 6

Alexa Padgett

Edited by Deborah Nemeth and Nicole Pomeroy
Cover Art by Sarah Hansen of Okay Creations

ISBN: 978-1-945090-18-9

For Kylie, my sister of the heart.

CHAPTER ONE
Teo

I strode across the short, jewel-green grass toward the other volunteers, ignoring my aching hamstring. *Dios mio.* The longer this injury lingered the greater its probability of destroying my chance to get out of Seattle. I'd clawed my way back to being the top player of my current team, the Seattle Timber. I'd played better *futbol* these past weeks than any of the pundits thought possible.

Words like *devastating* and *career-ending* were bandied across every sports network in Europe, my home country of Argentina, and here, in the United States, where I'd been traded eighteen weeks ago from Madrid. Already, they were clamoring to sign me back. My smile of satisfaction grew until the next twinge shot through my hamstring.

I'd worked too hard, rehabbed for months, to get on the shortlist to be traded to Milan, back to the soccer world's premier league, because I did not wish to return to a team that threw me away when I needed them—twelve years together and they dropped me at the first sign of injury.

More than a sign. The malingering pain might keep me from the world championship, let alone the World Cup.

I shortened my steps and picked up my knees, trying to pace my strides and not tug the weak muscle further. So far, even after all these weeks, no one within the Timber organization—or, more importantly, the press—asked about Mariana's profession. In fact, there'd been surprisingly little coverage of the woman staying in my condo. I'd been lucky, and I paid through the nose, for her

1

constant presence the past few weeks. My father's billion-dollar conglomerate's vast reach proved useful in both keeping Mariana's identity quiet and getting me the best care.

Mariana's fingers worked miracles, and I'd recovered near full function in my leg again—hence my fantastic play these past weeks. My scowl grew. I only had one more month on Mariana's calendar before she returned to her practice outside of Buenos Aires.

"Teo. Glad you could help us out with this," Noah, the Timber's assistant general manager, said. "I think you know everyone here except maybe my sister, Preslee. She used to play—"

"For Northwestern." I smiled, pleased to see such athletic talent on the pitch. "You have one of the best records for shots-on-goal of any player."

She smiled back, her eyes a pale green. *Ojos bonitos*, fringed with dark lashes under high-swept angel brows. After a long moment of perusal, I settled on her eyes as her most appealing feature. Not to say her long, toned legs weren't gorgeous, because they were. So was her glossy, short black hair, her thin, pert nose, those full lips. A beautiful face—one I would like to study more without with her brother hovering nearby.

I reached out, pleased to touch the soft skin of her hand. Mm, *una mujer encantadora.* Yes, she made this pit stop in my career better.

"Thanks for the compliment, but it's been a long time, and I haven't played since my junior year of college."

Her voice...*Santa Maria de Santa Fe.* Her voice raised chill bumps over my skin. I had never heard such richness before.

I wanted to ask her why she quit playing soccer, ask her anything that would allow me to hear her voice again, but defensive coach Kent Streeter clapped his hands to get our attention.

"We have five groups working today and tomorrow. You'll stick with your same partner for the duration of these camps. So, here we go. Teo, you are paired with Preslee."

I nodded, trying not to smirk at my good luck. The rest of the guys were paired with teammates or one of the female players from the local university that Preslee had played at six, maybe seven, years ago. I was more than happy to spend time with Noah's pretty sister.

"They paired us together because I'm out of practice," Preslee said, her voice apologetic. "Noah said if I suck, you'll be there to pick up the slack."

My hamstring cramped again, causing my stride to hitch. I scowled, breathing through the irritation. Preslee must have thought I was irritated with her comment because she rushed on. "I won't suck, though, I promise. I've been going through my old drills for the last couple of months, since Noah asked me if I was interested in helping, and I've always enjoyed working with the kids."

"I'm sure we will work together fine." I gritted my teeth, wishing there'd been a way to cut these camps from my schedule—not because I didn't like the kids. I, too, enjoyed their enthusiasm for the sport. No, my hamstring ached from morning practice, and Mariana's warning proved correct. I needed more rest to ensure my continued good health. I bent down to touch my toes, careful to keep the stretch easy, as Mariana showed me. Unfortunately, my new position pulled my attention away from Preslee's tight *culo* accentuated in those shorts.

Maybe I could talk Mariana into staying longer. I needed her. No way I wanted to share my concerns about my leg with Timber management. That would kill my trade possibilities, and I refused to stay in the United States.

Not if I wanted to add that last, elusive *copa* to my accolades. And I wanted the Euro Cup more than I wanted a hot fling with my sexy camp partner.

"Are you okay?" Preslee asked, a small frown marring her smooth brow.

"Why wouldn't I be?" I asked.

"You seem to be favoring your right leg," she said, cocking her head and narrowing her eyes.

"It's fine. Just a little stiff from practice this morning."

I studied her face, wondering how she picked up on my secret.

"Sure thing. I didn't mean to make you upset," she mumbled, her cheeks staining red as she attempted to tuck her too-short bangs behind her ear. The back of her hair was close-cropped—shorter than mine. The style suited her, bringing out her high, rounded cheekbones and making her soft eyes seem even larger under those dark brows. In fact, the cut proved shockingly feminine.

Short-haired women had never appealed to me before. I preferred to run my fingers through long locks while I kissed luscious lips or pounded into a soft, willing body.

Preslee's body—athletic and sleek—filled my head.

I cleared my throat and looked away, trying to remove the inappropriate thoughts about my assistant GM's sister. I might not be perfect, but I didn't like short-term affairs. My father cured me of those years ago.

"Um, well, I'll just go grab my water from my bag."

I wanted to hang my head, but instead I tracked Preslee's progress toward the metal bench lining the edge of the field. She was the first woman to catch my attention in months—since before that sweltering night game in Paris when Lavelle, frustrated by our large win, slide-tackled me late. He received a red card, I tore my hamstring.

I clenched my jaw so hard my teeth ached. One bad play. That's all it took for me to lose one of the most prestigious jerseys in the game. Well, that and my harsh criticism of another striker on the team. I should have kept my mouth shut, but the kid's drug habit made his play erratic. Winning was my goal. Period.

The kid, seen as a victim of my anger toward the organization, stayed and took over my role. He still had a drug problem, only now other players were speaking up—but only because he'd caused the team to plummet in rankings. I hated the losses of my former teammates nearly as much as I hated practically sitting out this year.

The hours were ticking away on the tail-end of my career, and the trade to Milan was my last shot at reaching my Euro Cup goal. My goal to prove to Madrid they never should have cut me.

Guilt washed over me. Preslee thought I didn't like her. Her long legs, the same pallid color of most of the people in the Northwest, slid out of her tiny black shorts. The lack of sun in this city weighed on me, making me sluggish. I'd never been interested in playing in England for the same reason, but I hadn't been given a choice about *this* move, thanks to the extent of my injury. In fact, I'd been lucky to stay in the pros after an opposing player's illegal slide tackle.

With effort, I swallowed down my bitterness. My trade to the US slapped at my reputation, demoting my accomplishments and career, though some critics would say I needed even deeper cuts at my ego. That's because they didn't know my story, and I wasn't about to enlighten them if all they saw was the spoiled son of a business mogul.

I might've wanted to gnash my teeth and beat my chest against the injustice of the entire situation, but I wouldn't. I couldn't. Not if I wanted to play for Milan this year and next, proving my worth to myself, thumbing my nose at my mother's plans for me and the media's has-been write-ups.

With a sigh, I headed toward Preslee, needing to make amends with her. Her eyes touched on me before skittering off again. Her hands fluttered up to her hair, touching it briefly before she headed toward the small, white goals we'd use with the kids today.

"I'll help you set those up," I said. "I'm looking forward to working with you."

She sucked in her lips and nodded. "Great. I've got these. I've already stretched." She looked pointedly at my leg, her eyes flashing back to mine. "Never can be too careful after injuries like *ours*."

I narrowed my eyes at her retreating back. She trotted across the grass, those short shorts rippling in the light spring breeze to show off a bit more of her smooth thighs. She maneuvered the goal posts and set out a series of bright orange disks to demarcate the space between the various drills we'd use for practice.

I put my foot up on the bench and leaned forward, trying not to wince as I reached down to grab my toes. Better, but not enough mobility. I jogged around the track, enjoying the warming of my muscles. Back at the bench, I extended my hamstrings, pleased with the easing of the muscle.

Preslee materialized beside me. "Stretch before and after each workout." She spoke low, something I appreciated now that other players were entering the field. "And soak in a hot tub, then get a deep tissue massage to ease out the lingering kinks."

"I assume you're speaking from experience."

She nodded, looking out over the field. She refused to meet my gaze. A damn shame because her eyes were worth gazing into.

"I pulled my hamstring my freshman year three months before the state championship. The team hired one of the best sports physical therapists in the country to rehab my injury. Once it healed, I played."

One question bubbled forth—the most important one. "And you won?"

She turned to look at me, delicate black brow raised. "Of course."

More questions surrounded Preslee Jennings. She'd fallen off the soccer circuit a year, maybe two, after that great win. One game she just wasn't there—and she didn't return.

Before I could ask her what happened, sound erupted from the gates, and within moments, the kids tumbled into the arena, a chattering and giggling mass of energy.

———◆———

We'd reached our last weekend of camps for the spring.

Three weeks of enjoying Preslee's subtle sense of humor, her eye for talent—not to mention her athleticism—now over. I sighed, realizing that while my hamstring would appreciate the end of these long, grueling days, I was going to miss spending time with her. Well, after today and tomorrow.

As usual, Preslee headed out into the sea of young bodies, most of which only came up to her waist. She greeted each child, taking time to ask a question or two, listening intently to their answers. I smiled, still marveling at her ability to engage even the most troubled youths.

"She's great with kids," Noah said.

I nodded, still watching her, tension creeping up my neck as I wondered if Preslee's brother was here to warn me away from his sister. Not that I'd communicated with Preslee outside of the camps. I'd considered it, but Noah couldn't know that. He gave no indication of concern as he leaned his arms against the metal railing that snaked between us.

"I wasn't sure she'd actually like being on the pitch again." Noah seemed to talk more to himself than me. "The way her soccer career ended…"

"An injury?" I'd pulled up an article whose headline said Preslee was in an altercation that led to the end of her collegiate soccer career. I'd scoffed and closed the browser, frustrated with the lack of clear-cut reporting.

"A career-ending one," Noah said on a sigh.

Shuddering at those words, I turned to watch Preslee, too, as she high-fived one of the girls. Another of the younger children wrapped her arms around Preslee's waist, hanging on tight. Preslee laughed as she slung her arms around the girl's shoulders. I couldn't help the smile that bloomed across my face. I liked

8

Preslee. More than I should.

Noah tapped his fist on the metal, his eyes focused on his sister as she began to line the kids up into their first set of drills. One of the other players called his name, and Noah trotted over before I could ask him any more questions about Preslee.

But her past—hell, her present—choices weren't my business. Best if I left her alone…even if she was one of the first women to hold my attention in years. After Vivi, I promised myself to focus on what mattered—that would be soccer. Winning. Earning *la copa* and the accolades that went with it. Anyway, I'd never met a woman worth the consequences a long-term relationship imposed. I liked looking at Preslee, even working with her, but I remained uncertain about whether starting a relationship with her would be worth the fallout.

Probably for the best this was the last camp. Milan. My goal to play there was closer now after one of the sports networks wrote about my healed leg and the explosiveness I demonstrated during training camp.

My agent had another conference call scheduled for Thursday this week. I'd asked to be in on this one—I wanted to get this deal sealed and delivered.

Preslee, as delightful and sexy as she was, didn't fit into my long-term plans.

I finished my stretches, trying not to wince at the continued pull in my hamstring. While I'd miss Preslee on the pitch, I needed to put her from my mind. My agent's call this morning confirmed Milan wanted me on their club roster—the healthy version of myself that I'd managed to show the world, anyway.

CHAPTER TWO
Preslee

Teo's dark hair, almost blue in the sun, fell in a riot of messy waves. Unlike many of his contemporaries, Teo was clean-shaven, showing off the strong line of his jaw and his firm, pink lips that quirked just enough for me to know he caught me staring. His eyes were a greenish hazel, and filled with humor as he assessed me with the same intensity.

A man with a reputation for being focused on the field and off. Not much broke that focus—at least from what I'd read. His dating history, at least per social media, appeared sporadic, which made me wonder if he needed the extreme focus or if he'd been damaged by past relationships, too.

"Nice day today," Teo said before sipping from his water bottle.

I watched his throat muscles contract, annoyed by how sexy I found everything about him. Even the way he drank water.

Much to my growing disgust, my crush had intensified with each passing week. I clenched my hands into fists. I didn't want to date, I reminded myself.

"It was," I said. "Excuse me. I need to talk to Noah about something."

Teo nodded. I felt his gaze on my back as I walked across the field. A small woman slipped onto the field, her long, dark hair bouncing with each step. Brenna Lansing. She reached into my hair and released the clip, fluffing my short bangs.

"You looked like you were having fun," she said.

"I was. Have you seen Noah? I want to ask him a question."

"He walked into the stadium earlier. Maybe he's in his office?

I'll wait for you at the car. It's colder than I thought. I've got your bag. I'm glad you're doing this, Pres. It's a pleasure to see you so happy this month."

I nodded, my eyes darting back to where Teo stood, but his back was to me now as he talked with one of the assistant coaches. I tried not to let the disappointment swamp me.

* * *

The next day passed much the same. We broke this round of children into two groups to ensure they had time to work on both midfield and forward skills, which we flipped at the midway point of each session. One of the girls, Tenada, struggled with her coordination, let alone any dribbling skills. Today, tears pooled in her eyes because she couldn't master the basic tenet of kicking the ball with the side of her foot.

Teo stood with her, patiently pointing to the part of her foot he wanted her to use. Tenada shook her head, frustration pulling at her mouth. Teo spoke to her, placing his hands on her shoulder. She lifted her leg up and pressed against the part of her cleat she wanted to kick with. Dropping her left foot, she pushed off her right foot and took a group of tiny steps, keeping the ball between her feet. When she shook her head again, I walked over.

"Do you think a hands-on demonstration might help?" I asked.

Teo, looked up, surprised by my voice, no doubt. I'd made a point of avoiding him as much as possible today.

"By all means." He swept his hands out in front of me to the open pitch.

Anxiety and uncertainty spiked through my belly, but I

cleared my throat. "You don't want to do it?" I asked, trying to hide my concerns. I didn't like being on display. Not anymore—I understood how much I still had to lose.

Tenada looked up at me, her large brown eyes imploring. "Please, Preslee, will you show me? I just don't get what he's saying."

Like I could turn down the sweet child.

"Go stand down by the goal." I sighed. "I'll come in slow."

Once Tenada got into position, I started with the small steps, the ball moving between my feet with the precision I used to take for granted. With effort, I forced my way through my clumsiness, lengthening my stride, keeping the ball at the optimal distance between my sprinting cleats.

Head up, I maneuvered around one group, then another, turning in a circle, maintaining complete control of the ball. I lifted my left leg, planted it firmly, and kicked hard with my right. The ball sailed into the back corner of the net. I put my hands on my hips with a nod. Not a bad shot. Tenada must've thought so, too, because she squealed and clapped, causing more heads to turn toward them.

"Do it again!" she shrieked. "I want to see you do it again."

I shook my head as the rest of the players and coaching staff were all moving forward, descending on me. This deluge of attention caused my heart to pound as I glanced around, expecting to find Oren, my ex-boyfriend and reason I didn't date, somewhere nearby, cracking his knuckles.

Thankfully, we were finished for the day, so I hugged all the kids, making sure each took a new water bottle with the team logo I'd asked Noah to purchase. I watched them go, a wave of longing slamming through me. Since I'd renounced dating years ago, I'd never move past my single status and create a family. Raise a child or two.

Brenna hugged a folded fleece jacket over her arm, which she extended when she saw me. "You left this at home. Thought you might want it."

I slipped my arms into the sleeves, grateful for the warmth. "Thanks."

Brenna tipped her head toward the net. "Can you do it again?"

"Do what?"

Brenna rolled her eyes. "You used to practice that bend-it thing for hours. You know. That movie."

I shook my head as my lips quirked. Soccer, well sports, really, had never been Brenna's thing. She used to go to some of my games, but she'd never bothered to learn terminology.

"Bend It Like Beckham."

"That's it! Can you do that still?"

I shrugged.

Brenna clapped her hands under her chin. "Try it. Please? The last kick was cool but I like it when it curves into the back of the net."

"I don't want the players and coaches watching me."

Brenna waved behind me. "Most of them are gone. The kids are loaded up on the buses. Just you and me, kid. C'mon. Try it again."

"Fine." I waited another minute, drinking my water, as the last of the coaches cleared the field. Then, I grabbed a ball and set it up where I wanted it. After running in place for a minute to rewarm my legs, I eyed the ball, then the goal. Deep breath, focus. Line up and kick. My cleat made a satisfying thunk against the side of the ball, which sailed through the cool evening air and slammed into the back of the net.

"Sweet," I yelled, pumping my arms.

"Still got it," Brenna said, laughing.

"I wonder if I can do it again." I trotted toward the goal and grabbed the ball.

My second shot was more on point than the first. Brenna clapped as we both laughed. I couldn't believe I'd given this up, cut myself off from the joy of a good sweat and the high of a perfectly placed kick.

"Bet you can't make it five times in a row," Brenna said.

"Dunno. The first two felt good. I still have some technique."

Brenna rolled her eyes. "You have better skills than half the professionals." When I scoffed, she wagged her finger. "I'm not the only one who thought so. So, prove it, Miss Soccer Star. Do that three more times."

When I nailed that kick, too, I hooted, racing toward the goal like I'd won the World Cup.

"You're on fire," Brenna shrieked.

"If I do this, you're buying me dinner at Formaggio's."

I lined up the ball and slammed my foot against the leather casing. Another perfect kick. Damn, this was fun.

"Fine," Brenna called. "But if you miss, you have to go out tomorrow. *To the bar.*"

My feet stuttered to a halt. I shouldn't have told her about that. Why had I told her about overhearing Teo and his team-mates discussing their last night of camp—and a start-of-season happy hour yesterday? Well, I knew why. I liked him, the same

14

soccer star most of the world lusted after. The youthful longing irritated me, but like a deep splinter, I couldn't force it from my irritated skin.

"I should be able to tell you my secrets," I muttered. "You're supposed to be my best friend."

"I am. Which is why I know you haven't dated in six years. Holy crap, Preslee, that's most of your adult life."

"It's my life, and I don't feel like dating."

Brenna's hands slid to her hips and she jutted out her jaw. "So you're not willing to admit you like him? That you want him to fantasize about you as you're fantasizing about him? Or is it that you're too afraid to ever go out with another man?"

Frustration burbled up from my stomach. "I'm not afraid, and I'll date when I'm ready."

Brenna scoffed as she set the ball in front of me. "Fine. It's not like you have anything to worry about. You'll kick the ball into the net and go back to your boring, loveless life."

One of the problems with knowing someone for over twenty years was the ability to press on the sore spots. I spent most of last week bemoaning my sexless life, and Brenna threw it in my face. I gritted my teeth and sucked in a breath, focusing on the ball and where I wanted the shot to go.

Go back to your boring, loveless life. My life was neither boring nor loveless. I had a large family, one I adored and who adored me. I loved my position as viola player in the symphony and occasional singer with one of my brothers-in-law's bands. I had a great condo near downtown. I was content. At least I thought I was.

I pulled my leg back and slammed it into the ball. I missed not just the bend but the entire net.

Not because I wanted to see Matteo Romero de Cruz again. No. That would be foolish.

———————

"I can't do this," I murmured. I'd said those four words over and over since Brenna concocted this insane plan last night. I stopped walking as my eyes darted around the street. I rubbed my clammy palms on the boiled wool of my trench coat. I straightened the asymmetrical collar, fingering the ivory edge.

Not even this, my favorite article of clothing, soothed me, gave me the confidence I desperately needed. Sure, I was back to wearing clothes that fit me—the *haute couture* I used to take for granted—but this time the clothes didn't bring confidence. Just a sour gurgle deep in my belly.

My shoulder and calf muscles tensed at hearing a catcall from down the street. Brenna grabbed my hand, and I turned to her, surely looking like a deer realizing the pain exploding within caused fatal damage. Imminent danger stalked me in the form of physical intimacy, thanks to Brenna's meddling.

"He wasn't whistling at you. You're standing in the dark. Get a grip, Pres."

"This is a terrible idea. I don't know why I let you talk me into this."

"This is what you get for losing the bet. I'll walk you to the door. See you in safely."

"I should never have let you talk me into that either."

"But you did."

"I'm not letting you talk me into things anymore."

Brenna smirked. "Good luck with all that."

"You should stay and help me out."

Brenna wrinkled her nose and shook her head. "Nope. I don't think so."

I gripped her hand hard enough for her to wince. "Finding out I can't bend it like Beckham five times in a row means I have to go in there alone?"

She extricated herself from my grasp. "Yep. That's what you get for overconfidence."

"To get even, you want me to die of mortification," I muttered.

"When did you get so dramatic? You started the bet."

"You're the one who bet I couldn't *five times in a row*."

"Whatever." Brenna turned me toward her and placed her hands on my shoulders. "You look hot. No one will be able to say no to you tonight, Siren Lady." Her light brown eyes tracked up my legs to the edge of my trench. She nodded at my waist cinched by the belt. She pulled one side of the coat to show off more thigh on the other side. Standing on tiptoe, she brushed my bangs off my forehead.

"How are you getting home?" I frowned, darting a quick glance around the pedestrian-lined street.

"I'm meeting up with some co-workers down the street." She pointed in the direction of a pizza place and a wine bar. Knowing Brenna, she could be at either. "No more excuses from you."

"I'm not going to a bar by myself. That's against the buddy system."

"I'm walking you to the door."

"Then you're by yourself. That's also against the buddy system."

"I can see my friends from here." Brenna turned and waved.

17

"They're sitting by the window and will be able to see me the entire time I walk down the street. Stop making this so difficult. You don't have to pick up a guy, Pres. But you need to get over your fear that all guys are like your ex."

I didn't want *a guy*. I wanted one man. Teo.

All because I listened to Brenna. Her eyes sparkled, her bright red lips tipping up as she straightened my coat at my neck.

I sucked my lower lip into my mouth, worrying the edges with my teeth. If I didn't do something soon, Oren would win. I couldn't give him the rest of my life. He didn't deserve even a single thought.

"Shove me in before I change my mind."

"You'll be fine, Pres. Just do more than you're comfortable with but less than is stupid."

"I don't know where that line is."

"No one does." Brenna hugged me, hard and long as she always did. "Love you." She kissed my cheek then opened the door behind me and pressed against the small of my back, giving me no choice but to step forward. Otherwise, I would've fallen over the threshold and embarrassed myself. I turned to scowl at Brenna, but I only caught a glimpse of her retreating back.

Tonight, she wore jeans and a long red cashmere cardigan and her favorite pair of black stiletto boots. I didn't like the idea of her walking around town alone, and not in those boots. I turned to head after her, needing to ensure her safety, when a man's hand slid across my back, making me jump.

"You coming in, sweetheart?" His kind eyes focused on my face, not my exposed legs.

Brenna had disappeared into the growing evening crowd.

With a sigh of resignation, I pulled the door shut behind me.

I glanced around, taking in the dark-wood bar top with its brass fixtures. The wood floors gleamed with the reflection of the soft pendant lights that hung over the thirty or so tables. Larger versions sat over the raised-booth tables. A mix of about twenty people, some young in ripped jeans and university shirts, interspersed the more sedate professional crowd.

My eyes focused on the only profile that gave me goose bumps and hot flashes rolled into one tidal wave of desire. Teo sat about halfway back in one of the high-backed wooden booths, his hands linked loosely around his beer glass. One of his teammates said something, and Teo tipped his head back, laughing, accentuating the clean lines of his throat and jaw.

Then, as if he felt my stare, Teo turned, and his eyes snapped to mine. My heart pattered in my chest. I couldn't do this. I turned to go only to find my way blocked by a new group of people. The laughter and excitement in the rooms suddenly felt suffocating.

I tried to fight my way back to the entrance as another round of people tumbled through the door. Giving up, I edged with tentative steps toward the bar and sat in the first seat available. Here, at least, I managed to assert a little personal space. Most people knotted together, filling up the empty booths while others sidled toward the pool tables in the back.

"Never seen you in here," the young bartender commented. He looked familiar.

"Do I know you?"

"Yeah, I was a year behind your brothers in high school. You're Preslee Jennings. We all knew you," he said with a wink. "Your voice remains legendary."

The nasty gurgling in my stomach ratcheted up. "I don't sing anymore."

"You play the viola with the symphony."

Double crap. If this guy was familiar with my career, then my hanging out in a bar would get back to my brothers. Just what I needed. Eighteen months younger than me, Nate and Noah took overprotective to the extreme. They had reason to, of course. Ever since Oren…I cut off the thought.

"Thanks. Great to see you again." My face flamed with embarrassment. He didn't introduce himself, and I didn't ask.

"Well, what would you like to drink? We cater to all tastes."

He was flirting. I patted the short hairs at the back of my head to cover up my shiver of dread, wishing I knew how to handle this. Whoever said dating was like riding a bike never rode a bike or didn't date. Probably both.

"What do you recommend?" I asked. I slammed my lips together, hard, refusing to flirt back. My shoulders tensed. None of this interaction felt right.

"Something smooth but with a bit of a kick." He sucked in his lip. "Vodka?" He looked at me, shaking his head a little. "No, you're not a Moscow mule kinda gal. Less kick. You want an appletini? They're popular with the ladies right now."

"I'm not much into cocktails. A shot of vodka sounds great." God, I hope he didn't hear the quaver in my voice. "Just give me a hard cider. Whatever's local."

The bartender smiled as he moved to a tap, pulling my drink.

He slid the pint glass across the bar toward me. I picked up the glass, ignoring my shaking hands, and took a huge gulp. I loved cider, the clean bite and crisp tang. But even with the anxiety-stifling effect of a good drink, I still had to will my throat to open so I could continue to breathe. Nerves blasted through my system, in part because the seat I settled on to meant no view of Teo, the only person I knew in the room—sort of knew—besides the bartender, whom I didn't *really* know. Even if we attended the same high school.

I didn't like crowds. I didn't like loud, drunk men, specifically.

To cover my rising apprehension, I drank deeply, my eyes scanning the boisterous crowd for Teo's shiny black hair. For whatever reason, I felt safer because he was in the room with me. That didn't often happen anymore, and I enjoyed the feeling. Part of why I'd started looking for him—turning him into a sort of talisman.

I took another large swallow as I turned to face the crowd. The cold, fizzy drink slid from my mouth to my knotted stomach. Teo was no longer at his table. The other two men there were chatting with blondes. Sisters from the look of them. I watched as one of the men ran his thumb up the skin of the girl's bare arm. To block my shudder, I gulped again, downing the rest of my drink. I turned back to the bar and smiled, licking my lips as I raised my gaze to the bartender, who was back in front of me.

"Another."

"I don't think it's smart for you to pound back anything, even if cider has a low alcohol content," the bartender said, his brows pulling down with worry. "Your brothers would kill me if something happened to you."

"It's the best idea I've had. The bad idea was thinking a man like Oren cared about me."

I just mentioned my ex-boyfriend, and I wasn't quaking in

a ball of fear. Brenna'd been right; getting out forced me to face part of my fear. "My ex-boyfriend," I said, feeling something important ooze out from my chest. Possibly pride. Yes, pride. I pushed another twenty on the bar toward him.

"The rest is for you. It'll be my last for a while. Promise." I smiled and winked as swiped my finger over my heart in an X.

He poured me another drink, his mouth twisting with reluctance. I picked it up to sip when a hand skimmed over my shoulder. I tipped my head back farther, surprised by my lack of fear. I peered up into the perfect features of Matteo Cruz. Teo's dark-lashed eyes studied my face, their typical hazel coloring shifted darker, filled with the same concern now etched into his forehead.

"Hello. Enjoying your freedom, I see." I smiled.

"I suppose. But I like the kids. Their enthusiasm for the sport brings back some of mine."

"I used to adore soccer." I sighed, shaking off the memories once again. "The camps were fun."

"You don't appear to be drinking for pleasure, Preslee," Teo said.

"I'm not." I smirked at him.

His lips flipped down as his dark eyes flicked from the glass to my face. Heat suffused my cheeks as I wondered what he saw. Not the models he dated infrequently.

I was just a woman. Pale skin. Freckles across my nose. Eyes too big for my face. I knew every one of my flaws. Oren catalogued each for me over our three-year relationship.

I sat up straighter, trying to ignore Teo's disappointed stare and my pounding heart. I poured the rest of the drink down my throat and set the glass on the bar. My head spun with the effort.

I gripped the edge of the bar. "Brenna won't let me come home until eleven."

"You two fight?" I'd introduced him to my roommate and BFF when she brought some sandwiches and sports drinks I'd purchased from a nearby deli for all the kids and staff at camp. Those kids deserved more than they got.

"No, not really. That would require putting up any real resistance."

Teo's lips curled up in that smile I loved. It wasn't his full one—just enough to let the person know he found the comments amusing—the same one he used during photo shoots. Noah mentioned Teo had two this weekend for different sports magazines.

"You're a pacifist."

I wrinkled my nose. "Just lazy." I hiccupped. Thirty-two ounces in my stomach in under ten minutes. My stomach gurgled, reminding me I hadn't eaten dinner. Too early, I'd said. Hell, it was still happy hour.

"Your friends are staring at you." I waved my hand toward the booth he vacated. "I'm sure they want you to join them and their cute little blondes. I've got an agenda tonight." I'd sit here for another couple of hours, then head home. I'd lie to Brenna, tell her I'd kissed a man. Not that I would because Teo didn't seem into me now like he had at the soccer camps, and I was too nervous to attempt seduction. Not that I'd ever had to seduce anyone before.

Six years of not dating meant no seduction.

Teo glanced past me toward the bartender. "She's done." His tone turned implacable, the set of his jaw more so.

He ruined my image—the one I'd built up in my head and

heart—of him. I'd expected kindness and patience like he gave the kids. That's what drew me to him. We'd chatted amicably as I helped him set up the cones, clean up the goals. But we'd been working then. Now, he acted like a possessive date, and I didn't like it.

"That's not your decision to make." I slid off the stool and managed to stay on my feet. I barely wobbled once I grabbed onto Teo's shirt. God, he smelled fantastic.

He cupped my cheek, tilting my head up so that my eyes met his. My gaze tangled there, lost in something deeper and lovelier than I'd anticipated.

"What are you doing here?"

"I'm drinking." I smiled cheekily, but I dropped my gaze. I didn't want him to see the secrets swirling in there tonight. One bubbled close to the surface: I wanted Teo. To touch me, hold me, love me. I wanted him to help me forget why I dreaded being in public, being near a man. I cleared my throat. "And forgetting."

"If I ask you nicely, will you stop?"

His slight accent slid into his words, further fuzzing my brain. I shivered as heat sensitized my skin. The mere idea of him conversing in Spanish, murmuring soft words in my ear, caused my belly to clench with need.

"Why do you care?" I asked. He never sought me out during the clinics we worked together. He conversed with me while on the pitch, but I'd assumed I remained as invisible to him as I appeared to be to most people. He left the stadium with a date that first weekend; the next set of camps I darted off early to go to my mom's house avoid seeing Teo with the petite redhead again. I hadn't wanted to see them together, to let jealousy take hold of me.

But he didn't leave with a woman this past weekend. I'd made a point to gather my belongings so that we walked from the arena at the same time.

Panic warred with excitement as Teo stepped just a little closer, his body blocking out all the other people in the bar.

"I'm worried about you. It's barely past seven and you've tossed back two drinks. At this rate, you'll end up on your back for some *pendejo* who's not worried about anything other than an easy lay."

Teo's dark brows drew down into a scowl as he spoke, the lovely light in his eyes darkening to something hard and angry.

"Perhaps that's the point."

"You're not that kind of woman." Teo brought his hand up to brush my bangs back. "Who hurt you, Preslee?"

I eased back from his hand, biting my lip against the cry of disappointment when he dropped it and his other hand on my hip. For a moment, we'd almost shared an embrace.

"The better question is who hasn't." I tossed my head, wishing momentarily for the long, thick mane I took for granted in college to make the action seem more natural. I'd cut my hair into a pixie style years ago. While I loved that I could roll out of bed with my hair needing nothing but a light tousle to look good, I missed the reassuring weight on my shoulders and the high ponytails. I missed the soothing evening brushing ritual. I even missed the tangles.

I didn't miss the way Oren held it in his long fingers, the first time to tilt my head to kiss me like he wanted—hard enough to draw a cry from my mouth that he cut off. But like everything with Oren, those first months faded into something darker and more painful, and my hair represented his ability to pin me in place, hold me helpless and pathetic while he raised his fist again. Cutting my hair severed me from the naïve girl Oren never actually loved.

My nostrils quivered as I clamped my lips together hard. No more thinking about Oren. He was in the *past*.

CHAPTER THREE
Teo

I studied Preslee's tumbling bangs as they tangled in her lashes once again. She looked as though she considered blowing them away but managed to stop herself.

I reached up and brushed the hair from her eyes, my fingers settling once more on her cheek, sliding down to the corner of her mouth. The mouth I'd wanted to kiss for the past couple of weeks. No, kissing was too tame for what I desired. I wanted to plunder those pink, soft lips, delve deep into her mouth and learn her taste. Learn her secrets.

"I see it here." I returned my thumb to the corner of her eye.

She flipped her lips up into a smirk, trying to hide the fear flooding her eyes. "I don't think so."

She slid back a little, wobbling as she let go of my shirt.

"Damn these heels and damn Brenna's crazy, half-baked ideas. This is exactly what I deserve for stepping out of my shell."

I was pretty certain she was unaware she'd spoken aloud; her voice was barely above a whisper, but I heard every word. She tightened the belt of her trench almost as if she didn't want me to see her dress—at least I assumed she wore a dress. Her coat hit mid-thigh without so much as a peak of another color or fabric under the nubby white wool.

Oh, *Santa Maria*, Preslee better be wearing clothes. Not that I minded the idea of undoing the coat to see smooth, soft skin, but I didn't want any of these other people to catch even a glimpse because…*mierda!*

The kid at the bar watched our interplay, even as he opened

beers and mixed drinks. I didn't like the hungry look in his eyes each time his gaze drifted over Preslee just as I despised the latent desire in my teammates' gazes.

I rocked back on my heels as possessive jealousy flooded my body, cranking up my adrenaline. Hell, I wanted this woman. The timing could not be worse, but there was no way I'd leave her to another man's mercy.

With a negligent wave of her hand, she said, "Since you're colluding against me, it's time for me to leave. Enjoy your night."

In an impressive move that few strikers pulled off, Preslee spun on those high-heels and disappeared into the still-growing crowd. Scowling, I walked back to the table with my teammates, intent to let them know I was leaving. Since they'd watched my interaction with Preslee, they were quick to wave me off.

"Make sure you get her home in one piece, Teo," Kevin said. "None of us wants to face Noah's wrath if something happens to his sister."

Garland shuddered. "Better you than me. Not only will Noah be angry, but Preslee's frigid. Barely looked at any of us." The blonde on his arm snuggled in closer, giggling that she was hot. I left them to their new friends, tamping down the vicious anger Garland's words evoked. Something about Preslee's large, watchful eyes told me she had reasons for the standoffishness Garland had mentioned.

I found her outside the building, hand slapped flat against the cold, rough bricks, muttering about what torture devices her shoes were. When she wobbled, I slid my arm around her waist, steadying her. She started, a small yelp falling from her mouth. As she turned her head toward me, she snapped her mouth shut, but her brows pulled down in displeasure.

"I told you I don't need your help." She sighed. "I'm going home. I promise."

I nodded as I lifted my far arm. "You might need your purse, though. I assume it has your keys."

Her cheeks suffused with heat. "Yes. Thank you. You can get back to your fun."

I should. My focus needed to be on my trade. That's how I picked back up the tattered pieces of my career. Then Preslee glanced up. Just a peak of those big, watchful eyes, and I couldn't leave her alone. "I'd prefer to see you home."

I kept her purse in my far hand, not trusting the way her eyes darted toward it. I wrapped the strap tight around my wrist, just above the platinum Tag watch the company gave me three years ago in exchange for lots more money and the use of my image on multiple billboards and magazines throughout South America.

Her body coiled tighter, preparing to lunge, which would only end badly in those heels.

"You just said the heels hurt. Let me help."

Preslee's defiant gaze turned into one of longing, and she nodded, moving out from under my arm. Those stilts did do amazing things for her legs, turning her already supple muscles into tight, sleek calves. I wanted to run my fingertips over that soft skin. My tongue, too.

Damn my need to keep her brother happy and my trade options open. Because right now, the satisfaction derived from those reasons proved hollow.

"I don't live far," she said.

"Then let's get you home."

"I'm going." She spoke to me over her shoulder, veering off to the left. I hurried up next to her then shortened my stride to match hers. I'm sure I looked ridiculous: my long legs taking short steps while her small, black handbag slapped into my other leg. Preslee stood five-seven without the heels, but I was over six-three in my bare feet. Even in the sexy footwear, the top of Preslee's head only came to my nose.

Preslee's heel caught in a crack in the sidewalk. As she staggered, unbalanced, I yanked her upward, plastering her to my chest. Holding Preslee was a taste of joy I never expected.

"While I love how your legs look in those shoes, these heels aren't the practical."

Her chin wobbled. "Put me down. Please."

I jerked my gaze from her mouth back up to her eyes. With great care, I set her on her one-heeled foot. I held her arm as I bent to pick up the other stiletto. Crouched at her feet, I guided her foot into the shoe. I couldn't resist the temptation to run my palm up her calf. She hissed, her hands falling to my shoulders.

Glancing up at her from under my hooded lids, I smiled as the deep pull of the attraction raged between us. Giving in to my craving seemed smarter with each thick heartbeat.

Preslee shifted and her coat parted. My mouth turned drier than a desert.

"What are you wearing?"

She glanced down and groaned. Her bright red strapless dress—though dress might be a generous label—started low on her breasts and ended two, maybe three inches below her ass.

"Holy mother of…" I gasped. The dress she wore…. but, no, it wasn't the dress that lit me up as much as the *body* in that dress.

I choked, unable to get more words from my mouth.

She stiffened as I stood up in a smooth, lithe motion. I pulled the edges of Preslee's coat together, my eyes drifting around to make sure no one else viewed *my* prize. A strange growling sound ripped from my throat.

Preslee stepped back. She stumbled again and before I considered the action, I ducked my shoulder, catching her low in her belly.

"What are you doing?" she gasped. Her shoe fell off again. "I'm burning the damn things. They've gotten me into more trouble than I can handle," Preslee mumbled, her hands scrambling for purchase along my back.

"I'm taking you home. You can't walk through Seattle like that. You're barely dressed." I winced at the pain in my hamstring as I bent and snagged her stiletto in the same hand as her purse, my other hand on the back of her thighs to keep her coat in place. She braced her hands on my back.

"Put me down."

"No. Not until you're safe, inside."

"I don't want to be on your shoulder."

I'd damned us both to the fallout to come because no way— *no way*—anyone else would see Preslee in this getup. "Sweet *Santa Maria*, Preslee. Don't argue with me. Not now."

Her struggles yanked my shirt upward. She gasped.

"Are you wearing those Hugo Boss boxer briefs?" She whispered. "The ones that say BOSS across the tush in bright blue letters?"

I chuckled. "Ah, you saw the ad."

"Everyone in the world saw the ad. There are at least three billboards here in Seattle with your rear end plastered across them."

True. And since I didn't particularly care for the ad or the fact that women eyed me as something delightful to lick, nibble, or devour, I ignored Preslee's comments. But, part of me wished I hadn't put on those boxer briefs tonight. They'd become my nemesis and, once again, I would not live that photo shoot down. Though, the global billboards did increase my popularity within the sport, something I needed right now.

My long stride ate up the distance, but Preslee grew quiet. Too quiet. I hoped she was thinking about how much she wanted to run her fingertips under the elastic of my underwear, how much she wanted to touch and taste my skin. Because that's what *I* was thinking about her.

Even though I shouldn't.

I couldn't have her—in large part because of how much I wanted her. She divided my focus away from the pitch, which meant away from my trade to Milan. Another week, two at most, of negotiations and everyone should be satisfied.

And I'd be flying back to Europe. Where I belonged.

I crossed the street, stepping off the curb and then back up the other side, jostling Preslee in the process. When I adjusted her back onto my shoulder, she snapped the boxer's elastic, eliciting a grunt from my chest as a delicious heat built in my belly.

"You're not as sweet as your brother led me to believe," I muttered, frustrated. "Do you do this every weekend?"

"No way. I haven't been in a bar in years."

"Glad to hear bars aren't your scene."

"Nope. I prefer watching *Gilmore Girls* reruns."

"Now *that* I can believe," I said, a smile in my voice and plastered all over my face. "You and your girlfriend snuggle in close with a pint of ice cream, don't you?"

She lifted her head from my back, but I couldn't see her face. "You mean my roommate? We don't snuggle."

I stopped walking. This time, I craned my neck to look at her face. Preslee's eyes were wide open, a little glassy but devoid of deception.

"She's *just* your roommate?" I asked, desperate for the truth. Frustrated I'd thought otherwise.

"Yeah. I mean, Bren's been my best friend since first grade."

I licked my lips as another obstacle between my desire to have Preslee fell away. I needed more reasons to keep my distance, not less. My breath expanded my whole chest, causing Preslee to shift and squeal. Her arms flailed for a moment before her hand gripped my butt.

My mouth went dry with need. "Stop that," I snapped.

"I need a place to rest my hand, what with your caveman behavior and all." She tried to sound irritated but the extra squeeze gave away her game.

"I think hard cider makes you downright naughty, Preslee."

"I think you're right," she said, the laughter escaping.

I remained quiet, considering my options. She needed to get home, give us both a chance to cool the sexual tension burning between us. But first, I must know why she waltzed into the bar in a sex-me-up dress.

"You going to tell me why you're wearing that?"

"Nope." She sighed, leaning her cheek against my back. Her neck probably had a crick from lifting it so long.

"I deserve to know, now that you've manhandled me." I

relished bantering with Preslee, enjoyed these moments with her more than I had the last hour with my teammates. Especially now that I knew she wanted me, too.

"You ogled me and your hand is next to my girlie parts, so we're totally even." If a voice could blush, Preslee's just did. Oh, I liked her contradiction of bold yet shy. Part of it was the liquor, I knew, but the other part was Preslee stepping out of her self-imposed shyness.

My hand slid up another inch, desperate to see if her body was as warm and inviting as I hoped it would be.

No. Noah's sister, the woman he begged, cajoled, and even threatened us to treat with respect, lay draped over my shoulder and down my back, alcohol-logged and, if her eyes were any indication, desperate to forget some memory. And here I stood, in the middle of the street, feeling her up. I shook my head, trying to dislodge the fog of lust that continued to build there.

We were mere blocks from my building. I walked toward it, rethinking my original plan of offering Preslee a cup or three of coffee and then calling her a car. But no, not in that dress. I'd drive her home when she was sober. And wearing my sweat pants.

I ignored the doorman and the two elderly ladies in the lobby. Preslee lifted her hand off my back to wave—probably the reason no one called the police. I pressed the button on the elevator panel and breathed a sigh of relief when the doors opened. The ride up ended too soon, though I spent the entire time wrestling with my desire to put her down, to feel her up or to call quits on the evening. Preslee remained silent, heightening my awareness of her and my internal drama.

I set her on her feet once we were inside my place. I reached around her and flicked on the lights. She squinted in response, her eyes filled with a deep sadness that made my chest ache.

"I don't like seeing you like this, Preslee." I wanted her eyes bright and cheerful...or full of lust as she looked up at me.

"Like what?" she asked. "It's not like you know me well." She forgot she was only wearing one shoe and started to tumble down with a squeak. Her flailing hand managed to grab hold of my shirt. *Riiip*. We glanced down to see three of the buttons ripped from their holes.

"Umm...sorry?"

I glanced up, shaking my head in amusement. "You could've just asked me to take it off."

Heat colored her cheeks. For a long moment, she stared at my shirt. Just when I thought tears would spill over her lashes, she inched forward so that her breasts touched my chest. The heat of her body bled through my thin undershirt. She tilted her head back, desire clear on her face.

"Take it off. Please."

I studied her eyes, not liking the desperation building there. "You're drunk."

She shrugged. "Mostly not."

I eased back from her, groaning at the loss of her warmth. "I don't sleep with drunk women."

She smiled, but the flash of teeth didn't cover her drooping confidence and the fear spiraling through those beautiful eyes. "That's great. I don't want to sleep."

Mierda. She tested my self-control. I pushed Preslee down onto the couch, where she sprawled. Her trench opened further, and my eyes focused on the gaps, tracing the pale skin exposed, especially those toned legs. My jaw firmed, and I turned my head away.

She would regret the events of the evening by morning. As would I.

She sighed. A soft rustling noise accompanied her opening the trench coat. "That's a real shame. I'm way more adventurous after a couple of drinks." She shrugged out of the boiled wool, and I got the first full frontal of the dress.

I groaned, low and loud. "You're trying to kill me."

"You're the one with all these silly rules."

"Morals." My hands balled into fists to keep me from reaching for her. "They're morals. Having them makes me ethical." And kept me from being tied to a woman who wanted me for what I could provide, not for the husband and lover I could be.

She kicked off her other high heel before pointing her toes, making the most out of her legs before tucking her feet under her *culo*. She leaned her head into her palm. "You're the one who brought me back to your place."

I stepped back, hands shoved into my pockets. "I don't know where you live." I hadn't asked because then our evening would end. Better to torture myself than lose her already.

"I could've told you."

"I'll make some coffee." I turned away, unable to look at her in that dress any longer. I burned for what she offered, which would get me in trouble with Timber management. At this point, I might not find a diplomatic way out of my current predicament. I shouldn't have approached her, and I shouldn't have picked her up.

But then, I didn't *want* to back out or away. I wanted Preslee more with each passing second.

36

CHAPTER FOUR
Preslee

And that was it. Total dismissal. *He doesn't want you, Pres. Time to move on.*

I wasn't drunk, but I sure as hell wasn't sober. Rejection in this state proved bearable. Six years ago, my life crumbled to pieces. Going out tonight was supposed to make new memories. Sexy, better ones.

That's why I intentionally missed the shot. Not that I'd admit it to Brenna, but I'd wanted an excuse to see Teo again. I wanted Brenna to give me that push when my self-confidence flagged, as it had tonight before I stepped into the bar.

I closed my eyes. "Where's your bathroom?" I asked.

"First door on the left."

I walked down the hall as I held the tattered ribbons of my pride together. I closed the door and managed to lock it before I slid down onto the floor. I buried my face in my hands and tried to control my breathing.

After a long moment, I stood, angry with myself and with Brenna. A quick glance in the mirror showed red splotches covering my face, as if I'd been crying. Thankfully, even in my tipsy state, I didn't go *that* far. At least not much.

I turned on the faucet and splashed cold water on my overheated skin. Black lines of mascara dripped down my cheeks to my chin. Attractive. Another reason not to wear eye makeup. Mascara wands caused the most injuries to the eye each year. I looked up the statistic after Brenna poked herself in the eye back in high school. Put me off the stuff, usually. I dabbed at my cheeks with some folded toilet paper, crumpling it before chucking it in the garbage can.

I turned toward the door but lost the tiny bits of courage I managed to maintain. My shoulders slumped, and my chest tightened. I wasn't ready to face Matteo. Not with my face like this. My eyes slid to his shower curtain—a brown paisley, more attractive than I would have anticipated for a single guy. Sure, he made excellent money, thanks to his fat contract here in Seattle, not to mention his sponsorships, but his place appeared minimally furnished—at least the living room and the tidy dining area I'd glimpsed on my way into the bathroom. Perhaps a gift from a previous girlfriend? That might explain the hair spray and other toiletries in the linen closet next to the towel rack.

I'd made a point of finding out his current relationship status after I saw him with the redhead. They were just friends, Noah had said. The Internet concurred. Teo told multiple news outlets he helped her out while she was in town. He was not seeing Mariana romantically, and had no plans for a long-term relationship, he repeated to a local reporter just yesterday. Which meant he just didn't want *me*.

I leaned my head against the door, ignoring my desire to take a long, hot shower and wash away the last embarrassing hour of my life. But, no, that would have to wait until I got home.

Pep talk time. After Oren's attack, I'd needed to give myself reasons to get out of bed. Transferring to Brenna's university in Oregon and sharing her apartment helped, but I'd needed to remind myself many times each day I was safe. Oren kept his distance as per the restraining order, and I deserved to live my life.

Squaring my shoulders and ignoring the thrum of blood in

my unhappy brain, I started the process: I didn't *want* to get involved with any man. A relationship with Teo would be even more dangerous because he was a professional soccer player, a media darling, and I refused to compete for my man's attention.

Teo would never be the right person to appreciate the dress or the toned body underneath. Sure, that meant weeks-worth of fantasies down the drain, but I could handle it because I was tougher than Brenna gave me credit for. I'd survived this long, and I would continue to do so.

Just get through the embarrassing situation out in the living room and never see Teo again. I breathed deep and let the air trickle out slowly. *Never again.*

I ran my fingers through my short hair, a nervous habit, as I opened the door. I walked down the hall, my eyes focused on my shoes and trench next to the couch. I sat down and slid my feet into my heels, my Achilles tendons screaming in protest.

I stood, barely wincing, and slipped my arms into my trench coat. Buckling it, I headed toward the door. Teo met me at the edge of the living room.

"Thanks for getting me home and the… never mind. I'm just going to grab my purse and go."

CHAPTER FIVE
Teo

Preslee's face looked like one of those antique porcelain dolls my grandmother collected: white, smooth skin pulled taut over fragile bones. The freckles dusting her cheeks and nose kept her from looking cold and fake.

I hesitated. If I touched Preslee, she might break, just as one of those dolls had.

"Preslee." She turned fast and slammed her nose into my chest. She made a little sound, like a newborn kitten, before she staggered back. Her eyes darted around and crimson stained her cheeks. I wanted to believe Preslee's thoughts circled back to how good we'd be together in bed—no doubt we'd be combustible—but her actions showed her embarrassment.

When she lifted her pretty eyes to mine, hurt welled there, causing my chest to burn. She thought I'd rejected *her*, not the situation. I never considered how she'd perceive tonight's events.

I scrubbed my hands over my head and cursed my parents, Noah's request, my position in the Timber organization, my history, my desire to play for Milan. All those warring needs meant hurting her, and she seemed unaware of how hard I resisted the need to pull her into my arms this second. Just as I had since I first saw her in the bar tonight.

"I—I need to go." She twisted her fingers as her eyes darted around again.

She wanted to leave and hate me for being an uncaring asshole. God, if she only knew how wrong she was about that. Her brows drew together when I rubbed my fingers through her hair.

40

Soft and glossy. I wondered why she kept it so short, well above her ears, the back even shorter than mine.

"I don't have any plans." I smiled. She glanced away.

"Well, I do." Her voice turned rigid, her shoulders back like a soldier's. Something cold and hard wedged itself in my chest.

"Are you going back to that bar?"

"No."

"But you're not going home?"

She sighed, wilting into herself. "I don't know. But thanks for thinking you needed to take care of me."

I couldn't help my narrowed eyes as I considered that sexier-than-sin strip of cloth visible between the rough edges of her trench coat. Her entire trim, pale thigh gleamed beneath the red like a petal to be plucked, kissed... wrapped around my waist as I drove into her willing body.

"You mean you might not go home right away? Like, you plan to go out again in *that* dress?"

She crossed her arms over her chest, her trench gaping enough to give me a view of those luscious breasts. *Santa Maria.* Nope. No way she was leaving.

"What I choose to wear isn't any of your business."

"I just made it my concern."

"Unmake it," she snapped.

"No."

She twirled around like she wore four-inch heels all the time—in the bedroom maybe? I groaned. The thought of Preslee in four-inch heels and nothing else kept me a step behind, trying to catch my breath. She stalked toward the door.

Like that, was it? Oh, the fallout from her night of revelry snaked deeper than she'd yet imagined. People recognized me, even here in Seattle. And I'd caught a glimpse of at least one lens and another cell phone camera while we spoke outside the bar. Those same people—fans—must have snapped pictures of me carrying her over my shoulder. I'm sure at least one of them took pictures of Preslee laughing while she grabbed my ass.

Those pictures might cost me dearly—her brother would extract his pound of flesh as would my mother—but the pain was worth it because Preslee and I were linked together now.

Something I could not undo. Nor did I regret my actions, something I was still mulling over.

"You don't have your purse."

"I know."

Desperation set in as she neared the door. She couldn't leave. How could I fix this current mess?

"How are you going to get home without your keys?"

"I'll just sleep somewhere else." She shrugged, but her eyes darted away.

Her hand closed over the doorknob. Before she could pull the door open, my hand, splayed flat above her head, slapped the solid panel of oak.

She turned and faced me, and her embarrassment morphed into a sizzling anger. "Get out of the way," she snapped.

"You're planning to go out and hook up with some random guy, aren't you? That was your plan for the night?"

"No, that *wasn't* my plan. I had a very specific plan, and it's all been shot to hell." Her eyes were greener now.

She cleared her throat, the delicate tendons standing out in sharp relief against the elegant curve. "Now I'm onto plan B. Unfortunately, because you're being difficult, I'm leaving my phone and my keys with you. So, if I get stranded or end up dead, that'll be on your conscience."

She knew how to play dirty. Of course, she did—she grew up with two younger brothers. I would've smiled if thoughts of other men seeing her in that band of sin didn't rip at my guts. I loved the way the dress clung to her, but I didn't want to share that eyeful of gorgeousness with anyone else.

"You threw back two drinks in minutes. You aren't currently fit to make decisions for yourself."

"Get out of my way."

I leaned in so that my mouth skimmed her lips. "No."

She huffed, her eyes dilating as the anger spiraling through her turned to lust. My body answered her unspoken question. *Mierda*, yeah, I wanted the same. Wanted more than that, which proved a problem. I shouldn't start a relationship with Preslee Jennings. Not with the mess my family had created, not with my work connection to her brother. Not while I was actively working to be traded to another continent.

When she stepped back and bowed her head, I relaxed, my hands dropping to my sides in an unaggressive posture. Faster than I blinked, Preslee grabbed my pinkie finger and brought it back. *Dios mio*. That hurt. She slammed her other fist into my gut. Unprepared for her attack, I slid sideways, shocked and out of breath.

Preslee opened my front door and bolted down the complex's hall. I shook my head before I followed her, but I had time: Preslee's heels were too high to run in and her dress made taking a decent step impossible. She didn't make it to the stairs before I caught her.

"That was mean, Preslee. Mean." I lifted her up by her slim waist so she once again dangled with her feet off the ground. I held her with ease even with those mile-long legs of hers.

"I wouldn't resort to such tricks if you'd just let me out." She shouted as she twisted, pressing her breasts to my chest. I liked the feel of her, and I wasn't a saint. I tightened my arm around her middle, cutting off her air supply but, more importantly, stilling her delicious rubbing. I needed to think.

She flailed her head, not willing to make this any easier, as I hauled her back into my condo. I threw the deadbolt in place.

"I don't like you at all, Matteo Cruz."

I chuckled. "You like me just fine, Preslee Jennings. That's why you're angry."

"Nope, not anymore. You've manhandled me more than I can stand."

"You like being manhandled." My voice dipped deeper, closer to the fragile skin on her ear. I wanted to lick it, nibble the lobe.

She threw her head away from me and glared, her chest rising and falling at a rapid rate. "No, I don't. I haven't liked it since my ex-boyfriend slammed his fist into my face. Puts a damper on the whole you're-bigger-than-me thing."

What the... *fist* to her face? I let go so fast she stumbled, her ankle giving out in those ridiculous heels. She slammed against the door, managing to stay upright as she gripped the molding. As the shock morphed into pain, she squealed, bending over to clutch her ankle.

The view of her back... my eyes climbed the miles of slim, pale calf and thigh. Her coat rode up, exposing the bottom of her dress. *Another inch. Please just ride up another inch.* Just a mere breadth of cloth raised would show if she wore panties.

I wanted to see her naked flesh, wanted to feel her heat against my hand.

"Really?" she cried, standing. I blinked, trying hard to clear the daydream from my mind.

"Do you need to sit down?" My voice turned raspy and my heart pounded as if I sprinted the length of the pitch and back.

"Yes, asshole, my ankle hurts." She turned toward me, tears leaking from the corners of her murderous eyes.

"Broken?"

She tested it, wrinkling her nose as she put weight on it. "Not broken," she decided.

"I'll get you some ice," I stammered.

"I'd prefer just to go," she sighed.

"Ice first. Your ankle's already swelling."

"This day just keeps getting better and better."

I took her hand, the small contact more intimate because it wasn't calculated. I led her into the kitchen and set her at one of the barstools.

The skin around her mouth turned white and the pulse in her neck dashed faster than a sparrow fighting a windstorm.

"We're in The Cosmopolitan, right??"

"Yes."

I put ice in a baggie, wrapped it in a towel and stepped close enough to press the towel to the bruise.

"What floor?"

"I'm on the twenty-first."

She closed her eyes and leaned her head back.

"When did he hit you?"

She looked away, making me feel like a total dick. She didn't want to talk about her ex.

"Six years ago."

"That's when you quit soccer."

"I didn't quit. I couldn't play."

I sucked in a breath with a string of curses. Dirty ones that left the guy in question ball-less and skinned alive.

My pulse sped up as I said a silent thank-you that she came home with me. She didn't know I'd watched her every day we worked together. Within a few hours, I'd keyed in on her quiet vigilance. Her skittishness escalated when the other guys from the team gathered too near, joked with her for more than a few moments. Even the way Brenna watched over her now made sense.

"Did he go to jail?" I scowled. I needed to know justice won out.

"No, he didn't. I pressed charges, but the only witness left after he hit me. Never to be seen or heard from again. A perfect he-said-she-said example of how fucked up our justice system is."

I blinked at her harsh expletive.

"He's still around?" I growled.

"Well, I attended Northern then. I have no idea if he's still there or not. Considering he was three years older than me, it's unlikely."

"He was your boyfriend?"

She threw the ice and towel into the sink. Her mouth twisted and her eyes shuttered. I turned away from her before I did something stupid—like take her into my arms to try to wipe that look off her face.

"You want all the details? Here's the short version: We were engaged. I couldn't believe such a charming, urbane man would pursue me after we met at a party a few months after school started." Her lips pressed firm again. "We began dating at the end of my freshman year. He continued into the MBA program and was in his last semester. I didn't realize he'd planned to use my connections—my family—to step into the cutthroat music business. Until he found out I wasn't as much of an in with them as he'd hoped."

She swallowed hard, her eyes dull and far away. I couldn't resist the need to touch her. I ran my thumb over her cheekbone, enjoying the warm silk of her skin. She glanced up at me, and I slid into the pain and self-recrimination that swirled in her beautiful eyes.

"Preslee." There weren't any words for what she'd been through. She stiffened her spine, and I worried she'd snap.

She shivered and wrapped her arms tight around her waist. "I remember those first two punches. He wrapped his hand in my hair, holding me still as he pulled his fist back."

Dios mio, her story. Her finger rose and traced along her cheekbone. With her eyes were closed, she couldn't see the horror coursing through me. Preslee might be tall, but her bone structure was delicate. Most men outweighed her by at least fifty pounds; I had to be closer to eighty.

She'd trusted a monster, and he'd tried to destroy her.

"My soccer teammate found me on the floor. I guess I passed out where he left me. She drove me to the clinic. Things snowballed from there."

Rage roiled through my stomach when her eyes, those pale

green eyes, lifted back to my face.

"He got a slap on the wrist. He was smart. He played it like our disagreement escalated, and I turned into a raving maniac."

"He hurt more than just your flesh, Preslee."

Her eyes flashed and her mouth firmed. She pushed out of the chair, forcing me to drop my arms. Forcing me out of her life. "Thanks for helping me relive a super-fun night!"

Pieces of her personality snapped together. The lively, happy glimpses that slipped through during those camps, before the rest of the guys showed up, stood out. Her immediate withdrawal when others came into her space. How she leaned on Brenna for emotional support.

"You weren't so quiet before, were you?"

She laughed, but the sound turned caustic, like a rusty saw through metal. I gritted my teeth.

"I've never been outgoing, like you, but I was a vocal performing major. My broken ribs ended that along with my soccer scholarship. I switched to music. Different school. I've played the viola since I was four, so I could handle the coursework."

I winced. A man broke her ribs and bruised her face. Such a recovery would be long and painful. I sucked in a breath.

"Did you love him?"

Surprise swirled up through her eyes, a deeper green than usual. "I don't know. I'm not sure I believe in love. For me, anyway."

"And there's been no one here."

She considered me, her eyes sliding across each of my features. She slid back into the chair, wincing as she banged her ankle.

"Thanks for the ice."

CHAPTER SIX
Preslee

"Please don't leave," Teo entreated. "I didn't mean to make you uncomfortable."

I shrugged. "I have trust issues."

"You were willing to trust a stranger with your body tonight."

"That's not what I planned."

"And I call B.S."

For a long moment, our eyes locked in a battle of wills with his practically begging me to elaborate. I refused to be the one to capitulate this time. Sure, it was easier, but there were moments where winning the battle of wills wasn't just important—it was imperative to survival. Teo had a strong, magnetic personality, like Oren.

I wasn't ever going to let a man dominate me—not in personality and not in a relationship. Not that I had a relationship with Teo, but this was a back and forth, a battle of wills, and I couldn't lose. Not if I wanted to meet my gaze in the mirror tomorrow.

"What about asking a man to dinner or a movie?" Teo asked.

"Um, no. I don't plan to ever trust a man with my heart again."

"But you would let some man touch you to get past your issue?"

My breathing escalated and my gaze flew to his.

"No."

The word came out barely louder than a breath. Teo moved closer, cupping the back of my neck. I inhaled his scent, my jangled nerves smoothed out. I curved into his heat.

"You let me touch you."

I'd told him too much. Probably because of the alcohol in my system. "I need to go home."

"You wanted me to be the one to make love to you." Something built in his eyes. Something warm and beautiful.

I eased back, wincing at the pain in my ankle. "Your ego is pretty impressive, Matteo. Must be the hella good soccer player vibes."

"You knew I'd be at that bar tonight."

His accent—with its direct line to my libido—thickened.

I refused to meet his gaze, refused to admit I listened to everything Teo said. Just like I wouldn't tell him he was the only man I yearned after in more than six years.

He stepped forward and pressed his thumb into the middle of my bottom lip.

"What if I told you I've noticed you, Preslee? What if I told you I admire your strength? Even before what you told me today. What if I told you I wanted to ask you out, but I worried you were a lesbian? And if you weren't, then I had to consider your brother's reaction."

I smirked at that. "Because I'm always with Brenna?"

He nodded. His fingers feathered across my cheek, down my throat to the pulse beating way too fast in the hollow there. He caressed the spot.

I picked up my purse from the barstool and settled the strap on my shoulder. I tipped my chin up so that I would appear more confident.

"I've wanted to run my tongue over your pale skin. It's living velvet. Your eyes are so big, watching. Always watching." He paused. His voice softened with regret when he continued. "Now I know why."

"You don't know me." Anger bubbled up, diffusing the drugging pleasure his earlier words lit in my chest. My past didn't define me. I wouldn't let it.

He stepped forward and used his palms to tilt my head up to meet his gaze. "I know you're intelligent. I know you were hurt, betrayed. I know you're trying to get past it. I know you're a better soccer player than most of the ones helping with the clinic. I know you're beautiful in athletic shorts, shin guards, and cleats, when your face is covered in a sheen of sweat."

I didn't want to be seduced. Wait. Yes, I did. That's exactly what I wanted. Just not now. I eased back, giving myself enough space to think. He held me in a gentle grip.

"I wanted to hold you. Kiss you. Make you burn the way I do every time I think of you."

I snorted and tried to turn my head, but he held me firm. His steady, warm gaze caught mine, staring deep to pull out the last few secrets I refused to reveal.

"I don't want you to lie to me," I whispered, my voice hoarse. "I don't want your pity."

"It's not pity, Preslee. I want you. Do you know how hard I worked to deny that earlier when you were coming on to me? I want nothing more than to sink deep into your body."

He leaned in, rubbed his nose down the contour of my cheek. I inhaled sharply at the touch, my head spinning from his warmth and his scent. He continued to brush his nose down my neck, pausing at my erratic pulse at the base of my throat. His tongue dipped into the hollow and I gripped his forearms to keep upright. I'd forgotten how potent desire could be, my body flushed and needy.

I closed my eyes as Teo's lips continued across the skin exposed above my trench coat. He pulled me closer, one of his hands settling on the outward flare of my hips, the other continuing to rub small circles on my scalp.

Teo's lips halted at the corner of mine. My chest rose and fell in tight beats. Teo pulled back a little, rubbing, seeking, learning. One corner of my lips to the other. I inhaled his scent; let it surround me, drench my senses. Whimpering, I brought my hands up to his cheeks. I held his face while I pressed my lips to his, just like I'd dreamed.

My first kiss in years. It was rich. Deep. I opened my mouth and let the tip of my tongue touch his upper lip—a tiny swipe to taste more of him. Teo's arm at my hips tightened as he tipped his head. His lips opened and his tongue slid across the seam of my lips and into my mouth, pulling me deeper into the kiss, deeper into his arms. My hands slid from his cheeks into his hair, my fingers buried in the silky strands as his tongue swirled across mine.

He pulled back as he licked my upper lip. My thigh muscles clenched as I met his passion-filled eyes. I slid up on my toes, ignoring the throb in my ankle, needing another one of those drugging kisses to burn out the last of my fears.

He complied, and this kiss flamed hotter, deeper. His hand splayed across the dip in my spine, pressing me tight against him. I could feel his passion in the firm ridge straining against his jeans.

I wanted more. I wanted him to devour me. I kissed him with all that pent-up desire.

"Holy hell, Pres," Teo said, dragging his mouth from mine. We were both breathing hard. "I've never had a kiss like that."

"Again," I whimpered.

"Pres, there are things I need to tell you."

"The redhead's your girlfriend?" I asked. I bit my lip…thinking of the petite beauty who'd met him at the stadium.

He shook his head before dropping his gaze to the curve of my neck. His lips pressed there, a soft brush that imbued a depth of feeling from him I never anticipated. That little caress sent shockwaves through my system.

"I can't, Preslee. This is killing me, but I can't do this to you. Not with my current situation." He stepped back again, his eyes so dilated, they were black. His chest heaved.

My eyes darted around, frantic to understand what the hell just happened. Teo rejected me *again*.

CHAPTER SEVEN
Teo

I poured her a cup of coffee, the simple task not as calming as I expected it to be. That kiss—that was *un beso increíble*, cementing our connection. A terrifying and gratifying realization.

Now that I'd tasted her, not having Preslee would be even more painful. My rock-hard erection and thundering heart battled for the prize of greatest source of discomfort. I scrubbed my hands over my face, into my hair.

I sighed, wishing the breath could release the tension from my body before I moved around the kitchen counter to meet her. I smiled at her flushed cheeks and cautious eyes. I wanted her like this, next to me, under me. Always.

The word slammed through my mind, sending it spinning. *Always.* I wanted Preslee Jennings always.

But I couldn't have her. Not if I wanted to achieve the dream I'd set for myself when I was twelve.

"You deserve honesty and respect. I want to give you both."

She managed to take hold of the coffee mug I handed her despite her shaking fingers. Dread thickened in my stomach.

"I'm assuming you failed to do so, then?" Her voice, still husky with our passion, slid from those kiss-swollen lips. I clenched my fists to keep from ripping off that ridiculous excuse for a dress and screwing her senseless on my dining room table.

This woman continued to impress the hell out of me, her voice controlled, her emotions tucked somewhere deep inside. Her eyes were steady, but her pulse slammed against the delicate column of her neck.

The key rattled in the lock, and my stomach dropped out of my body.

"Honey, I'm home!" Mariana's voice rang through the space.

Preslee's eyes snapped to mine; they widened and darkened. "You lied," she bit out. She turned to face the living room, her movements jerky.

"Where are you going?" I asked. She couldn't leave—I'd just discovered how much I wanted her.

"Away from you."

My heart rate tripled. The look in Preslee's eyes slayed me. She *couldn't* think I was with Mariana. Not like that. But I couldn't tell her the truth. I cursed as Mariana strolled into the kitchen.

"I came by the bar after my….Oh. Shit."

Preslee turned to look at the smaller woman. Mariana wore a tiny tee under a beige corduroy jacket and a pair of low-rise jeans. Her flaming hair spilled around her temples and cheeks in thick tendrils. Her boots were fashionable because Mariana was always put-together.

"Hello. You were at the soccer clinics," Mariana said, leaning against the counter.

Preslee nodded, managed a smile that didn't come close to her eyes. "Nice to officially meet you. Now, excuse me."

Mariana turned her gaze to me, eyebrows raised in a what-the-hell-do-I-do look. She took my not-subtle hint and skedaddled down the hall toward the spare room where she was staying.

"It's not what you think, Preslee," I said, my heart slamming against my chest as though I'd sprinted the length of the pitch twice.

"Oh, I think it is."

"Listen to me," I said, my voice urgent. "Mariana and I aren't…." What to say? An item? Together? She lived with me, at least through the game this next weekend. I needed her nimble fingers to work through the layers of too-tight muscle after the practice and games. The hell with it.

"Whatever you're thinking—"

"Don't." Hysteria bubbled up in that single word, and watching Preslee break a little ripped at my heart. I stepped closer, needing to comfort her. She staggered back, crying out as her weight hit her swollen ankle. "I can't hear you reject me again. Like the first *two times* weren't enough."

"I'm not with Mariana. We're not together."

She looked up at the ceiling. A tear slid from the corner of her eye as she laughed. She sounded shattered. "I knew better," she muttered.

My heart slammed into my ribs. She preceded to cut me out of her heart, her life.

No, that could not happen. So much for my secret. Even though Preslee's brother was technically my boss, the man who held sway over my potential trade to Milan, I'd already considered giving that up to be with Preslee, in a theoretical sense anyway, so how was ensuring the demise of my dream by telling her how bad my leg was any different?

It was, though—I'd lose my last thread of hope for winning the European title, for participating in the premier league. All that fell away as Preslee closed her eyes, her face a mask of regret and disgust.

"Goodbye."

I wrapped my hands around her shoulders; her heat seeped

through the wool of her coat. I tried to reach her, make her see that I was serious. But she wouldn't meet my eyes. She wouldn't turn.

"Mariana is my—"

"I don't want you near me. Don't touch me." Her cracking voice pummeled my aching chest.

"You can't leave like this." My voice turned hoarse, an improvement over the clipped tones I used before. "Let me call a cab at the least."

"No need. I live close by."

"You can't walk."

She turned and met my gaze, her beautiful eyes dulled by her incorrect assumptions. She swiped at her eye with the open palm of her hand. "You told me no. I've told you no. Now *back off.*"

She opened the door and staggered out into the hall. I waited until she entered an elevator before running to the stairs. I jogged down as fast as I could; my heart pumping as I worried about her in that tiny dress, walking through the Seattle streets with her sprained ankle.

Bursting through the stairwell, I tried to slow my breathing as I walked near the elevator bank. She wasn't in the lobby. The elevators opened and an older woman walked off with her tan Pomeranian.

Tension flooded my shoulders when she didn't get off the next elevator. I ran to the doors, shoved them open into the night.

I ran up a block, dodging the crowd as I searched for her nubby white coat.

Nothing.

I slammed my fist against the building, ignoring the pain radiating up my arm from my battered fingers.

The look she gave me when Mariana walked in. Like I was lower than slime.

Why hadn't I told her I worried I wouldn't focus on my career if she and I started dating? That I couldn't be with her for a few weeks and get traded? That I didn't want to hurt her, but, more, I feared she would hurt me, too?

My cowardice—my concern about my professional future—caused her to leave. Plain and simple.

My head fell forward between my shoulders, as heavy as my heart.

I'd refused to listen to his explanation. Maybe there was a reason for the beautiful redhead to be there. And maybe I continued to remain a naive idiot. No one acquired a live-in friend. Unless the friend came with benefits of the sexual persuasion.

"Did you hear me, Pres?"

"Yeah. Men suck. I'm tired, Bren. I'm going to bed."

"Want me to get you up in the morning? We can do breakfast before you spend the day with Abbi?"

I considered Brenna for a moment before I shook my head.

"I'm about to text Abbi to let her know I'm not feeling well. I'll see you tomorrow." I pulled off the hateful shoes and carried them toward my room.

Brenna reached out and grabbed my hand, holding it tight in her smaller one. "Teo doesn't know how great you are, Pres. He's just some random douche."

He was neither random nor a jerk. Hell, he stopped me, even after I threw myself at him. Not once—I closed my eyes and shivered—but twice. I groaned. The whole situation mortified me.

Brenna would happily march up there and get in his face if I told her anything more. She protected me with a tenaciousness I didn't want. But because I didn't know how to rein her in, I no longer tried.

I'd never gotten to be the independent person I dreamed of being, like my oldest half sister, Lia. She'd blazed her own trail, much to our mother's frustration. I respected the hell out of Lia for living her life the way she wanted. One day I hoped to do the same. If I could figure out how. Right now, I needed to crawl in my bed and force today to cease to exist.

"I'll be out here if you need me."

"Thanks."

"Love you, Pres."

I closed my bedroom door before pulling off the trench. I hung it in my closet, but I dropped the dress on the floor, sneering at everything it represented. I slid on a pair of boy shorts and a cami—a much more comfortable outfit—and climbed into my bed. I pressed my flushed cheeks into my pillow, refusing to cry.

I texted Abbi to let her know I wouldn't be at her place for our spa afternoon.

Abbi: *What's wrong?*

Preslee: *Coming down with something.*

Abbi: *You need anything?*

Besides a do-over for this horrible day? For all of them since Oren hit me?

Preslee: *No. I'm good. I'll catch up with you soon.*

Abbi: *K. Holding you to that.*

Light filtered through my curtains, and I rubbed my eyes. The night proved fitful, but I finally dropped into sleep after three. Now, my clock read ten. I never slept in so late.

After lying in bed for another few minutes, I pulled the pack from my bedside table and popped my birth control pill. I only remembered to take it consistently if I made it the first task of my day. While I might not be sexually active—and after last night I probably never would be again—I liked the shorter, more controlled periods the medication provided. Without the help, I was sporadic and spotty.

I leaned back against my pillow and shut my eyes again, only for them to spring open when I imagined Teo's hands on my cheeks, the tender way he kissed my lips. His eyes darkened with the same frantic desire I'd felt just before they slid shut.

I managed to screw up again.

I stood, grimacing at my swollen ankle. Hobbling to my bathroom, I swished water in my mouth then brushed my teeth. The red suede heels were still on my bedroom floor. I picked them up and took them to my closet. Instead of dropping them back into their box, I threw one as hard as I could. It struck the dry wall and stayed. I glared at the hole, fuming, before I turned back to my bathroom.

Deep blisters oozed at my heels. I bandaged them and washed my face before limping into the kitchen. I picked up my phone from my nightstand on the way. I found a bunch of texts and even five missed calls.

Abbi: *You went out with Teo Cruz last night?! WTH? Is that why you didn't want to come over today? You could've just said you were too busy getting loved up by a soccer stud.*

Noah: *If you don't respond to this in the next five minutes, I'm coming over there to make sure you're okay.*

I sent a group text back: *I'm fine. At home. In my own bed. I twisted my ankle last night, and Teo carried me back to my building. That's all.*

And I'd stick to that story.

Noah: *Brenna said you went to a bar last night. By yourself. What were you thinking? I'm so glad Teo was there to cart you home. But did you have to grab his ass?*

Preslee: *That was an accident! I nearly fell off his shoulder when he bent to pick up one of my shoes. You're embarrassing me! Leave me alone, Noah. And leave him alone! I'm serious.*

Noah: *You sure I don't need to pound in his face for taking advantage of you?*

Preslee: *Yes! Nothing happened.*

Much as I wanted to turn off my phone, I went through my voice mails, trying not to wish too hard Teo had called. The calls were from various media outlets asking for comments about the pictures. I deleted all the messages.

I made myself a cup of tea before I picked up my iPad and typed in Teo's name. There were five different pictures of us from last night. I touched my fingers to his perfect profile.

He hadn't contacted me.

I wanted him to. I wanted him to say I misunderstood his response to me. That he wanted me. That we should be together forever. That we'd make a whole passel of cute little soccer and music prodigies.

I forced myself to turn off the iPad and sip my tea. I needed to respect his silence—his lack of interest.

Still, this newest rejection hurt. Badly.

———◆———

When Brenna came home, she shoved my feet out of the way and sat on the other end of the couch.

"Ouch!"

Her face fell and she picked up my swollen ankle, rubbing it with her thumb. "I forgot. I'm sorry! Want some ibuprofen?"

She nudged me when she came back and I rolled over, took

them from her hand and swallowed them.

"You've been here all day?"

I didn't bother to respond.

"I'd bully you into going out, but I'm broke," Brenna sighed.

"Aren't you working full time for that software place downtown?"

Brenna made a face. "They downsized. Since I was the newest employee, I was the first to go. So back to temp work and part time gigs for me. Yippee."

"I'm sorry, Bren. I know you liked that place. What can I do?"

"Well, I'd trade just about any sexual favor for Chinese tonight."

I shook my head, pressed my hand to my aching stomach at the thought of food. Or sex. I planned to give both up forever.

Brenna narrowed her eyes, ready to argue. She turned my pale face toward hers. "Sweetie. Brenna's here to make it all better."

I shoved her hand away and leaned against the throw pillow. "Order whatever you want. My treat," I sighed.

"Movie? I'll just microwave popcorn while we wait for the Chinese. Want some Lo Mein?"

I shrugged. I wouldn't watch whatever she put on, and we both knew it—just part of the ritual to try to get me back into a semblance of a real person. Brenna went to the kitchen. She closed the microwave door and then the corn began to pop.

She brought the bag back and picked up the remote. The smell of the popcorn hit my stomach hard. I stood on wobbly legs and managed to make it to the bathroom where I retched up the water and tea I managed to drink earlier.

"I'm *so* kicking his ass." Brenna stood in my doorway, hands on her hips and scowl on her face.

I stood on quivery legs and managed to brush my teeth. "It must be a virus. If I'm lucky I gave it to him, too."

"I haven't heard about anything going around."

"Probably something I picked up from all those kids last weekend."

I walked to my bed and sank into the mattress.

"You never go to bed this early."

"I told you, I'm sick."

"You're freaking me out," Brenna replied, yanking at the oversized sweatshirt I threw on a couple of hours ago. "Guys are such assholes. They don't deserve to make you this upset."

"I'm not upset. Just tired. Maybe sick. I'm sure I'll feel better after some sleep."

Brenna still looked worried.

"I'm getting in bed. My purse is sitting on one of the barstools. Grab what you need for your Lo Mein. Shut the door, please."

"Are you going to cry?" Her voice, filled with compassion, brought the tears to the surface.

"Only if you don't leave."

"I'm going. We'll get you through this."

I nodded. She closed the door with a soft click. The TV switched on. My phone beeped. A text from Teo. Really? How did he get my phone number? Right. The volunteer roster at our clinic. But it took him *all day* to contact me. Wait. He had a photo shoot today. Why was I just remembering this?

I hesitated for a minute before opening the message.

Teo: *I couldn't find you last night. I need to know you're okay. Even though I know you don't want to talk to me.*

I typed back the only important part of the entire situation:

I'm fine—well, as fine as I can be since I'm embarrassed and ashamed of my behavior. Do me a favor. Please don't contact me again.

His response was instantaneous. *Mariana is staying with me, but we're not dating. Can I see you to explain?*

I snorted. That would be a big, fat no. My willpower disappeared whenever I saw Teo. Being in the same room with him when he tried to explain how he and Mariana weren't dating— with my history, I'd probably believe him and end up on the cover of some terrible gossip magazine.

My heart ached as I typed, *there's nothing left to say.*

———◆———

Brenna knocked on my door the next morning.

"You planning to get up?" She poked her head into my room. I lay in bed, feeling groggy and anxious.

"No, I have the day off."

"I'm seriously worried now. You never miss an opportunity to practice. We're going to the clinic."

"I'll take myself."

Brenna held up her phone and waved it. "Your appointment's in half an hour. Let's go."

I glared, but Brenna crossed her arms. "I'll stay in the waiting room, Miss Independence. You can get an X-ray for your ankle, too."

I agreed because my ankle still ached. Brenna had managed to find the pair of crutches she'd used when she broke her leg a couple of years before, and I hopped into the clinic's waiting room. After a short wait, I was escorted back where the nurse practitioner diagnosed me with dehydration from the virus I contracted.

"This one's been making the rounds. Shouldn't last too much longer."

"Good." I sighed. "I don't like to vomit."

"I don't know anyone who does," she replied cheerfully. "Now, let's get that ankle X-rayed."

As I suspected, my ankle was sprained—I'd need the crutches for a few more days at most.

I went straight to my room when I returned to our condo, glad for the break from Brenna's hovering.

I called my half niece Abbi. She and I got along well, and besides Brenna, she was one of the few people I was comfortable talking to.

"Hiya, Pres. How's it going?"

Maybe calling her was a bad idea. I didn't want to make Abbi sad. "Tired. I picked up a virus from the kids. Are you still in Seattle?"

"Yeah, until next Sunday. We're all congregating out at Mom's place this weekend. Want to come hang out?"

"You don't think Lia will mind?"

"She wants you to come. She loves you just as much as I do. You know it's your mom she's still working to get along with."

I made a noncommittal noise in the back of my throat.

"Briar and Hayden are coming over on Saturday. Asher bought some huge smoker-thing he's excited to try out. He mentioned a whole pig. I *so* hope he was joking."

"Clay will be there, right?"

"Yep. Want me to ask him to bring a friend?"

I groaned. "No. You all freaked out over a picture a couple of days ago. I'm not interested in repeating that."

"You mean striker Teo?" Abbi asked.

Abbi wouldn't judge either Teo and me as harshly as Brenna had. "Yes. I crashed and burned all in one night."

"Ouch. How are you doing with that?"

"I'll be okay. I didn't sleep with him, so that helps." Some.

Except it didn't. I'd needed to feel desirable, wanted. What *man* turned down sex? I scowled. A moral one, apparently.

"You don't sound like you're fine," Abbi said. Silence stretched, and I knew she was probably worrying her lower lip, in the right corner like she did when she was thinking or concerned. "Want to come up to my place? I don't have classes until this evening."

Abbi lived a couple of floors above me. One of the perks of being in the same building was we tended to spend quality time together. "No, I'm probably contagious."

"You really liked him."

I blew out a breath. "More than liked." Admitting my feelings eased a little of the ache. "He's great with the kids at the soccer camps. He's funny and thoughtful. Plus, he's an amazing soccer player. Have you seen his legs?"

Abbi giggled. "I'm pretty sure the whole world's drooled over his legs. And his booty in that ad outside our building. Total hotness."

"It's my fault." I sighed. "I've never wanted a sweet, boring man. Oren played football through college. I liked all those sexy muscles."

"First off, Oren was a weak excuse for a human. A strong man

69

wouldn't hit a woman."

I knew Abbi understood my continued standoffishness. She'd had to deal with her own personal hell last year when her ex-boyfriend dosed her with GHB and then took pictures of Abbi in compromising positions with three different men.

Only after she met Clay did Abbi tell her side of the story. I was proud of her and the foundation she helped set up to work with other victims of date rape and cyber bulling.

"If Matteo Cruz didn't want you, that's his loss. A big one. You're fun, Pres. Not to mention ridiculously talented. Asher's frantic to work with you."

I grunted. "He tricked me onto the last one."

Abbi laughed. "It's turned out okay. That song's gorgeous. Who knew an electric viola could sound so cool? Doesn't Teo have a game tomorrow? Maybe he's busy prepping for that and he hasn't had a chance to call."

"Ugh. You just reminded me. I'm playing the national anthem with a group from the symphony, so I guess I'll have to face the music so to speak. I'll make up for spa day next week."

"Awesome. I'm looking forward to seeing you, Pres. It's been too long."

CHAPTER NINE
Teo

Two Days Before…Right After Preslee Left

Mariana met me at my condo's door, my breathing still ragged from running after Preslee. Exhaustion weighed on me. All I wanted was a hot shower, a cold beer, and my damn hamstring to quit hurting.

"I'm sorry about tonight, Teo. Your lady friend didn't look happy to see me." Mariana wrung her magical hands, together, and I resisted the urge to tell her not to break those precious fingers.

"Timing was pretty terrible," I conceded.

"She doesn't know about me? I mean, that I'm your sports therapist?"

I shook my head, rubbing my thigh. "Her brother is my assistant GM. I didn't know what to say."

Mariana pressed her lips together and dipped her head toward my leg. "Still tight? You're going to speak with the team trainer?"

"I mentioned it to Streeter." But only in vague terms. Some soreness, I said. "Can you work on the muscle?"

Mariana shook her head. "It's more than tightness. I'm concerned there are tears in the muscle. Tiny ones right now, but if you don't rest and rehab properly this injury could very well be career-ending."

Those words again. Fear and anger spiraled from my chest to my stomach, making every muscle in my body ache more. "I'll talk to the trainer." Dammit, the timing was terrible—sure to spook the front office in Milan. If I left soon, as I'd need to if I wanted to be on Milan's roster before the injury had the chance to rear its ugly head again, I'd never get to try to smooth over the mess I'd made with Preslee.

Maybe that was for the best. But her leaving, thinking I was *un pendejo,* didn't sit well with me. In fact, I wanted to call her, make sure she was safe. Try to explain why Mariana was staying with me.

"Let's see what I can do to ease the discomfort. But then I'm outta here."

I nodded, disliking the bitter taste in my mouth.

Mariana touched my arm. "I have to go, Teo. I can't lie to your team about your injury. I can't participate in this anymore." She sucked in a deep breath, her dark brown eyes lifting to meet mine. "I'm going to get on a plane tonight. That gives you time to tell your coach, your management before I call them tomorrow."

"Is this about your license?"

"In part. But also because you love to talk about your morals."

I pulled my lips into my mouth. "You're right."

Mariana smiled. "But it's time for me to beat it because you don't like that I've backed you into a corner." She laid her hand on my tight shoulder, her voice softening. "I hope I didn't mess up your chance with her."

True to her word, Mariana zipped out of my condo and headed back to her practice an hour and a half later. I watched from my living room windows as she stepped into the car driving her to the airport.

———◆———

The chatter in the locker room the next morning annoyed me

nearly as much as my aching leg. I hadn't slept well last night, worried about Preslee's well-being as I was. I slammed my bag into my locker, scowling when my water bottle fell out and rolled onto the floor.

I had to wait to get in to practice this morning so I could find one of the soccer camp rosters. I'd find Preslee's number there and call her, explain. At least try to, because I simply couldn't take Preslee thinking I was a cheater.

I was not my father. And in the case of womanizing, I never would be.

"We need to talk."

I turned, unsurprised to see Noah Jennings behind me. His stance shifted, becoming more aggressive, and his brows pulled low over a masculine version of Preslee's nose. I nodded, having expected this since the picture of me carrying Preslee hit the web sometime during the night.

"Here or in your office?"

Noah blinked. He should know by now I wasn't a typical soccer player prone to tantrums when inconvenienced or questioned. My father owned a soccer club in Argentina, and I'd worked in the front office when I could. I understood how quickly the rumors surrounding me and Preslee, even my place on the team, would escalate if we spoke here, in the locker room—part of the reason I guided him into inviting me to a semiprivate location.

He turned on his heel, and I followed, feeling like the naughty schoolboy about to get chastised by the school principal. I just managed to shut the door when Noah snarled, "What the hell was that with my sister?"

I settled into the chair, my expression neutral. Good. We'd

deal with Preslee first. But I knew I had to talk to Noah about my hamstring—soon—before Mariana called. "She downed a couple of drinks. I helped her home."

"She never would've asked you to touch her, Cruz. She doesn't *like* to be touched."

Noah ran his hands through his hair, scrubbing at the back of his head, his eyes filled with sadness.

"Because of what that *imbécil* did to her in college?"

Noah's gaze slammed back to mine, his eyes widening. "She told you about Oren?"

I nodded. "I made her coffee. We talked a while."

I didn't tell him she flung the story at me in anger. That was between Preslee and me. At Noah's blank look, an idea began to form. I leaned back in my chair, suddenly feeling much more chipper than I had even ten minutes ago.

I'd overslept this morning and been late to practice. Mostly because I spent another night trying to figure out how to broach the subject of my hamstring with the Timber staff. If they believed I'd lied to them, not only could that nix the Milan deal—which deteriorated to a wisp of a dream now that Mariana planned to step forward—they could trade me to some C-league team in the middle of nowhere.

That couldn't happen.

On top of my concerns with my future in the sport, my frustration that Preslee wouldn't listen to my explanation ratcheted up.

Mierda. I wanted her. *Mi pene* remained unhappy with my decision-making, and the rub-off in the shower didn't improve my short temper.

I'd planned to scam Noah into giving me her address so I

could send her flowers and make up for last night. I hated knowing I added to her hurt—she deserved affection, caring, not the actions of her ex-fiancé. Since Preslee and I were already linked in the local press, and since I only wanted to be traded to a quality team like Milan, Preslee Jennings had just become my best ticket to staying in Noah's, thus The Timbers', good graces.

"She doesn't like to talk about that."

"Didn't think she would. *El cabron's* the reason she lost her soccer scholarship?"

Noah nodded. He tugged at his bottom lip as he leaned against the corner of his desk. "She loved to play almost as much as she loved to sing. But three broken ribs kept her from doing either. She just…quit, which is unlike Pres. She's got this stubborn streak."

"Not so good on the listening when she's made up her mind either," I muttered, still feeling the sting of her walking out of my place.

Noah's smile filled with rueful amusement at my tone. I shifted, stifling a groan. My lack of attention at practice this morning meant I turned sharply to get out of the way of a defenseman and I tweaked my hamstring. I needed a hot shower and Mariana's magic-finger massage before I'd be able to function properly again. But Mariana was gone, and the muscle wasn't back to one hundred percent, and I had to figure out how to tell Noah I'd kept my concerns from him.

"We all thought she'd play on the national team. That didn't happen. She never said anything, but she must have been disappointed."

I nodded. "Preslee's rusty but her fundamentals are fantastic."

Noah sighed, rubbing a hand through his short, dark hair. "I love the sport, but I never had Pres's talent. She spent hours in the yard with me every week, working on my skills. I never received the scholarship options she did, so I decided to go front-office." Noah lowered his brows and glared. "I didn't mean for her to get hurt when I asked if she wanted to help with the camps. I wanted her to take back another piece of what Oren beat out of her."

"She told me she switched to viola and doesn't sing anymore, either. Because of the attack, I presume."

Noah studied me intently. "Pres said nothing happened between you two. I know you took her home—I saw the photo at the door of her building."

I started, shock turning immediately into satisfaction. She lived in my building. No wonder I never saw her outside that night. I exhaled slowly. *Mierda.* I'd been worried about her limping home in that incredibly sexy dress.

"She told you a hell of a lot about herself. And she was laughing in the picture where her hands are on your, er, back."

Ah. Noah's wasn't angry with me; he wanted information, too. The satisfaction spread, and I fought down the urge to grin. "She groped my ass. After she popped the band of my boxers. She also told me she wanted to have sex to see if she could do it again."

Noah cleared his throat. "I don't want to hear you talk about sex and my sister."

"I didn't sleep with her." I leaned back in my chair, annoyed Noah thought so little of me.

Noah shook his head, eyes filled with concern. "What could she be thinking?"

"She said something about not being able to handle intimacy. I guess that goes back to your comment about not liking to be touched. But here's the problem." I leaned forward. "I think I hurt her feelings when I turned her down."

Noah's scowl turned blacker than my shins after a game. "Well, shit."

"Yeah."

"She doesn't need you dragging her through the tabloids. The last round almost killed her."

A growl built in my chest, but I swallowed it down. "Last round?"

"You didn't google her? There are pages of articles and social media stuff. Oren's family's well-off, Pres was a well-known figure on the college soccer circuit. Her vocal department has national acclaim, and Pres was one of the top students. She'd been asked to sing in some major markets, consider a recording contract. Media like a kick-you-when-you're-down story."

I scrubbed my hands over my face, hating what her ex took from her. What her brother thought I'd do to her. "I took her home. Now she's mad at me. Thinks I rejected her."

"Did you?"

"Are you kidding me? Your sister's incredible." I shook my head, thinking about her life since college. "Maybe I'm not good enough for her."

"That's supposed to be my line. There's a girlfriend back home?"

"Seriously? You think I'd try to destroy the trust with my significant other just to sex up your sister?"

Noah waited. I sighed. "She told you I have a friend staying with me."

Noah narrowed his eyes. "She didn't, but that pisses me off. Is the woman staying with you that redhead—a friend with benefits?"

"*Dios mio*, no. She's…" Great. My opening. "My hamstring's been tight. Mariana Nigella has been working on it. She's a sports massage therapist." I paused. "She's going to call in later today to discuss her treatment suggestions."

"How tight?" Noah switched gears to team management.

"Not too bad, but I wanted to be proactive, make sure I didn't reinjure the muscle. Mariana came up from Buenos Aires to visit and she stayed a few more days because I asked her to evaluate an ache after the preseason game last week."

All true, though I skewed my response so that I looked more proactive, more forthcoming. I forced myself to hold Noah's gaze.

"You can't be seen in pictures with my sister and have her name linked back to you if there's another woman, Matteo." His voice quieted and firmed. "You can't drag her down there again."

I narrowed my eyes. That was it on my leg? The injury that could cost the Timber their highest-paid athlete? That might cost them an international trade?

Wait. This was good. Better than I expected, actually.

"I didn't drag her anywhere. I took her home."

"And now pictures of the two of you are everywhere. We've been fielding calls from local and international media asking for more details."

I sealed my lips. Speculation about me being traded to Milan remained high, for which I was thankful. Making that trade would finish my career on my terms—as one of the sport's elites. I'd spent more than two decades of my life striving for that—and if I could just maneuver through the rest of the trade talks, I'd make it back onto the world stage. The front office there would want to know where my head was, and it must be in the game.

Originally, when I saw her in the bar, I wanted to see Preslee home, make sure she remained safe. But now...I'd created an international story *just* when I couldn't afford one. And the one to get hurt more in all this was Preslee.

Noah stared at me again, his green eyes so different from Preslee's.

"What do you want me to do? Because I know what I want—I want to see your sister again." I wanted to rub my hamstring. I wanted to throw something. Instead, I sat in the chair, my leg muscle seizing in painful jerks.

"When I walked in this morning? For you to stay away from my sister. Far away. Pres has been hurt. She needs to find someone who'll take care of her, no matter what she tells you about being able to take care of herself." Noah leaned back in his chair. "Now? I don't know."

"What changed?" My leg cramped again, and I gritted my teeth, forcing my body to stay still.

Noah leaned forward, his arms on his desk. "You said you wanted to see her. You haven't even asked about Milan."

I sucked in a breath. "Have they called?"

Noah's eyes narrowed. "Yeah."

———◆———

A white coat down on the sidewalk caught my attention as I looked out my condo's windows later that evening. Preslee. My heart rate kicked up.

No, not Preslee. The hair was too long.

Mierda. I needed to speak with someone with perspective, who understood the risks associated with me linking my name further to Preslee's. Time to call my father.

"Dad," I said in Spanish. "I need to talk to you."

"Of course."

"I need your complete discretion."

Raul chuckled. "You mean you don't want me to tell your mother."

I waited, letting the silence grow between us.

He sighed. "I love you, Matteo. I'll do what I can."

"I needed to hear that. Because there's a woman here."

"Ah. The one you carried home."

My father enabled google alerts on each of his players and me. I would have been disappointed if he hadn't known about the pictures. "Yes."

"She has quite a sordid history with men, son."

"You mean her ex-fiance? He beat her, Dad."

"I cannot approve of public intoxication, Matteo. With your mother's struggles—"

I gritted my teeth, hard, and swallowed down my retort about my father's affairs. I wasn't one to pick a fight, and I wouldn't fling his indiscretions in his face. Being married to Lucia Aranda Romero de Cruz would've been hell for any man.

"You wish to further a relationship with her? Even knowing she might trap you as your mother trapped me?"

When I was six, my father told me my mother got pregnant with me before the wedding to ensure my father married her. At the age of twelve, my father explained he only stayed married to my mother because she threatened to take me away from him if they divorced.

Preslee's eyes filled my mind. Interesting that's what registered first, before her sexy legs, slender waist or perky breasts. Before, even, her impressive singing voice I'd yet to hear.

"I like her."

"What about your plan to play in Europe again?"

I sucked in a deep breath, but some truths had to be faced no matter how challenging—and devastating. "I'm not sure my hamstring will allow that."

"Mariana said she did not give you the news you hoped for." Raul sighed. "Speak with Jorge and your trainer."

"I did. Today."

"And?"

"I had more tests run through the Timber's trainers and doctors today. No visible damage, so I'm cleared to play tomorrow."

"What did your agent say?"

"That I wasn't helping my chances with the trade."

"But it still may happen."

I clenched my fist, hard, needing to believe in the possibility. "We're working on it."

The silence stretched as my father digested the words that were still bitter on my tongue, a stone-weight to my gut. Like I was giving up an essential piece of myself with the acknowledgment that I may not make it back to the Euro League.

"Tell me about your young woman."

I smiled, grateful he didn't push me on my leg. I wasn't sure how to handle that situation. I filled him in on our soccer camps, stressing her need to help troubled kids ran at least as deep as my own.

"So, when do I get to meet her?"

I chuckled, thinking about my father's reaction to Preslee. He loved beautiful women, which is how he'd ended up shackled to the woman who'd birthed me... and why he spent the next thirty-plus year cultivating more mistresses than most men owned shoes in their lifetime.

"Once I know you can't steal her."

My father's booming laugh poured out of the speaker as I clicked off the phone.

CHAPTER TEN
Preslee

"Let's go." I pulled my bag over my shoulder, settling it with more care than necessary. My shoulders ached from my three-day bout with illness, and I still moved with an unsteady gait thanks to my twisted ankle.

"You don't have to do this, you know. You just got home from rehearsal. You look tired."

I scowled. "Six other musicians are expecting me. Tonight's performance has been set up for months, and I'm not willing to screw over my colleagues. Now, are you coming or do I need to call Abbi to be my and-one?" I crossed my arms over my chest.

Brenna's expression soured. "You could get sick again."

"I'm playing the national anthem, Bren. And Noah got us spectacular seats as a thank-you for my help with the camps. Go ahead and say it."

She took my hand, her eyes searching mine. "But you'll have to see Matteo, and he hurt you."

I sucked in a shaky breath. "I'll see him again sometime anyway." Not totally a valid statement, but bravado appealed more than collapsing into a blubbering puddle of emotions. "Might as well do it now."

I stalked to the elevator, refusing to let Brenna see the embarrassment and rejection crash over me yet again. I wasn't sure what would be worse: Teo acknowledging me or pretending I didn't exist.

We were greeted at the back entrance by a man I'd met during the camps. His name was Kenneth. I couldn't remember his job title, but he seemed to ensure everyone was where they were supposed to be.

Kenneth strode down a concrete hall, flashing a badge at the employees and security guards we passed. My heart thumped when he led us toward the team offices.

"Where are the rest of the symphony musicians?"

"Your brother can fill you in." Kenneth's brow puckered as he knocked on the thick wooden doors. They swung open to reveal a harried woman with salt-and-pepper hair. Her name might be Wendy. I wasn't sure because I only saw her in passing during the clinics.

Taking in my viola case, she gasped. "Oh, thank good gravy you're here." She gripped my arm with desperation, tugging me farther into the space. I dug in my low heels.

"Whoa! What's going on?"

"Major change of plans."

Teo strode over, looking way too edible in his soccer shorts, tight-fitting jersey, and cleats. Even his shin guards looked attractive. Damn him. Annoyance gathered in the pit of my belly.

"The rest of the musicians were in a car accident on the way here," Wendy said.

"What? Are they okay?"

"Nothing too serious, I don't think, but a broken cello and two pulverized violins. Noah's on the phone with one of them now."

"Being sick benefited you." Brenna patted my arm. I left the symphony hall earlier than I probably should have, stating my need to nap before the game tonight. "Otherwise you'd have been in that car."

"Wait!" I cried. Teo's gaze met mine and I couldn't breathe.

"I—you want me to play by myself?"

"You've got this, Pres," Brenna said. "This is way easier than your part in 'I Do Not Love You.'"

Wendy turned to gawk at me. She looked me up and down, her lips pursing as she took in my dark slacks and long-sleeve, cowl-neck sweater with its frayed asymmetrical hem. A favorite of mine, thanks to its softness and emerald green color. "You play with Asher Smith?"

I nodded, feeling numb. Teo's eyes widened. "You said you don't sing anymore. After your broken ribs."

Wendy considered. "Maybe start with the fiddle then sing."

"Viola," I replied. No one cared about the difference, but it mattered to me. "And I'm not singing."

Brenna clapped her hands together. "Oh, *come on*. I haven't heard you sing since the barbecue last summer. She looks so skinny but she has a set of lungs on her," she loud-whispered to Teo.

"You still sing?" Teo asked.

"No. I don't do live performances." I glared at Brenna.

"You are tonight," Wendy dragged me forward toward an office. "We're paying you," she said before turning from me to speak into a walkie-talkie. "I found a singer. Call up the announcer and tell him Preslee Jennings is singing the anthem."

"No, I'm not." I kept my voice firm. "I'll play the viola. Like we agreed. For symphony promo."

Teo's fingers touched my cheek. I closed my mouth, but not before a soft gasp slid past my lips. "You don't have to do any of this if you don't want to, Preslee." His accent licked over my skin, burning and soothing me at the same time.

"Don't give her an out, Matteo Romero de Cruz! Someone

must sing the national anthem."

The woman sputtered before she banged her head against the wall. "Could this day get any worse?"

"Come on, Preslee," Brenna urged. "It'll be fun!"

My eyes met Teo's. His thick lashes got me every time. I sighed. "Would it help you?"

He shrugged. "We don't play the game until the anthem's sung or played."

Brenna moved forward to stand at my elbow. "You know all the words, and it's not like you haven't done this before."

Teo's eyebrow went up, but he waited patiently for me to make up my mind.

"No," I whispered, wrapping my arms around my waist. "I can't sing." I didn't tell them why.

"Fine. Just the viola. God, I hope you can pull this off." Wendy looked me over critically. "You can't wear that. It looks like a funeral outfit."

"It's standard symphony dress," I said, offended.

"Your brother has some extra jerseys in his office," Teo offered. He leaned in so I could smell his spicy body wash. "A souvenir," he whispered, his breath warm against the fragile ear of my skin. My entire body vibrated, heating up. I glanced up at him in askance. "I'm glad you're here."

"Bring the jersey, Cruz, and back off the talent. I need this to work." Wendy scowled.

Teo smiled again, the one that devastated my defenses, before striding toward my brother's office. One of the trainers and another man—an assistant coach, maybe—eyed me with various levels of interest. I cringed back into Brenna, who squeezed my shoulder.

"It's fine, Pres. You can do this." Brenna's cheeks bloomed with color and her eyes gleamed with anticipation. "Oh, I'm recording this. Your performances are always electric."

Teo's scent drifted around me, relaxing me. "Here's a jersey. Do you have anything to put under it?"

"I wore a long sleeve white shirt under my sweater," Brenna said. "I'll give it to her so she doesn't look weird in her dress blouse."

"Excellent!" Wendy clapped her hands together with a finality that reminded me of an executioner's drum. "Twenty minutes until you're on!"

I took the shirt, fingering the large C on the back. Teo brushed my bangs back from my forehead.

"Why are you up here?" I asked.

Teo raised his chin toward the two men who were still watching us. "I needed to be cleared for tonight's game. Because my hamstring has been tight. That's why Mariana was at my place. To help me develop a therapy plan."

I flushed bright red and dropped my gaze from Teo's. Confusion built and slid through me, making me light headed. The pretty red head wasn't his girlfriend—just as he'd told the press. So…what did that mean?

"Come this way." Teo led us into a larger room with a couple of sleek couches, chairs, and a low coffee table. "You need anything?"

"Water. Thanks."

Teo shut the door behind him to give us some privacy. Brenna clapped her hands and jumped up and down.

"A solo. I love your solos!"

"I don't want to do this." I started to shake, the fear from that night when Oren told me I'd better not try to put my slutty self out there, to let other men see what was his, washed over me, and I placed my hands on my knees to keep from collapsing.

"What's wrong?" Brenna rubbed her hand up and down my back in soothing strokes.

"Oren said…"

"Oh." Brenna imbued so much into that one word. She continued to soothe me until the black floaters drifted away from my vision. "It's been years, Pres. I'm sure he's over it. This is a great opportunity."

I scowled at her. "That I don't want and don't want to chance." I swallowed, a thick sound weighted by the garbled emotions filling my throat. "I could've just said I wouldn't play at all since I was supposed to be part of a group. But no, *you* pointed out I do solo stuff sometimes."

Brenna's mouth popped open. She whipped her sweater and shirt off, throwing it at me. "Excuse me! I wasn't the one who insisted on coming to this game so I could rub up against a soccer player."

I yanked off my blouse and threw it at her. She shoved her arms in and started buttoning it up. "That's not true. I don't rub."

"You still want him," Brenna hissed. She pulled her sweater back over her head while I turned her shirt right-side out.

"And if I do?"

"Then I'm a lucky man," Teo said. He leaned against the doorway. "Fabulous as you look like that, Preslee, I suggest you put on a shirt before you hit the Jumbo Tron."

In a huff, I yanked on Brenna's white tee. Teo stepped into the room, a fierce frown on his face. I scuttled backward. "What?"

He cleared his throat. "You really sing?"

I rolled my eyes. "Not often. And only for myself."

He studied me for a long moment, causing my cheeks to heat. "Wear the jersey. Please. See you on the pitch."

Brenna started. "I'll wait and go up with Preslee."

"I'll do that," Wendy said, bustling into the room. "We need you in your seat."

Brenna's mouth twisted in annoyance, but she left without another complaint. Teo's eyes burned into my skin, causing a rush of heat to ripple across my neck, arms, chest, but I focused on opening my case and tuning my viola.

Once I was satisfied with my instrument and my ability to play the piece alone, I pulled on Teo's jersey over Brenna's too-tight white shirt, disgusted yet thrilled to step out in front of a stadium of people dressed like this.

"Five minutes."

I handed Wendy my coat and viola case, before picking up my instrument and bow. She clutched both, mumbling about this having to work. I followed her up the stairs, trying to calm my nerves. She stopped a few feet from the tunnel entrance and pushed my hair back.

"Good thing you keep it so short. Ready?"

I shrugged. No. I hadn't had time to prepare for this. I stepped out onto the soccer field, a big fake smile plastered across my face. The drone of the crowd didn't change. The announcer point-ed out I was the electric viola player on Asher Smith's new single. That quieted the crowd, and within a breath, all that attention zeroed in on me.

Closing my eyes, I began to play. After the first few notes, I hit my stride, letting the music fill me. Oh, this felt good. I opened my eyes, blinking a couple of times, as I pulled the bow across the strings.

The entire stadium stood, quiet, their hands over their hearts. I hummed the tune as my fingers moved down the neck, then back up. My body swayed to the music. The crowd began to sing, as caught up in the music as I was.

This was electric. My fingers picked up speed, adding more intricacies to the melody. I kept swaying to the tune as the crowd's singing grew louder.

I'd missed this. I'd really missed playing to a crowd.

I hooked eyes with Teo, who watched me with unblinking focus. Holding his gaze, I finished the song, prolonging the note a tad longer than I should have because I didn't want to break eye contact. I bowed my head to the cheering crowd and stepped around the mic, my instrument and bow down by my legs.

As I walked toward my seat, Teo stared at me, his dark eyes gleaming with something I couldn't quite read. He smiled and dipped his head; an answering grin tugged at my lips. Yeah, I knew my way around a bow and some strings.

Brenna hugged me, bouncing up and down. "You rocked that, girl. The way you stroke those strings gives me *chills*. And the look between you and Teo at the end…you played that for him, huh?"

I smiled as I uncapped my water. Had I played for Teo? I shrugged. I'd performed well. That's what mattered.

"Your case is right here," Brenna said. "Wendy brought it over along with your coat."

I took both, stowing my viola at my feet and my coat in my lap.

The players took the field, and the match started. The Timber wore their home whites while the Grizzlies were in a strange combination of gold and swirling green.

Teo played forward, typically in the striker position. The Timber quickly gained possession of the ball, and he moved down the field with easy, loping grace. His footwork was better choreographed than any dance, but his head swept the field, looking for defenders and his teammates.

Teo made a quick pass to the left, and the ball sped just behind the feet of the defender, right to his teammate's cleat. My mouth popped open at the accuracy of the pass. While I'd been watching the ball, Teo darted around his opponent and took up position closer to the goal. No wonder Teo wanted to play for the premier European league. Those were probably the only players in the world who could keep up with him.

With a quick flick of his hand, Teo caught his teammate's attention, and the player kicked the ball toward him. Unfortunately, the kick wasn't as precise as Teo's, and a Grizzlies' defender intercepted the pass with ease. They began to work the ball down the field, toward the Timber's goalie.

Teo's face showed flushed resignation as he picked up his opponent and worked his way back down the pitch. Another few minutes passed with the Grizzlies getting closer to the Timber's goal, causing the goalie to step forward and intercept a lazy pass within his circle. As he punted the ball, I already knew Teo was in position to receive the pass.

I leaned forward, fascinated by his game acumen. He knew where all the players were on the field and he knew their weaknesses, preferences, dominating his opponents. I wondered if he'd be this attentive, this focused in the bedroom.

Brenna nudged me. "I need to go to the bathroom."

"So, go."

"Buddy system."

I sighed, standing. I pushed through the crowd and headed toward the steps. The collective breath I heard in the audience made me to spin back toward the field. Teo dribbled the ball, maneuvering between two defenders before he kicked off the side of his left cleat. The ball sailed over the goalie's outstretched hands and into the back of the net. I ran down to the railing, screaming with the rest of the fans. Teo turned to look toward my seat, frowning when his gaze hit my empty chair. His eyes scanned the crowd, disappointment pulling down his triumphant grin. I waved like mad, and his eyes met mine, just as his teammates jumped on him. I smiled and clapped, and his face lit up in a bedazzling grin before he disappeared under sweaty male bodies.

Brenna stood at the top of the stairs, arms crossed.

"What? I wanted to see the goal."

The rest of the game passed in a blur of almost-shots, though Teo got the closest with two more shots on goal. His hamstring didn't seem to bother him, and I hoped his problem was simply lingering stiffness. With his talent and ability to read the game, Teo outshone the rest of the American players, who, surprisingly, didn't let their own egos get in the way of improving their chances of winning.

Yeah, Matteo Cruz was a soccer force, and watching him lit the joyful fire of teamwork and desire to win deep in my belly. I placed a hand there, wishing I could run out on the field and play for ten, twenty minutes with any of the players.

Somehow, in six short years, I forgot how few and far between scores could be in soccer. Not that it mattered. I enjoyed watching the footwork and the explosiveness of some of the players. I stood, feeling exhilarated. Noah had been right—closing myself off from the sport hadn't reduced the pain of losing my chance at competing nationally; instead, I tried to amputate a vital part of myself.

As we were putting on our coats, an usher came to our row. "Ms. Jennings?"

"Yes?"

"Your brother is dealing with the media and said to tell you he's sorry he can't come out, but Mr. Cruz asked if you'd come down to the meet-and-greet. I'll show you to the waiting area."

"Um, okay. Sure." I fumbled my purse, then turned to Brenna. "Want to come with me?"

Brenna's eyes drifted to the field, the usher, then back to mine. "No, thanks."

I collected my viola. "If you're sure…" At her nod, I said, "See you later, Bren."

She kissed my cheek. "Be careful," she whispered in my ear. "He hurt you last time."

"Of course."

"He's an athlete so you know he's all about sex." She raised her brows high. "With someone."

I glared back, letting her know my position on that dig. "I'm ready," I told the usher.

The usher jerked his head, glaring at Brenna. My cheeks bloomed with color. He must have heard her comment.

"He's not like that," the boy said. His tag read Stephen.

"Who isn't like what?" I asked.

"Teo. He's not like that—using women. The media's making stuff up about him, I know it." Stephen's face suffused with color even brighter than mine.

"Um, okay." Our feet clopped along the concrete. "Do you play soccer, Stephen?"

He nodded, relieved by the change of subject. "Midfield. I've got a few schools looking at me, thanks to the Timber training camps."

"I helped with a couple. I played through most of college until I was injured."

"Really? What position?"

"Midfield. Like you."

"I've learned a lot from the camps, too. When Teo or Jorge set up the drills and stuff, we all learn tons. They're the best."

"Is Teo better as a player or a coach?"

"He's great at both." Stephen pushed open the door, holding it open for me. "You saw him out there. He's phenomenal. We're hoping he'll stick around and join the coaching staff here."

Noah had told me that part of the reason the front office picked up Jorge Valencia was because he was Teo's first coach, and the GM hoped Teo would want to stay because of him.

"Here you go."

"Thanks. Just wait here?"

"Yeah, this is the most private area. Only the players and some staff are allowed down here. Teo will be out soon." Stephen fidgeted for a moment. "Can I get your autograph?" he asked in a rush, the words tumbling over each other.

I blinked at him. "Sure."

"You play really well. I love that song you did with Asher Smith."

"Thanks. I just helped Asher with the melody—I didn't know he planned to put that on his album. Do you have something for me to sign?"

The kid glanced around, consternation dragging down his brow. He pulled out a crumpled piece of paper from his back pocket as I dug through my tote for a pen.

A group of players walked past us, and I flushed under their gaze. Why did being here make me feel so exposed?

"Do you know when Teo will come out?"

"The trainer needed to work on his hamstring, but he shouldn't be too long."

I signed Stephen's ticket and handed it back to him.

"Awesome! You're the first famous person I've met. Besides the soccer team, I mean. And you know Asher Smith."

"He's my brother-in-law."

Stephen's eyes grew wider. "Holy crap!" The boy's voice cracked, sliding too high in his excitement. "He's part of your family?"

"She doesn't play for just anyone, Stephen." Teo stepped close enough for me to smell the sandalwood from his body wash. His dark hair glistened, black from his shower. "She's never performed for me."

"I did today." I tilted my face up toward his. Brenna'd been right. I played for Teo, not the rest of the crowd.

The dimple appeared in his cheek as his teeth flashed, white and perfect. "So you did. And I enjoyed hearing you make that viola sing so sweetly." He narrowed his eyes at me. "I scored a goal for you."

"That was exciting. I almost missed it, though."

"Glad you didn't. Let's go." He tugged my viola from my hand and placed his other palm against the small of my back.

"Where?"

"Dinner?"

I sucked on my lip. "Is that what you want?"

"Besides you?" His voice, with that sultry Argentinian lilt I found so difficult to dismiss from my mind, addled my brain.

I scoffed. "You don't want me."

"Oh, I want you. Enough to suffer the consequences."

"What consequences?" Confusion and frustration welled up in my chest.

He stepped in, even closer, crowding my space. "Being with you is complicated."

I hiked my purse up my shoulder, smoothing down Teo's jersey. "You don't give clear answers. Okay, here's the deal. You and I almost hooked up. I unhooked when you turned me down and now you feel like you missed out on easy sex. Though I can't understand how you'd feel bad about it seeing as your living with that pretty redhead." I slammed my lips together to keep my chin from wobbling.

His light brown eyes were filled with sorrow. "I don't think you're easy. And what we're starting—it wouldn't be just sex. And I'm not—never was—sleeping with Mariana."

"She's *living* in your condo." I stepped back again, bumping into the cold, hard cement wall. I needed emotional space and that proved harder to get than physical distance.

"She's a friend, more importantly, a sports therapist, who happened to be staying with me, but she's gone home now." He ran his hands through his hair, creating mussed waves. Of course his hair was sexy when he was agitated. Everything about the man was sexy. So sexy it hurt.

Great. Now *that* song would play in my head for days.

"You're planning to go to Milan. Noah told me. You're leaving." *Me.* I didn't say that because there was no us, and I had no right to voice my frustration. I breathed in deep as I closed my eyes, trying to find an equilibrium that'd been lacking since my ridiculous attempt at romance last weekend. Talk about lessons learned. The third time proved the smack down I needed.

A bunch of cats and giving up on men, forever—a bleak future but at least my heart would never break again.

Brenna said I'd eventually realize men weren't worth the effort. She did casual one-night flings—keeping her partners out of her personal life and away from people she cared about. Maybe her idea about relationships was smarter than mine. Scratch the itch and move on.

I opened my eyes when Teo's fingers slid around my elbows, cupping them as he pulled me closer to his body. I struggled against him but mainly against my need. I wanted his touch; my body begged for it even as my mind rebelled. His facial expression grew pensive, his eyes too world-weary for a man his age.

"Maybe. Maybe not. What I do know is I'd like to get to know you better."

My heart hammered so loud, people must've been able to hear the steady thrum across town. I covered his mouth with my hand. "Don't say that."

He pressed a kiss to my palm as he stepped in closer. "Tell you the truth?"

"I googled you."

"I'd be disappointed if you hadn't. I did the same. After my conversation with Noah."

"You talked to Noah?"

"He worried about you after those pictures of us came out."

"He doesn't get to talk to my boyfriends," I said, offended. Teo slid in, placing his hand above my head.

"Boyfriend?"

My body quivered at Teo's nearness. Damn, my crush ratcheted up another notch as I stared into his dark-lashed eyes. "That's not what I meant. You don't want me."

"Really? Is that what my body's telling you right now?"

He pressed even closer, and I sucked in a shattered breath. "You said you didn't want to have sex with me."

He bit the tip of my ear, and I bit back a moan. "No. I never said that. I said I wouldn't have sex with you when you were drunk. And for the record, that dress was the sexiest damn thing I've ever seen."

He shifted so I was sandwiched between the warmth of his body and the unforgiving coldness of the concrete at my back.

Shock slithered through me because I remained relaxed, comfortable with the position and Teo's nearness. In fact, I craved more.

"Turning you away was next to impossible," he murmured into my hair. "I've craved your lips for weeks. I've loved your fierce quietness since you first met my eye. You have no idea how happy I am that you felt the same spark."

The smell of his body wash trickled from my nose into my head, circling my heart and warming my belly. He tipped my chin up, his lips brushing to the corner of my mouth. I trembled in his arms, willing him to do that again. Or to kiss me like he had before. To own me so I couldn't think—just give in. Instead, he ran his thumbs over my cheekbones with delicate strokes.

"I've done and been many things, Preslee. But I've never pined before." He paused, sucking his lower lip into his mouth. "When you walked out of my condo, that was so much worse than your punch to my gut. Which hurt, by the way. I didn't like it—the pining."

My eyes slid closed as I let his words drift over my skin, settle against me like a warm hug. Better than I expected.

He must have sensed my softening because his hands were on my arms again, sliding up and pulling me in closer. He leaned down so that his lips touched the sensitive outer shell of my ear.

"I need to know…you have to tell me…you came to the bar for me?"

My heart stumbled in its rhythm. An admission wasn't just leaving me open for hurt, it would rip me to shreds when this ended. And with his steely focus on the game, this could only end poorly. But still… I couldn't lie to him.

I met his eyes, kept my gaze firm. "I wouldn't have gone home with anyone else."

He nodded once as he leaned in, brushing his nose along my cheek. I shivered at his smell, his warmth, his touch.

"You want to see where we go, too. We can. We can do that, starting now." His fingers dug into the soft skin just above my elbow. I liked that he wanted me so much.

"What do you mean?" My voice wavered as much as my integrity. I didn't understand how he did this to me. I should push him away. Instead, my hands fisted in his shirt. I opened them slowly, intent to make the smart, if painful, decision. Teo lifted a hand and pressed it against mine. He leaned back down, nuzzling into my hair. His chest muscles relaxed.

I blinked, my world righting itself.

"I can't keep a level head where you're concerned."

"I don't understand what you're saying."

"I like you. I want to know you better. The world believes we're dating already, and I'd like the world to be right." His hands slid down my back, soothing and arousing all at once.

"For how long?" I whispered, voicing my biggest fear.

CHAPTER ELEVEN
Teo

I cupped her cheek, making sure her eyes met mine. "I don't know. I just…" I exhaled, shocked by how fast my heart beat. Telling my father about my desire to date Preslee proved hard, but this…having to convince her was more difficult than threading my way between three defenders.

I sucked in a breath. "Let's just see where this goes." I'd already weighed my hamstring, my possible trade, which was why I spoke with confidence when I said, "I promise you, you'll be the one to end this."

Preslee needed control—I understood why—and she deserved it. But if I ended up leaving, she wouldn't want the hassle of a long-distance relationship. In the meantime, I'd get to be the one to reintroduce Preslee to intimacy, something I very much wanted.

Her breath puffed out, and I waited, wanting nothing more than to touch her. Preslee's eyes darkened to a lovely emerald. She nodded and I slid my hand to the small of her delicate back, nudging her forward again.

"Now, will you go to dinner with me?"

Her eyes remained wide and a smile lurked at the corner of those pretty pink lips. "I'd like that."

Her voice softened with each word she spoke. I liked *that*.

Preslee nibbled more than ate. I rarely ate after a game—my normal routine entailed a light snack before bed then a huge, three-course breakfast next morning.

She sipped her wine and kept darting looks at me like she expected me to disappear. I curled my arm around her waist in a possessive gesture as we walked toward my car. Her free hand was stuffed into the pocket of her coat, her nose and ears pink from the thickening chill.

I took her viola case and purse, my fingers lingering on her shoulder.

"I'd like you to come home with me," I said. Well, I'd like to finish what we'd started at the bar, but saying so right now felt wrong.

Her eyes darted back to mine, lips parting in surprise. A frown followed, pulling her angel-wing brows down.

"I don't understand what's changed. Why this new seduction?"

"Nothing changed."

I sighed. Everything had changed. As soon as I told Noah about my hamstring, I knew my chances of wearing the jersey of my dreams shrank to near nil. But, also, that day Noah and I spoke in his office, I realized I wanted to date Preslee. No matter how much I denied the attraction, I couldn't shake my need to see her, touch her, again—a feeling I'd never experienced before. Because soccer always—*always*—took precedence in my life. It was my escape from my mother and it bloomed into my passion. Some said an obsession. Before, I brushed aside such comments as silly, but...since talking to Noah, my father, even my agent, all of whom showed surprise at how well I was taking my potential injury, I came to realize I did obsess about the sport.

"Except I've lost days I could've spent with you."

She glanced at her bag on my shoulder, at her viola in my hands. I trapped her by taking her things, but this wasn't the way I wanted her. I wanted her warm and willing, like last weekend.

"What about Milan?" she asked.

I shrugged. "My agent's working on it." And earning every penny I paid him. Somehow, he'd revived the trade discussion and the front office wanted to schedule time to talk with me. Satisfaction warmed me as I considered my chances. "Which means each day is more precious."

"I don't think this is smart." She spoke slowly, weighing out each word.

"Us, in a relationship, has always been a terrible idea. Then, I saw you in that dress last weekend." The lack of control over my desire for her irritated me. "Each time we meet, I want you more."

"I read about you—how you refuse to get involved with a woman for more than a few weeks during the season. Because that 'splits your focus.'" She folded her arms over her chest and glared.

I leaned in so that my nose almost touched hers. "That's because I never met a woman I wanted for more than a few weeks. More than I wanted another W in my column." Truer words I'd yet to speak. "Between us, we're exclusive."

"I won't be the other woman again." She slapped her hand over her mouth, her eyes wide as they darted around.

"You had an affair with a married man?"

"No," she whispered. "But with Oren...after the first time he hit me, he made it seem like I was clingy. Like I'd fastened on to him when he'd wanted to be free to see another woman, who corroborated that story." She twisted the edge of her coat, her agitation increasing. "It felt...I felt dirty."

She closed her eyes and tilted her head back. Her fingers fluttered to her other arm before dropping to her sides where she clenched them into fists.

No wonder Preslee didn't trust men. I gripped her cold hand in mine. Her bones were small, delicate. But not fragile. No, her calluses and the tendons there proved Preslee's diligence to her instrument. To survival.

"I won't push you to go for more than you're comfortable with. I can't tell you I won't get an offer to play elsewhere that would be better for my career, but I can promise that while we're together, we're exclusive."

Her eyes searched mine for a long moment, trying to delve deeper than I wanted her to go. "Why would you make me a promise like that?"

"I don't ever want you to compare me to that little piece of slime. I'm not Oren. I won't cheat, I won't hit you, and I won't leave you alone. At least, not for more than my travel schedule."

"Okay." She drew out the word. "You travel a lot."

"I do."

"Is that why you don't date? Because there really isn't enough time?"

I shrugged. "If you'll come up to my place, we can talk further." I opened the door to my car and waited.

Preslee settled her hand on the top of the car door and began to lower herself in. Before she did, she raised her gaze to mine once more.

"I still don't understand. Why did you push me away the other night, and suddenly want me now?"

CHAPTER TWELVE
Preslee

He glanced around, eyes narrowing at a spot behind me. "Please get in the car."

My first instinct was to scoot closer to him, my body responding to the tautness of his voice.

"Okay," I whispered.

I slid into the car's seat and he closed the door. Teo glanced over his shoulder as he trotted around the front of his silver sedan. Whatever was back there caused his muscles to coil, his steps to lengthen.

He drove with care, his gaze split between the road in front of him and the rearview mirror. Once we were in the parking garage, he sighed, a heavy sound filled with tension.

"I need to go to the lobby."

I frowned but nodded and kept up with his quick pace to the entrance of the condo. He headed straight toward to the security guard.

"There is a man out there. All in black. He followed us for a few blocks."

"Did you get a description, Mr. Cruz?" the guard asked.

Teo shook his head. "Too dark. But I'm sure he followed us, and I'm concerned about Ms. Jennings' safety."

I jerked, my gaze flying up to Teo's. He was equal parts worried and pissed. I pressed closer to his side, needing his physical reassurance.

The guard picked up the phone, already dialing. "We'll deal with this, Mr. Cruz."

Teo nodded and ushered me to the bank of elevators. "Up we go."

The emotions of the night caught up with me and I trembled, not just from the fear of being followed—and completely unaware of that danger—but the insidious voice whispering that Teo was playing me for a fool. This change in him was too sudden, too intense for me to trust it. More importantly, him.

"Maybe I should just go home."

Teo clasped my hand that picked at my elbow through Brenna's shirt. He lifted my hand and kissed my knuckles. "Hey now. None of that."

"I didn't know I was being followed."

Teo frowned. "I didn't either until he moved forward into the streetlamp's light."

"Do you think it was a fan?" I ask, searching for some thin string to hold on to.

Teo turned toward me, setting my viola on the ground. He placed both hands on my shoulders and met my gaze. "We may never know. But I do believe our security will look into it. Let us not worry more now."

He scooted closer until his hip touched mine. When I met his gaze, he dropped my hand and brushed my bangs from my lashes. He leaned down until his mouth rested just above mine. Cupping my cheek, he moved closer but once again paused. Our eyes locked, and I barely resisted the urge to press into him.

The elevator dinged and the doors opened.

"Riding in elevators is more fun with you." Teo tugged on my arm and pulled me from the car. "Let's talk. I know you have questions."

I licked my bottom lip, wanting to feel more than a brief brush of his lips against mine. Anymore and I might burn up.

Opening his door, Teo led me to his living room. The experience was surreal. Last time, I entered this place in clothes that revealed more than they concealed, hoping to finally *feel* again. Which I did, in the form of shame when Mariana showed up. This time, I wore black dress pants and a soccer jersey and wondered if I'd walk out of Teo's condo with my pride and heart still intact.

I settled into the corner of his sleek, modern sofa. It was beige, leather, tailored and much more comfortable than I remembered. I snagged a throw pillow and plopped it in my lap, facing Teo who still stood above me.

He tugged at his lip, his eyes dark with an emotion I couldn't name.

"What did you want to tell me?"

"May I get you a drink?"

I shook my head. He sighed and sank onto the couch next to me.

"My father seduced Lucia Arandas, the impossibly beautiful girl from the *villa miseria*. That's one of the slums near Buenos Aires."

"Oh-kay." I drew out the word. I clearly missed something because I didn't see the dots from his dad's affair to marrying a woman he didn't love.

"This gets us to the reason I turned you down last weekend. I don't date."

Teo pressed his lips together. "Lucia could not conceive again. As their only child, there have been expectations. High expectations from my mother. I quit trying to meet them around age

107

six when my father stayed home more. We spent time together, though my mother tried to get me to do activities with her instead. I remember a fight I overheard." He sighed, leaning his head back against the sofa. "She said my father bought my love, just as he bought the love of his female companions. That I would prefer to be with her."

I touched his hand, needing to offer some comfort to the child's feelings still buried within this beautiful man. "I ran into the room, threw myself on my father, begging him not to leave me."

"That didn't go over well," I said.

Teo shook his head. "My mother's face turned chalk white. She said if I didn't want her, she'd leave. She did. I don't know where she went for the next few months, but my father finally dragged her home, and she was a mess." He met my gaze. "She'd become an alcoholic."

I wrapped my fingers more tightly around his warm hand. He turned it over so our palms meshed.

"Living with the disease is difficult. She's been in and out of rehab programs for years, but she can't stay sober. My father blames himself."

"Why?"

"Same reason I do. My mother is difficult to be around, always needing everyone to prove their love. She's told me many times she hates me. That I ruined her life. That's when I turned to soccer. It was an outlet for all the terrible emotions in our house."

"So, he stayed with your mother? Er, Lucia?"

"Unhappily, and not so much for the business as for me—at least when I was young. He worked to build up other businesses, but the soccer club's been his passion, his place to help so many

108

young men like him."

"And your mother is okay with the fact he cheated on her?"

"No, she's never been happy about that." Teo's cheek bones stood out in stark relief. "That's why she drinks."

Teo dropped his head deep between his shoulders, his fingers lacing at the back of his neck. He lifted his head to met my gaze. "I may not agree with my father's decisions—I don't, in fact. But I hate being the reason my parents are unhappy."

"How are you responsible for their unhappiness?"

"I'm not. She's responsible for mine. When I started my career, I met a girl after a match. Vivi. She was from a poor neighborhood." He looked around, searching for something to steady him. "My mother found out and told me she'd tell all the papers about my girlfriend's 'trash family.' If I quit seeing her, my mom guaranteed she'd move them into a better house, pay her tuition. I cared about Vivi—not enough to marry her, then, which I considered briefly—but I didn't want her hurt because of me. So, I agreed. I also accepted an offer to go to Real Madrid."

"What happened to Vivi?"

Teo smiled, fondness lighting his face. "She finished medical school and works in some of the roughest neighborhoods in Buenos Aires, helping women like her mother."

"Do you talk to her? Still?"

Confusion and even some jealousy filled me at the thought of Teo talking to his former lover. I didn't have experience with such a situation.

"Sometimes. Her younger sister, Mariana—the red head—was my sports therapist."

I digested this newest bit of information. "Why her?"

Teo shrugged. "She's someone I can trust." He leaned in so that his lips whispered across mine once. Just once. "Enough talk for now, yes? I want to kiss you again, Preslee."

I met his gaze, enjoying the smoldering passion building there. "Yes, please."

His mouth returned to settle over mine, his lips gliding back and forth in gentle swipes until he settled me against his chest and deepened the kiss. His lips sought my passion, but he also sought forgiveness. He raised his head, his hands wandering down my back.

"I plan to enjoy each moment of this time with you."

Brenna sat at the breakfast bar when I entered our condo an hour later. Her eyes darkened and her scowl turned to a hurt expression. "Really? Do you care—at all—that I've been worried about you?"

Brenna cut me earlier with her comments about Teo wanting me for easy sex, so I ignored her texts. But Brenna looked so anxious now, I hugged her.

"I'm sorry, Bren. I should've been more thoughtful of your feelings. I'm fine. I'm home, all in one piece and it's barely eleven." I frowned, considering the man Teo saw trailing us.

"What's wrong?"

I shrugged, unwilling to fall into that pit of unrelenting fear as I had for years. In some ways, I still did. I refused to pursue singing because I feared Oren's retaliation. I declined all attention after he gave that exposé about my partying and loose, immoral living.

"Does this have something to do with Oren?"

I sighed, wishing Brenna didn't know me so well. I plugged my phone into the charger on the counter, needing something—anything—to do with the built up restlessness.

"Teo saw someone." I swallowed. "Following us. And I played solo tonight."

Brenna laid her hand over mine. "Which Oren warned you about."

I nodded. "And Teo's famous."

Matteo Cruz's entire persona, indeed his livelihood, depended on public perception. I wore his jersey while I performed and people took his picture or asked for his autograph at the restaurant. Another something to consider. Speculation about our relationship status skyrocketed immediately after last weekend's bar debacle.

Why hadn't I thought any of this through?

"Is he worth it?" Brenna's voice was quiet. "The fear you're feeling now—the second-guessing—I don't get it, Pres. Why now? Why *him*?"

I sucked my lip, worry warring with my desire. Teo made me feel safe even as he brought my body to levels of passion I never felt before—all from the touch of our lips. Yeah, I wanted to explore that more. Even if…I swallowed hard…even though he was an athlete. An internationally famous one.

More than likely, Oren had moved on, forgetting his vendetta against me. My fear was simply based on past experiences.

"I like him."

She stood abruptly and practically threw her teacup into the sink.

"Will this go anywhere? I read he might get traded to Milan. While worrying about you since you didn't even answer my texts."

I set my purse down in the bar chair.

"He took me to dinner. We talked. That's a distinct possibility." I bit my lip, hating how jumbled my feelings were. I wanted Teo—no doubts there—but the idea of him leaving hurt. And if the pain was this intense now, how could it not be worse if I spent more time with him?

"So, he's taking up with you now but will dump you as soon as he gets the call? Are you a consolation prize?"

"*Excuse* me?"

Brenna was on a roll and ignored my tone and my indignation. "You're behaving just like your mom did, Pres. You're letting your desires blind you to all the reasons this situation is *wrong*."

Of all the things Brenna could have said to me, she chose the most hurtful. I swallowed hard to keep the bile from spewing up my throat yet again. Love didn't mean a free pass. Actions still inspired consequences. Like my mom leaving her two daughters to start a new life with my father. Leaving those little girls alone for weeks because she feared their anger over the way she'd left.

Mom had been right to worry. Lia, my oldest half sister, still hadn't forgiven our mother. Not that I could blame either Lia or Briar. They'd almost starved waiting for my mother to collect them.

All the while, my brothers and I had lived, full-bellied and well-loved in a nice Seattle neighborhood.

Brenna hammered the point home when she flung her final salvo over her shoulder.

"What happens when Oren sees the papers? You *know* he'll lose his shit."

She slammed her bedroom door as I sank to the couch, forced to sit on my trembling hands.

CHAPTER THIRTEEN
Teo

"I didn't have a choice," I bit out, irritation fueling my tone.

"There's always a choice, Matteo." Roberto, my agent, sighed long and loud, to make a point about his irritation with me.

"Not once Mariana said she planned to call Coach and speak with him."

"That's what seduction is for."

I curled my lip. "Mariana is like a sister to me."

"And that's why I'm scrambling to pick up the pieces. Because you didn't have the balls to keep your therapist quiet."

My phone pinged, and I glanced at the screen.

I'm not sure dating is a good idea.

Disappointment crashed through me when I read the text. Brenna's beady-eyed glares came to mind. As soon as Preslee left, her friend must have pounced, adding to the doubt I'd sowed by turning her away last weekend. Not that I could blame Preslee for her doubts. *Mierda*, I collected them, too. Which was why I'd tried—and failed—to stay away from her.

"I have to go," I said.

"I'm not finished going over your choices," Roberto barked back.

"So far my choice is taking less money to go to Milan."

"Because that may be the best we can hope for at this point."

"Then make that best happen."

Roberto made a disgruntled sound, but I'd already pressed End. I read Preslee's message again, my heart sinking.

She was the one bright spot in being forced to play in the US.

I didn't want to lose her, too.

I called her back.

"Can we talk about this?" I said after her tentative hello.

"I knew I couldn't resist you if I heard your voice. That's why I texted."

Even those quiet words made my blood burn. The more time I spent with Preslee, the harder I found it to shake loose of her spell.

"I don't want to pressure you, Preslee." I sighed. "Actually, yeah. I do. Letting you leave earlier proved difficult." I clenched my free fist so I wouldn't press my hand against my straining zipper.

"Brenna thinks you're playing me." She hesitated, perhaps debating what to say. "Using me for some deeper purpose."

"Is that what you think?"

She remained quiet for a long moment. Maybe she wouldn't answer. Maybe I wouldn't like the answer she gave.

"I think, after tonight, I'd always regret not giving us a chance."

I leaned back on my couch, trying to get comfortable. "What are you doing tomorrow night?"

"I finish rehearsals at four."

"I want to take you out."

"On a date?"

"I don't date, haven't you heard?"

"Then what are we doing?" Her panic blasted through the phone's speaker.

My lips flipped up into a grin that must be too predatory to be legal. Oh, I liked Preslee flustered. "More than dating."

"I don't know what that means." Her voice took on a breathless quality that made me shift, trying to ease the ache in my groin.

"Right now, it means I'm taking you out on a date tomorrow.

And then I want to bring you back to my place. For more than a long, difficult talk and a few kisses, no matter how mind-blowing. You left too soon. I want you, Preslee. All of you. Tomorrow."

My smile broadened at the little whimper that slid through the phone. Perfect. She thought about me, just as I fixated on her. I clamped down hard on my teeth, refusing to ask her to come back up to my place. My months of celibacy were catching up with me. Fast.

She hesitated, and I wondered if she wanted to say more. When the silence drew out, I said, "It's getting late. Practice starts early. But I'm going to sleep better knowing I'll spend hours with you tomorrow."

"I'm looking forward to it."

"Dream sweet, *dulzura*."

"What does that mean?"

I smiled. "I'll tell you tomorrow."

"Fine." She sighed. "I'll see you tomorrow night. For our date."

"Our second date," I said. "And that you will."

I clicked off the phone and pressed the edge of the case to my lips, eyes narrowed in thought. Nodding at the strategy, I stood, stretched, and sauntered toward my bedroom, happier than I'd been in months.

———◆———

I poked my head into Noah's office. "I'm taking your sister to dinner tonight."

He held up a finger then waved me in, showing me the phone pressed to his ear.

"Of course," he said. "That's an interesting offer. We'll look it over once you send the details. No, without it in writing, I'm not sure there's anything I can do. You do that. Thanks."

He hung up and turned toward me, running his hands through his already disheveled brown hair.

"So...Preslee, dinner. Thanks for the heads-up."

"You okay?"

Noah tipped his head back and rubbed his eyes. "Didn't get much sleep, what with putting out the fire on the symphony players hurt en route here." He leaned forward, his eyes darting to the open door. "Can I tell you something in confidence?"

I shrugged.

"That was Joel Concha. He's making a play for our head coach."

I sucked the breath through my teeth. Bad news for the Timber organization. Joel ran the front office for one of the biggest teams in Europe—the one I used to play for.

"Think he'll go?"

"He'd be an idiot not to. And Coach isn't an idiot."

I swallowed down the bitterness of my current situation. If only I hadn't been injured, I'd be there, helping Joel make the decision about the best coach to take over the offensive coordinator position.

"What are you going to do?"

Noah leaned back in his chair. "Not really my problem. The GM and owner make that call. I got this initial one to feel out the organization—what we'd need in exchange."

Joel Concha always could sniff out talent. My initial surprise at him contacting the Timber dissipated. "A better full-pitch strategist will be difficult to find."

Noah leaned back in his chair. "Your name came up. I'd be willing to put in a word for you if you're interested."

My eyes flew up to his. He raised his brows.

"You know, if you wanted to make Seattle your home base for a while. Settle down a bit."

"Noah, I asked your sister to dinner, not to marry me," I croaked. The vise of public opinion closed in around me.

"During the season. When you never date."

"The season's gotten longer. Doesn't leave much down time."

His gaze shifted from calculating to eagle-eyed. "You said you cared about Pres. Right?"

"Obviously."

"Then just think about the possibility." Noah clasped his hands, and leaned in again. "Not many players get to go from player to head. You could do it—the team would be thrilled with the transition. And Jorge's still got three more years on his contract with us. The pay's multi-million. It's an excellent opportunity."

"But I couldn't play."

"Professionally? No. But you favored your left leg yesterday during the game. That hamstring isn't a hundred percent—you told me that yourself, and our trainer agrees. I'm just throwing out an option that could be mutually beneficial." He narrowed his eyes. "Unless you hurt my sister. Then I'm going to rip your leg off and beat you with it. End of career."

We stared at each other, his gaze full of promises. This is what I got for helping a beautiful woman home from a bar.

"Hey. Got a minute, Noah?" Pete, the offensive coach, asked. "Oops. Didn't know you were in here, Teo. I'll come back."

"No." I stood, my face stoic. I didn't wince or favor my left side—I couldn't give Noah anymore ammunition. "We're done here."

"Seems like I stepped in something. I can come back."

Noah smiled at Pete and motioned him in. "Teo wants to date my sister."

"She's hot. If I weren't married, I'd be interested in her." Pete grinned only to raise his hands and step back when we both turned to scowl at him. "Sorry. Jesus. You two are touchy. Preslee's a babe. And she has one of the best bicycle kicks I've ever seen."

"That she does," Noah said. "She taught my brother and me, but we could never match her. She's great with the long pass, too."

"I bet. I had no idea she played the violin, too," Pete said.

"Viola," I said.

Noah laughed. "Already got you trained, I see. Have you heard her sing yet?" he asked.

I shook my head.

"Maybe it's best she doesn't. All my friends were in love with her voice. Pissed me and Nate off no end."

I walked to the door, needing some space from Preslee's *loco* brother.

"Enjoy your time tonight," he called, still laughing.

It took all my self-control not to flip him off.

I straightened my tie. I hated wearing anything around my neck—perhaps my dislike of decent clothing came from spending so much of my life in soccer shorts and a tee. But I needed to do this date right. Not only did Preslee deserve a spectacular night out, I needed to own the media's reaction to us. Nothing wrong with setting the tone I wanted them to pick up on. I was going on offense early to counteract my mother's inevitable vitriol.

I cracked my knuckles then knocked. Brenna opened the door. She looked me up and down slowly before she sighed, opening the door farther.

"Your date's here, Pres."

"Hello, Brenna. How was your day?"

She shrugged before slouching back to the couch. "You know, the life of a partially employed software engineer."

I frowned. "There are many jobs for such positions here in Seattle."

She glared at me. "Which is why there are a bajillion coders in the city."

Once again, I managed to say the wrong thing to this woman. *Mierda.* I was off my game.

"Do you have plans for the night?"

"No," she grunted, staring at the TV.

"Hi, Teo," Preslee said from behind me. I turned to face her and my breath caught. She wore a light purple halter top outfit like the iconic white dress Marilyn Monroe wore. When she walked toward me, the skirt split to show the bottom was wide-legged pants. She paired it with some simple gold hoops and a necklace with a large purple flower that hit right above her cleavage. I managed to clear my throat.

"You look lovely." I raised her hand to my lips. At the last second, I turned her hand palm up and kissed her there, letting my tongue flick out and touch her pulse point just below her thumb.

119

She inhaled sharply, her eyes darkening.

"I brought you these." I held out the green lilies I'd been holding by my side. "They reminded me of your eyes."

She smiled. "Thank you. They're lovely. I'll just put them in water."

Brenna's eyes were heavy on my face as Preslee sashayed into the kitchen. Once she was out of sight, I dropped my gaze to Brenna's, catching the hurt in the twist of her lips.

"Why don't you order out—my treat. Noah mentioned you're a fan of Lo Mein."

Brenna pressed her lips together in a tight line and shook her head. I shrugged and stepped back, giving her the space she wanted.

"Good seeing you." I pulled my hands from my pockets and placed one at the base of Preslee's spine, just above the luscious curve of her *culo* as she joined me by the door.

"Yeah," Brenna said. "You, too."

She turned back to the television, not bothering to tell Preslee goodbye. I waited until we were in the elevator before I broached the subject. "Your roommate doesn't like me."

Preslee's angel brows pulled low before she smiled. "She doesn't like anyone I date. It all came to a head with Oren, obviously."

She played with the latch on her small silver purse. "Doesn't that bother you?"

"A lot. She's always been jealous of my time and where I spend it," Preslee continued, echoing her brother's words. "But I can't live my life for Brenna."

She looked at me from under her lashes as she moved farther back into the corner. She leaned back against the rail, causing her chest to thrust out enticingly.

"I'm glad you invited me to dinner."

"I'm glad you accepted. I like the idea of wining and dining you."

"Why's that?" she asked as the elevator dinged. I held out my arm, placing it at the small of her back as we stepped from the elevator. I loved the feel of her hips swaying in her high-heeled sandals.

"Because I like spending time with you."

"You could've bought me pizza to share in your condo."

"Ah, but then I couldn't show you off. And everyone deserves to see my beautiful, talented date. All the men tonight wishing they were me."

She regained her equilibrium and her lips quirked up. "I think the ladies are all going to want to gouge my eyes out with their utensils when they see you in that suit." She brushed her fingertip down my lapel. "I never understood the term suit porn before. But on you... Hmmm, I like."

I leaned in, inhaling her soft fragrance. "As much as I love this outfit on you. I've been trying to decide if you're wearing a bra since you stepped out of your room."

"You'll have to wait to find out until you take me back to your place after dinner."

I groaned. "That pizza is starting to sound like a better option."

The look she gave over her shoulder could only be classified as a smolder. "But then you wouldn't get to show me off."

CHAPTER FOURTEEN
Preslee

He drove to Altura. I laughed as he helped me from the car. "You remembered all this time?"

He brushed my bangs off my forehead. "Your brother reminded me it's your favorite. Let's go feed you some pasta."

I bit my tongue, unsure how to take his remark. So, he didn't remember me mentioning this place or was he being sweet to ask Noah? Either way, my mouth already watered. Pasta was my weakness.

Discreet—and not so discreet—cameras focused on us as we were seated at a table in the corner of the restaurant. I tensed, wanting nothing more than to fade back into the background. With a deep breath, I focused my attention on my gorgeous dinner companion. The waiter came up and asked if we'd like to hear the small-bite plates and drink specials.

"I'd prefer the wine pairing, please."

Teo nodded. "Same. Thanks."

"Would you like to place your order now or should I bring you the first glass of wine.

"I know what I want," I said, clutching the menu to my chest.

Teo winked. "Pasta?"

I smiled as I nodded. We placed orders for our meal before our drink order, then settled back in our chairs.

I tried to ignore a camera's flash.

"I'm sorry about them," Teo said, leaning in.

"It's fine. You're hot stuff." I winked.

But he refused to let me keep it light. "I know they make

you nervous."

I kept my gaze down in my lap. "Not them. I don't mind having my picture taken."

"You're worried Oren will see and react?"

I smoothed my napkin as I settled deeper into the leather chair, debating what to say. Noah must have given Teo the rundown on Oren's threats.

The waiter brought our wine and I smiled my thanks as he set it down.

"First, I need to say that I want to be with you. I've thought through what that means, and I understand I've once again put myself out into the media spotlight."

"Noah said you haven't sang in public or played soccer—anything that could gain you media attention—in six years."

"Because Oren didn't like when other men looked at me. He told me my clothes attracted the wrong attention or performing made men think I wanted sex."

I knew what that was—emotional abuse. I spent the better part of the past six years working through my issues. But I still hated how stupid I'd been to trust him, to let him break me down that way. He destroyed my confidence long before he kicked in my ribs and bruised my face.

My teeth slid out to nibble at my bottom lip. "It's part of why I got spooked. He called me after…after the lawyers came to an agreement and all the news stories. I didn't pick up the phone, but he left me a message. All it said was he didn't share."

I forced a smile. "As you said, that was six years ago. I'm sure he's forgotten me."

If Teo's long look was any indication, the attempt at good

humor looked as fake as it felt.

"I knew the drill when I invited you to dinner, Preslee. I'm here. You can ask anything of me. Your brother would help, too."

"This situation is my responsibility. I let him into my life. I don't want anyone to get hurt for me. Because of me."

Teo opened his mouth, but I cut him off. "The security at the symphony keeps an eye out for Oren, as does the security at our condo. Any time I go anywhere, I'm with someone else and I try hard not to be out after dark. Those were all the precautions the police gave me when I filed a restraining order. And so far, those steps have worked."

Teo picked up my hand and kissed my knuckles. "Sometimes you need to take the help you're offered because others want your happiness as much, maybe more, than you do."

I scoffed, but he just kept his gaze steady as he leaned in and cupped my chin, holding my face steady as he brushed his lips over mine. We both kept our eyes open, our breath mingling before our lips touched. Our eyes locked in an embrace as intimate as the brief lick from Teo's tongue against the inside of my bottom lip.

This kiss morphed into something different.

My feelings for Oren or any of my boyfriends in high school weren't in the same universe as the emotions ricocheting through me as I kissed Matteo Cruz.

I'd fallen hard for him while I watched him with the kids. His desire to see me home—and safe—softened my heart further, only to break it when he pushed me away. But now… I was willing to fight for a chance at happiness with him.

The waiter brought out our small plates and we settled in to our meal. Our talk remained on lighter topics—my brothers' youthful antics, mainly. We spoke of our favorite venues to play. Teo's skewed toward Europe while I liked some of New England's.

Two and a half hours later, I was drowsy and full, completey replete from the food and wine.

"Dessert?" the waiter asked.

I shook my head. Much as I liked treats, I wanted something else more. Teo's eyes locked on mine.

"We're good," Teo said. "The bill would be fabulous."

The chemistry built between us again—not that it hadn't been there before. Our dinner was fun, easy, but the mood shifted the longer Teo stared at my mouth. I picked up my wineglass and his pupils dilated.

"Come home with me, Preslee."

"Yes."

"I want to make love to you."

"You better," I whimpered.

"You aren't leaving my bed. For days."

"Okay."

Teo grinned as he tugged me up; he dropped a pile of cash on the table before getting up and quickly stepping to my side to pull out my chair.

I stood as he took my hand and led me to the exit. I lengthened my stride to keep up with him. "A little impatient, there, aren't you, buddy?"

"I've dreamed of us together. I want to run my tongue across your skin, right here." He raised his hand until the tips of his fingers glided down my neck. "This long line of your throat. I want

125

to hold your breasts in my hands as I kiss my way up your spine."

Teo stopped at the valet, who smothered a grin. I should be embarrassed the college kid heard Teo's comments. I wasn't. My breasts ached for the warmth of Teo's mouth.

The car ride took too long. My oversensitized skin grew hotter with each heartbeat. Teo held my hand the whole trip, placing my palm high on his thigh when he needed to turn into our building.

Once we were on his floor, he pressed me back against the wall next to his apartment door as he fumbled for his keys. I ran my hands up over his chest and nipped at his chin.

He dropped the keys. I sucked my lips into my mouth to fight back the giggle bubbling up. He bent picked them up. Straightening, he covered my body with his, his mouth hot and coaxing over mine as he kissed me and kissed me. I fumbled with the buttons on his shirt, giving up and instead pulling the tail from his tailored pants.

"Inside. Now."

Teo shoved the key in the lock and swung open the door. He picked me up with his free arm and deposited me inside. My bag slammed against the floor, followed by his keys. He kicked the door shut, his hands in my hair.

"Lock the door."

He looked confused, his head bent toward me.

"Lock the door. Please?" I gave him a gentle shove. Ensuring my secured privacy was one of the many precautions I took since Oren's attack. Not that I wanted to say that now to kill the mood. I sighed with relief when Teo turned to lock the door, and I kicked off my heeled sandals and yanked off my wrap. My fingers felt clumsy as I undid the pearl clasp on my jumpsuit. Teo turned back to face me as I lowered the zipper.

"I want you in my bedroom. If you undress here, I'll take you here."

I raised an eyebrow, the ache between my legs intensifying. "Where?"

"I might not make it past the door. I need you, Preslee."

I shimmied out of the top of my halter, and Teo's eyes widened. "No bra. *Santa Maria*, you're gorgeous."

I brought one of his big hands up to my breast, stepping between his splayed legs to give him better access to my overheated flesh. My jumpsuit slithered to pool at our feet. His breath hitched, his grip firming.

"You made me a promise."

"You have to learn to listen," Teo growled. He backed me up against the couch, hooking one of his large, warm palms just above my knee as he pressed me back. I clutched his shoulders, my hips tilting into his as I began to lose my balance. "Or not." His smile turned predatory.

He followed me down onto the couch, his teeth nibbling from my ear down to my collarbone.

"Make love to me, Teo. I haven't been able to sleep because I've needed you so badly."

"Oh, I like hearing that. And I intend to." He smiled again, his head pressed into my right breast. My panties were boy shorts, my favorite style, in the same soft lavender color as my outfit. They hugged my hip bones and Teo ran his finger in the slight gap over my stomach.

He sat up all the way and pressed his lips to my tight, pouting nipple. I drowned in sensations. My skin burned, plumped and primed. His fingers kneaded my breast, rolling the nipple between thumb and forefinger as he tongued the other. I speared my fingers back through his hair, needing him even tighter against my body.

I gripped the collar of his shirt and yanked down. He laughed at my impatience but helped me rid him of his button-down and T-shirt. He pressed his palm into my lower back. We both groaned when our naked flesh touched.

"You feel better than I remembered." I looped my arms around his neck and plastered myself to his front. One of his hands cupped my left rear cheek through my panties while the other slid back to my nape. He kissed me again. Then again and again. His tongue set my entire body singing with need. I moaned, writhing against him.

He took his time, drawing out the nuances of my reactions, testing them, testing me to see what I liked best, the amount of pressure against my skin I preferred. Once he found the point, he kept it there. His hand caressed my hips, molding the supple flesh to his hand. His lips left mine to trail down my neck. My pulse ratcheted up. He nipped at my neck before licking the pulsing vein.

My hands slid from his shoulders, down his back to his narrow waist. I gripped it tightly before I slid my palms over his hard abs. I let my hands drift upward into the springy hair on his chest, then slid my middle finger down to the V at his hip, to the waistband of his dress slacks.

"I like you like this. Covered in a flush of arousal."

He dipped his head and suckled at my breast again. My core clenched tighter, tiny pulses shivering through the sensitive flesh.

I gasped. He grinned against the cushion of my breast as he

slid over the smooth plane of my stomach. He pushed my panties down and cupped me through my short, neat curls. The tiny pulses there built.

"You seem worked up, Pres. What do you need?"

"To come," I gasped. I hadn't meant to say that. I meant to tell him I needed him.

"Spread your legs wider."

I gripped his shoulders and did as he asked. His hand slid up into my folds. Those tiny ripples swelled up into a tidal wave of need. I pressed hard into his finger, urging him on as my mouth slammed into his. My teeth caught his lower lip, and he growled into my mouth as he pressed a second finger into my tight channel. I moaned into his mouth, bucking my hips. He pumped his fingers into me once. Twice. The little pulses became thick, powerful waves as the orgasm slid over me. I bucked against him, twisting both into and away from the extreme pleasure. I tore my mouth from his and screamed his name.

The orgasm clutched and clawed through my whole body, deep and visceral. Finally, with a last shudder, I lay quiet, drifting, floating in a soft, sweet place I'd never before visited.

CHAPTER FIFTEEN
Teo

She woke in tiny increments. Her lips twitched as she snuggled down into the pillow. She turned and stretched, her long limbs pulling her body taut and thrusting her breasts into sharp relief. They were soft, pink-tipped and pouty. I drew my thumb across the upper slope of her right breast as her eyes flew open. I cupped the warm weight in my hand, my thumb rolling over the crest.

She smiled and scooted closer even as her body flushed with shyness. I loved this dichotomy of the temptress wrapped within a shy, intelligent woman.

"You carried me to your room?"

"Seemed more comfortable than the couch."

"I've never fallen asleep like that before."

"I've never been with a woman who fell asleep screaming before," I chuckled.

"That second time…you wore me out."

"Now I know how to sedate you." I winked.

The blush rolled over her skin down to those perky globes I still palmed in my hand. I leaned in and kissed the side of her warm neck. She smelled good, better now that arousal warmed her skin.

"I've never been so assertive either," she said, her lids drifting down to cover her sparkling eyes.

I pressed a kiss to her cheekbone. "I liked your need."

"Did you take the time to thoroughly check me out?"

"Of course. I've been checking you out in your clothes since I met you," I said with a sly smile.

"Hmm. I like that."

I nipped her earlobe. "I like you naked better."

She laughed and rolled over so that she lay atop my chest. She leaned down and kissed me. Her lips were warm. I gathered her closer, needing to feel her heat against my skin.

"I like you better naked, too."

I scowled, trying to control the blood pooling in my crotch. Nothing compared to the feeling of Preslee's eager body pressed to mine. I didn't have much self-control around her to begin with, and she quickly pushed me to my limit.

I brought her forehead down to mine. She trailed a finger over my stomach, swirling it around my belly button. What little blood remained in my brain sank to *mi pene*.

"I have a fantasy of you and me together." Her voice, soft but rich, like warmed cream, slid across my skin.

My lips parted. I lifted a brow to question her.

"At your desk. Me bent over it and you behind—"

I groaned, drowning out her next words.

"I'm not going to survive your passion, but your imagination is a bonus. If you want desk sex, I'm glad to offer my assistance."

My fingers were in her hair, my mouth on hers. I shifted, trying to find relief. She rubbed against me, and I thrust up in between her thighs. Her fingers fumbled with the waistband of the boxer briefs I'd slid back on after she'd fallen asleep.

I cupped her cheeks and gazed into her eyes, searching. "I want to give you my sole focus, as you deserve, but I'm not sure I can right now. The trade is still up in the air and Noah suggested—"

"Stop talking." She rubbed over me again. "Just focus on making us both feel good.

I hated the panic building in her eyes, but I wouldn't take this step without her complete acceptance of what we were doing. I couldn't let her think it was more...or less. Being with Preslee complicated my life, and yet here we were, tangled limbs and desire so strong I smelled it.

She nipped my lower lip. I crushed her to my chest, the moan ripped from deep within my chest.

I hooked my leg behind her knee and twisted so that I rose above her.

My lips found hers in a scorching kiss. I let myself slide deep into it, deeper this time than I had before. Still, my passion flared hot, consuming me, and I reveled in it.

She slid her hand back to my underwear, sliding it down in a slow, sinuous caress. Her soft touch excited me. Other women had undressed me, sure, but this was Preslee, and she wanted me naked and inside her warm, giving body.

I groaned into her mouth. Preslee smoothed her hands over my butt and down my thighs, the heat from her skin searing me.

My lips trailed over her ribs as she arched into me, fitting my thick erection against her hot center. She pressed her lips into my shoulder, licking and sucking the muscle there as she ran her hands over my abdomen. I loved her hands on me. I wanted more. So much more. I didn't want this to end. I nuzzled the underside of her breasts, chuckling when she squirmed against me.

Her hands roamed across my back, her fingers tracing the ridges and smoothing over the hollows. I moaned when she cupped my aching balls. I moved up to take her nipple into my mouth, swirling my tongue over the soft, pliant flesh. Her breathing escalated, and I slid my mouth to her other breast, my thumb and forefinger continuing to work her pebble-hard nipple.

She slid both palms to capture my erection. I pressed more firmly into her hands, sure I'd just found heaven. She explored my shaft to the smooth, soft tip, flicking her thumb over the bead of moisture there. I took her mouth in another kiss, this one pure carnality. Need streamed through my veins, screaming for release. The pleasure I received from her hands intensified.

She started when I pressed my thumb against the bundle of nerves at the front of her sex. I rubbed in deep circles as she slid her hands up and down my shaft.

"You're big," she whispered.

"You excite me." I groaned as she slid her fist down to my balls. Months since anyone but my own hand touched me. I was a poor substitute for Preslee. Pleasure crackled over my skin, and my balls tightened. "I'm not sure I can wait."

"Then don't."

"When you're ready," I growled.

"I'm ready now."

I slid a finger between her warm lips, and she arched into me, making some inarticulate sound of pleasure.

"You're beautiful all flushed and ready for me to love you."

"Please."

I pulled away to grab a condom, and my skin cooled. I bit my lip as the desire slid in big shivers up and down my thighs. I nudged at her entrance and she shifted upward, eager to accept me into her body.

I hissed as I pressed slowly into her tight warmth.

She cupped my cheeks, her fingers scraping over the stubble there. She rubbed her palm against the growth, mewling at the rough texture against her sensitized palms.

I leaned down, pressing my lips to hers. The perfection of our joining slid from my lips into my chest, burying in my heart. I pressed in further, and she adjusted, taking more of me into her hot clench. I pulled out, needing a moment to calm my racing heart and rock-hard balls.

The little minx arched up hard and fast, trying to get me to bury *mi pene* deep inside her. But that would end the pleasure too soon.

"Slow, Pres. *Santa Maria*, let's slow this down."

"Deeper. More."

"You're getting me," I growled as I kissed the edge of her jaw—that spot that lit her up every time. She arched up into me, crushing her breasts against my chest, her nipples hard points boring through my skin.

I trailed my lips across her jaw to her earlobe. I slid out of her body, sucking gently at the soft skin on her ear. She whimpered, her fingernails clawing at my arms. I bit her earlobe as I swiveled my hips, pressing my erection deep inside her body.

She bowed under me and moaned my name.

Damn right she did.

I pulled back and waited for her to open her eyes. Her lashes caught together before parting to reveal the green of a mature leaf. I loved her ever-changing eyes.

"Ah. Do that again," she whispered.

My breathing escalated as hers did. I shifted to ensure my pelvis rubbing across her sensitive flesh. She moaned again. I smiled as I bent my head, dropping a kiss on her nose and the arch of her throat. Sweat bloomed across our skin. Her legs thrashed as I pinned her under me, holding her still with my hips.

"I need..." She tilted her head back and tried to thrust her hips upward. She couldn't, and I loved watching her come apart like this. She trusted me enough to lose herself in her passion.

"What do you need?"

"You. More."

I complied. She pulled her knees up to take me even deeper. My next thrust was harder, less controlled, deeper.

"Like that," she whispered. My balls tightened further and my cock twitched.

I wrapped an arm around her waist when she bucked under me. I picked up the tempo, hammering into her willing body, my spine tingling. I slid my hands from Preslee's waist and placed them on her thighs, opening her to my pounding.

Her hands fell to the sheets, gripping and twisting, her knuckles white. She screamed as the orgasm ripped through her. This wasn't soft and sweet—this lasted longer than the last two. I slammed my mouth to hers with a ferocity I didn't know I possessed, and ravaged her mouth, plundering with my tongue as I sped up even faster. My movements weren't smooth now. I couldn't help it. I needed her, felt the orgasm building up my spine. I drew back and pressed deep, trying to breathe through the pulsing of my body.

I collapsed onto her, kissing her sweat-dampened temple. It took most of my energy, but I rolled, gathering Preslee in my arms so we stayed joined. She settled her head on my shoulder. I reveled in the contentment of the moment.

"Thank you."

"My pleasure."

She lifted her face enough to meet my eyes. Hers were back to a pale green, dazed. "Mine, too." She grinned.

I didn't try to resist the call of her lips into a soft and perfect kiss. She snuggled in closer, pressing another kiss to my chest as I smiled.

CHAPTER SIXTEEN
Preslee

Teo leaned on his elbow, sprawled across the mattress as he stared down at me. I blinked at the sunshine streaming through the windows. My cheeks flushed. We'd made love many more times, and even fulfilled my fantasy of taking him as I leaned over his desk. I smiled, enjoying the rehash nearly as much as the experience.

Teo was more inventive than my previous lover, and he took the time to be interested in my reactions.

"Hi." I shifted, unsurprised by the soreness between my thighs. Just the thought of some of our exploits the previous night made me shift again, this time with growing excitement.

"*Buenos dias.*" Teo leaned in and kissed me. I turned, trying to pull him on top of me. He held back, and I whimpered. He pressed another kiss to the corner of my mouth and leaned on his elbow, brushing the hair from my eyes.

"I love waking up next to you. So soft, warm, willing." He brushed a finger over the top swell of my breast. "But you're also a very bad influence."

Confusion turned into embarrassment. "I didn't mean to make you do anything you didn't want to do."

Teo threw his head back and guffawed. "I wasn't talking about our lovemaking, Pres. It's six thirty, and I must be at practice by seven."

"It is? Holy crap!"

I sprang out of bed, looking, wild-eyed, for my clothes. Teo's hand drifted up my back, curving around my shoulder so my back pressed against his chest once more.

"I'll make us breakfast."

He smeared a kiss across my lips before he slid into his boxers. I sighed, wishing I was Hugo Boss. Teo's butt put Greek sculptures to shame. And his back...all toned and muscular. I gulped. I *slept* with him.

"Dress, Pres. Now. Or we're skipping the day, and I'm tying you to my bed. Screw the fine."

My body warmed past the point of caution. "That's more an incentive than a threat," I said, breathless, as I stepped nearer. Teo's hand caressed my bottom as he walked past.

He groaned. "You are full of surprises. We'll make up for it later."

"Promise?" I asked, my voice barely more than a whisper.

"I'll pick you up as soon as I finish. From the symphony?"

I nodded, not trying to fight the grin spreading over my lips.

My morning attire turned out to be a problem. I didn't wear a bra last night, and I refused to put on day-old panties. For the first time in my life, I went commando, and I squirmed, feeling naughty.

Teo lent me a pair of his soccer shorts, which I folded over twice to keep snug at my waist, and a too-large faded T-shirt. I tied the extra foot of material to the side, going for an intentionally casual look.

The amused looks from one of the residents who entered the elevator a couple of floors below Teo's told me I hadn't quite pulled it off. Walking me to the door, Teo kissed me long and slow. He leaned down and whispered, "I'll be back in a few hours."

"And then?" I whispered.

The look he gave me from under his lashes made me suck in my breath.

Whatever we'd started proved more exciting than I'd anticipated. I slid into the dark condo and tiptoed to my room. I padded straight to the bathroom and turned on the light, blinking at the glare.

My skin was rosy, in a near-constant flush, thanks to Teo's sensual words and sexual prowess.

I settled on the edge of my vanity. I still didn't understand why he'd decided to date me. He was attentive, charming—the best lover I'd ever experienced. On the surface, there was no reason for me to worry.

But underlying the perfection of last night was the reality that he'd changed his mind once. And if he could do that so thoroughly, he could do it again.

CHAPTER SEVENTEEN
Teo

I slid through the side door Preslee told me the symphony members used, waved in by a security guard, who grinned broadly.

"She said you were coming by, but I still can't believe it. Matteo Cruz here in our building." He shook his graying head. "Can I get your autograph?"

I smiled and nodded, though I wanted nothing more than to stand there in the quiet for a moment and close my eyes.

"Any word on your trade? I mean, how will that work with Preslee?"

I suppressed the urge to squirm, not liking the uncomfortable feeling building in my chest. "No word. My agent is working with the Timber and Milan."

The team management perked up at the idea of paying me less—and shortening the contract to three years. I'd told Roberto to make it happen, and he was, but the entire process left me disappointed, almost dismal.

After signing his symphony program, I moved along the passage and massaged my hamstring, trying to ease the tension there. I needed another round of massage therapy. Our team trainer was good, but not as good as Mariana—which is why I'd paid her a large sum of money to treat me.

Maybe I could talk Pres into rubbing my leg for me. I already knew her fingers were magic.

I grinned and shook my head. I was worse than a teenager when it came to Pres. I wanted to spend all my time with her. Not even with Vivi was I ever so focused, so interested, in a woman. Was this normal? Not as though I could speak with my father about the matter and any of my current teammates. My former teammates from Real Madrid weren't speaking to me because they felt I should have kept my mouth shut—to stay on the roster.

Which meant I didn't know what to do with the myriad feelings bubbling up—euphoria and fear. Fear won out.

I glanced up and caught Brenna's scowl.

"Hello. I didn't expect to see you today."

She crossed her arms over her chest. "I'm sure you didn't. I was just leaving now that I asked her the question I needed answered." Her brows tumbled lower. "Because it seems like you'll be keeping her occupied for a while."

I laughed, an uncomfortable emotion bubbling up because I'd started something with just the type of woman I'd always feared—the long-term woman. I cleared my throat, trying to regain my equilibrium. "I care about her, very much. And plan to spend what time we can together."

Brenna sighed in defeat "You'll take care of her?"

I met her light brown eyes. This answer was simple. "Yes. She deserves the best."

Brenna's lips twitched up. "We agree on that."

"Is she finished?" I asked, needing to change the subject.

"Not quite. The conductor is yelling at them. You know, the opposite of a pep talk."

"Why does Pres work for the symphony? She likes to play the electric viola."

Brenna studied her nails. "It's relatively unique, and she's a hell of a player." She glanced up at me from under her brow.

"She's racked up quite a few inquiries to play. Big name bands. Offers for studio time."

I glanced down the hall, confusion warring with pride. "Why doesn't she do any of those?"

Brenna smoothed her hands down the lapels of her suede blazer. "Oren."

"Have you met him?" I didn't bother to hide my disgust.

"Yes."

"Pres is afraid enough of him to hide in a group of musicians?"

"Clearly," Brenna's voice turned curt. "And with good reason."

I didn't get a chance to say anything further because a mass of voices, mostly grumbling, approached, then flowed around us.

I spotted Preslee talking to another musician about halfway back in the crowd. She smiled, her eyes alight at the sight of me, and my chest ached with the need to pull her close and kiss that smile.

"Can I get your autograph?"

I turned toward a matronly woman in jeans and an oversized T-shirt. I smiled. "Of course."

"For my son. He's a huge Timber fan."

I nodded, mainly zoning out on all the comments as I waited for Preslee. My hand cramped before she materialized next to me. I handed back the latest paper and pen before turning toward her. I cupped her cheeks and captured her lips in a soft kiss.

"Fabulous to see you," she grinned, her eyes a sparkling mint green. "How was practice?"

I shrugged, annoyed by my aching leg and lack of clarity on the trade talks. "You ready to go?"

She glanced around at her colleagues, all of whom stepped

back, giving us a modicum of privacy.

"Yes." She leaned in, and I caught my breath as her chest brushed against mine. "Are you okay?"

"I'm better now that I'm with you," I murmured back, kissing her cheek near her ear.

She pulled back slowly. "Will you take me back to your place?"

I brushed her bangs back. "I'd like nothing more," I said, face and voice solemn.

"Let's go."

I took her viola from her and knitted the fingers of my free hand through hers. We said our goodbyes and walked quietly from the building.

"I wanted to hear you play, but Brenna ambushed me at the door."

Preslee's eyebrows rose and she glanced around. "Brenna was there?"

"She said she needed an answer to a question."

Preslee shook her head. "She never spoke to me."

"You know, I didn't see her when we were leaving. I was too caught up in you to notice."

She sighed, snuggling in closer. "I like the sound of that."

I dipped my head so I could whisper in her ear. "I like all the sounds you make."

Preslee's lips trembled before she failed to contain her mirth. Her laugh caused many to turn their heads to see who made such a gorgeous sound. I pulled her still closer and kissed the top of her head.

"Especially that one," I breathed into her ear.

"Let's just stay in tonight," she suggested.

I escorted her into an empty elevator car in our building. I pressed her back against the wall and kissed my way up her neck.

"Mm. That's nice."

"I care about you, Preslee." I brought her knuckled to my lips.

"That's sweet," she said with a flirty smile that did nothing to hide the building panic in her eyes.

I cleared my throat, as uncomfortable with the turn in our conversation as she was. "I owe you a real meal. The piece of toast I handed you on the way out the door doesn't cut it."

"You don't have to feed me."

I tipped her head up and pressed a kiss to her lips. "I want to. I like spending time with you."

This time, her smile was broader, more genuine. The grip on my chest that ballooned when I saw Brenna earlier eased. Preslee wanted me—to spend time with me—as much as I did with her. If we focused on that, on the present, we'd be good.

———◆———

Late that night, we lay in bed, facing each other, not quite touching. My body ached, as it should after the number of times we'd made love since picking up her clothes and phone charger after her rehearsal, but my hamstring wasn't one of those spots. As expected, Preslee's fingers worked their magic.

Brenna hadn't been at the condo, which relieved me and saddened Preslee. I hated the distance in her relationship with her friend, but Preslee told me Brenna was the one who'd pushed her into the bar last weekend. I'd never understand how women's minds worked.

"What time is your game on Sunday?"

"Four-thirty."

"So, tomorrow's free?"

"Mostly. Why?"

"I'm going to a barbecue. Want to come with me?"

I grinned. "Sure."

"It's at my half sister's."

"I didn't realize you had siblings other than Noah."

"Many. You know Noah and you've heard me talk about his twin Nate. They're about a year younger than me. I also have two older half sisters. And Lia's daughter, Abbi, is a few of years younger than my brothers."

"Quite the group. As I mentioned before, I'm an only child."

"Probably benefits to that. My oldest sister and my mom don't get along." She sighed as she rolled onto her back, her arm over her eyes. "That's my fault."

"I doubt you intentionally derailed their relationship."

"My mom left their dad to follow *my* dad to Seattle. She was pregnant with me when she abandoned Lia and Briar."

"That's nothing for you to feel guilty about, Pres. You can't fix a relationship that isn't yours."

"I hate that I'm the reason for the trouble between them. Lia's anger's justified, but my mom dismisses her feelings. If anything, I feel bad for Lia and Briar. And it taught me that every action has consequences. I mean, sure, it's nice for my mom to say she loved my father. But she left her daughters and husband for my dad and started another family."

This sharing showed her growing trust, which made that ache in my chest expand. I wanted this, but I didn't. It was too much intimacy. I wanted to stick to what felt good—right. The connection of our bodies. So, I slid in tight next to her, cupping her cheek. I kissed her again, and she answered with slow, lazy swipes of her tongue against mine.

"You do that well," she whispered when she pulled back. She pillowed her arm under her head and continue to gaze at me with an awestruck expression.

"Mmm, I can say the same for you."

She smiled. I settled my arm around her waist, pulling her closer, content to cuddle her naked body. These moments were just as special as our lovemaking—soft, quiet lulls between the bright flares of passion. I'd never lain quietly with anyone before, but now that Pres and I built these moments, these memories, I craved more of them even as I feared them.

Maybe I *could* find a solid, loving relationship. Maybe I didn't have to end up like my father. Uncomfortable with those thoughts, I refocused on Preslee.

"Tell me more about your family."

"Nate's a firefighter. He and Noah are close, mostly with each other, but they're protective of all their big sisters and even Abbi." She smiled. "They've been able to relax their constant watching now that Lia, Briar, and Abbi all have wonderful men in their lives."

"So, they focus on you?"

She rolled her eyes. "They smother me."

"You mean they love you. I want to meet Nate."

"You will. Soon if he has his way. We're going to Lia and Asher's today."

"You played the viola for Asher Smith in his last song."

"He's the sneaky one." But she smiled. "Lia's daughter, Abbi, my niece, is dating Clay Rippey."

"Rippey? His band just released its first album, and it's getting lots of airplay. He's a big deal."

She nodded, her mouth flipped up. "You're up to speed with the music scene."

I shrugged. "Hard not to know what's going on. The people you've mentioned are all over the radio, blogs, everywhere, really."

"It's intimidating," Preslee said. "Asher's going to try to talk me into doing a gig with him in a few weeks. He's playing at The Showbox with Simon Dorsey, whose older brother was Lia's first husband."

A thick, oozy feeling drifted out from my stomach, probably because I worried about this issue with Preslee. She didn't understand how wealthy I was, and I didn't want to tell her. "Did Lia divorce him for Asher?"

"No. Lia's not like that. Partly because of my mother, I'm sure. Doug, Lia's first husband, died. He had a neurological disease. Lia was a wreck for years." She paused, brows pulling that porcelain skin into tight ridges of consternation. Her eyes clouded with what I guessed was a pained memory. Before I could ask, she cleared her throat. "She met Asher at a concert a little over a year ago. They connected." Her little sigh told me how romantic she found the story.

"Your relatives have great taste in men."

She shook her head, her eyes sparkling. "Correction. The men have great taste in women. Briar's married to Hayden Crewe."

I whistled. "I'm intimidated. That's quite a talented list. Do they get together and jam on the weekends?"

"Sometimes. It's funny because they're all so super talented, but Hayden and Asher don't do well with letting the other be in charge. Clay and Simon just laugh at them and do whatever they want."

"Do you sing with them?"

"I've helped Asher and Hayden with harmonies. But I never wanted to be on their albums. I'm still upset with Asher for going against my wishes with the viola."

"Will you sing for me sometime?"

Her eyes met mine. "Sure. I love singing. It's what I always wanted to do." She smiled a little sadly. "Or be a professional soccer player. But I gave up that dream when I lost my scholarship. So, I'll live that one vicariously through you."

"That must've been hard for you, losing your dream. But you created another, right?" I ran my hand from her ankle, up over her hip to the dip at her waist. Touching Preslee made me burn for more. "So much talent hidden inside your body."

She smiled a little, but her eyes muddied with another memory. "You're pretty talented yourself," she murmured as she rubbed her soft, warm breasts against my chest. I tightened my arms around her, willing to let her drop the topic. For now.

"Mm, so are you. I better bring my A-game."

She rested her head against my chest as I wrapped my arm around her narrow waist. She felt so right snuggled into my side, sharing my heat.

"They'll like you because I like you."

I dropped a kiss on her temple, her bangs clinging to my lips as I pulled back. "Bet I still get the third degree."

"That's what families do. My half sisters and Abbi want to make sure I'm safe and happy. So do my brothers. Which is why

148

Nate will call me on the drive back from Lia's place, all angry he didn't come out to grill you himself. Doesn't matter that Noah knows you."

"I guess it's good I'm taking your family in doses."

"Nate and Noah are a lot to take in. Thankfully, Nate's in Uruguay this week. Vacation," she added at my look. "But you passed Noah's bar, which is high."

Again, I fell silent, wrestling with emotions I wasn't sure how to handle, much less control. Preslee gazed down at me, her concern more evident with each passing moment.

I kissed her again, softly. I rolled over, my weight on my elbows and my hands holding her face still. I stared into her eyes, which were bright with desire. She pressed up into my aching body with a soft moan.

I could understand why my father focused on sex—it was an escape, both mental and physical, from the demands of his day-to-day life. I stilled, not liking the direction of my thoughts. But Preslee slid her hand into my hair, fingers tugging me down to her lips.

"I want…" Preslee began, hips shifting with restlessness.

"You got it," I growled.

———◆———

After a long shower, I collected my keys, wallet, and phone from the dresser. Then, because I couldn't resist, I tilted her face so our lips met, tongues tangling in a lazy dance of promises of more, later. I swiped my thumbs along her cheekbones before stepping back. Preslee sighed—a sound full of longing—as she grabbed her tote and slid her sunglasses onto her head.

She remained nervous throughout the drive north, which surprised me. She asked me to stop so she could pick up some wine.

"Lia likes red," she said as she stared at the bottles lining the wine shop.

"I know just the bottle. We'll take a few. Do the guys prefer beer?"

Preslee nodded. I grabbed a cart and she followed me.

"What about Briar and Abbi?"

"They follow Lia's lead. She knows more about wine than the rest of us."

I found the bottles I wanted and then went to the refrigerated section. "Any style of beer?"

"Um, Asher likes ales. Hayden and Clay like darker kinds. Stouts, I think."

I pulled out a couple of six packs and added them to the cart. "Need anything else?"

"No. Lia likes to cook. She'll make way too much. She always does."

"I like your sister already." Preslee's eyes widened when the cashier announced the total, but I just winked and offered my credit card.

"Th-that was very sweet of you." Preslee twisted the sleeves of her light-weight sweater over her hands.

"One of the benefits of dating a rich man."

She stopped outside the store doors, her porcelain skin paler than usual. I couldn't see her eyes behind her big, fashionable glasses. "Please don't say that again."

My heart thudded out a harsh rhythm behind my ribs. "I'm

just pointing out that having money helps."

"I'm not with you for your money, Teo."

"You're with me for my body."

"More so than your money." She let out a small laugh, softening at my joke. She helped me load the wine into the back of the car. When I closed the trunk, she turned back toward me and lifted her sunglasses, her eyes focused, serious again. "Oren's family called me a gold-digger. I-I can't do that again."

I pulled her into my arms. "I never thought you wanted me for anything less than me."

"Thank you for saying that. And to clarify, I'm with you for your personality and insanely gorgeous—"

"Ass?"

She snorted. "Eyelashes. You have swoon-worthy eyelashes."

"I think you just insulted my manliness."

"Your legs are pretty good, too." She winked. "Do you run or something?"

I swatted her *culo*—the one I thought about too much—as I opened the door. "I like your playful side, Pres. A lot."

She waited until I settled in the car before she turned to me. "You dropped hundreds of dollars on a case of wine, Teo. I just…it's a lot to take in. I mean, I do well enough to own my condo, but—"

I pressed a kiss to her twisted lips. "Relax. I'm happy to do it, and I can afford to. Plus, I own the winery so I get some of it back."

"Oh." She looked out the window. "One of your dad's businesses?"

"No, it's mine. I'm not interested in plastic widgets and sugar prices. When I was home, playing for the national team, I needed a break so I took a drive. I ended up on this derelict winery in the Mendoza Valley, and I met this older guy out tending these grapes. Most of them wilted because of the drought, but he refused to give up. He told me how the land passed down through his family since Argentina was settled. But without the wine, his passion, he wouldn't be able to keep the acreage. I could tell he loved the land, so I offered to pony up the money for half the business. We used it to upgrade the irrigation system. It's very cool. High tech. With the grapes ensured enough water, we've increased yields. We've both done well."

"I play dead people's songs for a salary. Don't you see how this is so different from my world?" She settled her sunglasses back onto her nose.

"No, not really. Because you also create your music. I've heard it, and it's fantastic."

She smiled, but tension returned to ring her mouth.

"I didn't mean to make you uncomfortable, Pres. Consider it a suck-up gift."

She shook her head, her sunglasses making it hard for me to read her expression. I needed to tell Preslee my net worth. Just not yet. If the millions her family banked made her uncomfortable, then my personal accounts—let alone my father's vast wealth—was sure to cause another round of insecurity.

I never once considered my money a detriment, even when my mother used it as a weapon against my relationship with Vivi. Now, however, relief swept through me, making me even more grateful for meeting Preslee the way I had. She knew me as a soccer player, one with some well-paying endorsements. She thought I lived comfortably, brought in extra cash by posing in my underwear. Which I'd only done after I ascertained I could give my endorsement money to Vivi's practice in Buenos Aires.

Because of the way our relationship developed, I knew Preslee's feelings for me were genuine, not heightened by what I could give her as my father had suggested. Which was pretty much anything and everything she'd ever wanted. And then some.

Preslee gripped her fingers, twisting her hands in her lap. "I don't like the idea of us being on unequal footing. I wonder what I bring to this.... Because you already have great style."

I picked up her hand and kissed her knuckles, trying to cover my smile.

"I can't play the viola. Or sing. And your timing for headers is better than mine."

She snorted but clasped my fingers tighter.

"You give in so many ways, Preslee. Noah told me about your work with domestic abuse victims at the shelter. Then there are the soccer kids. I'm really proud of you."

"Thanks."

My comments made her uncomfortable. She didn't like to discuss anything even remotely related to Oren, and I understood, sort of. But I wished she could see herself as I saw her.

"So, you'd freak out if I told you I have more money than Asher and Hayden put together?" I asked, trying to get a bead on her feelings. Plus, I couldn't let this go on too long—she'd think I misled her, and Preslee didn't trust easily.

Her lashes slid down to cover her eyes. "I know your parents are wealthy."

"They are. But so am I, independent from them. My endorsements bring in way more than my soccer salary, and playing in Europe, being from Argentina, makes me a global brand." I shrugged, but I felt anything but nonchalance. "I own the winery in Mendoza, and I've been thinking about buying one here." I hadn't, not until the words were out of my mouth. Being near my vineyard, taking Preslee there to sip wine and wander the paths…a fantasy I'd make a reality. "I like learning about viticulture."

"Turn here. It's faster."

I turned, even though the GPS wanted me to continue for another few miles. Preslee kept holding my hand as she leaned forward and canceled the route.

"Do you really make more than Asher and Hayden?"

"Yes."

She blew out a breath. "I'm going to need to process that."

"Because of what Oren's family did to you?"

"In part. But because money means responsibility. I hadn't realized that until I started spending more time with my family."

"But it also means security and power."

She was back to knotting her hands in her lap.

She told me where to turn next and within a few more minutes, we were pulling up in front of a large house. I smiled at the place; it felt homey, not too showy though the neighborhood and lake beyond proved its steep price tag.

"What has you so concerned?" I asked.

"That power part."

"Because Oren's family used theirs to hurt you."

She nodded.

Mierda. Preslee was right to worry. My parents were more ruthless than Oren's family and twice as likely to wield their influence.

CHAPTER EIGHTEEN
Preslee

"Holy shit, Pres! You're dating Matteo Romero de Cruz! He owns like half of Argentina and tons of stuff here, too. He's not just rich and obviously sexy as hell, he's a major player."

Lia narrowed her eyes. "What kind of player?"

"Not like that." Briar waved her arm. "I meant power player. As in lots of money. But he's also a soccer phenom."

Abbi's phone rang and she stepped away to take the call.

"I know. I don't like that part. It makes me uncomfortable."

My stomach churned. I set down my glass of wine, still untouched. I rubbed my temples with my hands. Everything I learned about Teo made me wonder why he'd want to spend time with me.

"Stop it," Lia said, her voice gentle. "He cares about you, and you're more than good enough for him."

I blinked at her, shocked.

She sighed. "You are. You're smart, talented, and kind."

"Don't forget gorgeous." Briar toasted me with her glass. "You always look so put together. Even in jeans. I mean, look at you today. It's all comfy but sexy—and that scarf. Good thing we're related, otherwise I'd hate you."

"The most beautiful of us. Don't you dare tell Abbi I said that."

"Tell me what?" Abbi said from behind us.

"That Preslee's the prettiest woman in the family," Briar said.

Lia smacked her arm, spilling Briar's wine, causing Briar to yell, "Hey!"

"No wine for you," Lia hissed.

"You're right. Preslee is the prettiest. But that isn't why Teo likes her. Let me try a sip, please. I promise to give it back."

Abbi picked up my glass. "Mmm, that's lovely."

"Give it back." Lia held out her hand.

Abbi rolled her eyes at her mom before turning back to me. "He's hot, Pres."

I nodded. "I didn't realize he was so rich until we were on the way here and he dropped so much money on beverages." I shoved my hands into my pockets. "I mean, I read his dad owned some businesses and a soccer club, but Teo was supposed to just be a soccer player."

"He's that, too. Doesn't seem like he cares about your middle-class background," Lia said. "Hell, we all came from that, except Teo, maybe." She glanced at Briar who nodded. Lia shrugged. "So he grew up überrich and you didn't. Abbi's right. He wouldn't be here if he didn't care about you. I wouldn't let something as silly as money get in the way of your feelings and happiness."

"I'll drink to that," Briar said.

The rest of the afternoon passed with the usual Asher and Hayden squabbling and Lia soothing. I enjoyed the time with them more because of their acceptance of Teo—and that I deserved to be with him.

My favorite exchange occurred right after we arrived. Asher hugged me. "Miss you, sweetheart. You coming to my show? People are asking for our song."

"Sure they are. Especially since you *already* told everyone I was playing with you."

I scowled at him, but Asher smiled, all slow and devastating, as he added a little shrug. "What can I say? Hope springs eternal, and I like singing with you. You've got nearly two months to prep for the next one," he added with a wink.

"Next one?" I huffed, tucking my bangs back and stepping closer to Teo. "There's no point in getting angry with you, is there? This is Teo."

"Ah, the man with great taste in women and wine," Asher said, smiling.

Now, the sun had long since set and the car felt intimate, but my concerns about the exchange earlier reared back.

"Did you have fun?" I asked Teo once we were back in his car, heading back toward downtown.

He brought my hand to his lips. "I did. One of the best afternoons I've spent in years. Thank you."

"I'm glad you came with me," I said, shyness making my voice soft.

He glanced at me from the corner of his eye, his lips quirked with a knowing smile. I hooked my leg under my other knee and faced him better.

"Briar says you're stinking rich *and* super famous." I bit my lip, wondering if I should have brought that up.

"And what did you decide about that?" Teo dropped my hand; his knuckles whitening as soon as he gripped the steering wheel.

"I don't understand why you'd want to be with me when you could have probably any woman you wanted."

"I have the woman I want. Or, I should say, I plan to have the woman I want. That's you, Preslee."

Warmth blossomed behind my breastbone. "What a nice compliment."

"I'm sincere. Stay with me tonight?"

"Yes."

"Do you need anything from your apartment?"

I nibbled my lips. I packed a couple of outfits yesterday because I wasn't sure what I'd want to wear today, depending on the weather. Seeing Brenna's closed, angry face—the last look she threw at me—helped me decide.

"I think I'm okay for tonight. I just don't have anything to sleep in."

Teo's smile formed slow and wicked. "That's just the right thing to wear to bed."

"Have you always been so sensual?" I didn't like the idea of Teo saying such things to another woman, let alone touching her as he did me.

His brow pulled down. "I don't think so. You bring out feelings in me I didn't know were there."

"I like it," I whispered.

He sent me another sly smile. "I'll make sure you do."

———◆———

The next week passed in a blur of practices and rehearsals, a couple of games and lots of time spent in Teo's condo. I wasn't sure how to jettison my worry that I was just a way to pass the time until he was traded. Though, from what Teo said during his call with his agent, the likelihood of the trade was deteriorating with each passing day.

He hung up his phone and bowed his head. I hovered in the doorway between his bedroom, an awkwardness I'd never felt before oozing from my pores.

"You can come in here," he said. "I assume you heard?"

"Y-yes." I twisted my fingers into my sweater. "Is that okay?"

He looked up at me, a frown tugging at his brows. "Why wouldn't it be?"

"It's just…you have to be disappointed."

"Milan wants me to have another physical in two weeks."

I settled next to him on the couch. He cupped his hand under my knee and tugged me closer. I pressed my cheek to his shoulder and wrapped my arm around his waist. With each breath, I relaxed into his side more.

"And then?"

"If everything looks good, I'll sign papers."

I nodded, unable to speak. He'd go. He'd never hidden his goal from me, but the ache in my chest expanded, making breathing more difficult.

Teo's fingers slid up my hip to my waist. "Did Oren take his bad humor out on you?"

"He yelled when he was upset."

Teo tipped my chin up and met my gaze. "I'm not Oren."

I shook my head.

"I won't hurt you."

I nodded.

"I want you to come to my game. Please."

"I'd like that."

Teo remained quiet the rest of the morning, holding me for a while before he had to get ready to go to the stadium. My heart ached for him—I was too well-versed in giving up dreams not to understand the turmoil he must be feeling.

At the same time, Milan kept the talks open, stringing him

along more than any player liked, but not closing the door. Which meant if his next physical was good, he'd go.

We didn't discuss what that would mean for us. If there would be an us if he were traded. Instead, I kissed him as I exited the elevator at my floor and smiled.

"Good luck today."

"Wear my jersey?"

"Of course."

He stepped forward, blocking the elevator doors from closing, and kissed me again. "I'm glad you'll be there, Pres." He stepped back and let the door slide close.

Sucking up my courage, I entered my apartment, shoulders braced for Brenna's scowl. Instead, I found her sitting listlessly on the couch, watching *Four Weddings and a Funeral.* My stomach fluttered at the sight of Hugh Grant. He only made an appearance in Brenna's life when she was struggling to come to grips with some terrible blow.

"Hey." I settled onto the cushion next to her.

"How was your weekend?" she asked, not looking up from the screen.

"Good." Way better than good, but I didn't want to tell her that.

Brenna sighed.

I turned toward the television and watched a few minutes of the movie. "Want to tell me what's going on?"

Brenna shook her head. She pulled the blanket up tighter under her armpits and scowled at the screen.

"Um, 'kay. I'm going to grab something to eat, and then I'm going to get ready for Teo's game."

"Have fun." Brenna's voice was listless.

"Do you…do you want to come?"

She picked up the remote from the cushion next to her and paused the movie. She turned to look at me. Her eyes were bloodshot and her nose red. My chest ached at the sight of her recent crying bout.

"Do you want me to? I mean, I know you're mad at me, and I don't want to make the situation worse."

I snatched up her hand and squeezed her fingers. "I want you to come. You're my best friend, Bren. I miss spending time with you."

She leaned over and rested her head on my shoulder. "I've missed you, too. If you want me to join you, I'd like that."

Balancing my time with Teo and Brenna might prove precarious, but both were important to me. I'd figure it out.

———◆———

This game, like the previous one, kept me on the edge of my front-row seat. After settling in, I looked up at the JumboTron to my own face. Though dread swirled through my stomach, I smiled and waved as the announcer said, "Looks like our favorite player's girlfriend is back to cheer on her man. Maybe, if we're lucky she'll sing for us soon."

Brenna's sullen pout also hit the huge screen, much to my dismay. Almost as much as the announcer calling me Teo's girlfriend. We hadn't defined our relationship—in part because I was afraid to ask him what he wanted or where we stood.

As soon as the camera crew moved on, Brenna leaned over. "Oren's going to hear about this."

I shrugged. What else could I do? Not much, really. Sure, dating Teo meant stepping back into the limelight—a place I thought I'd left for good. But not dating Teo…my skin warmed at the thought of his touch, his kiss, and the feeling of his long, hard length sliding into me. Yeah, not going to happen. I needed him. More, I wanted him. And, for the first time in years, I wanted more than I feared.

Teo turned from the lineup and threw me a kiss. I smiled as I pretended to catch it and smack in on my cheek.

I planned to keep the wanting more than the fear. Forever.

Teo took his position for the opening kickoff, eyes focused on the ball, brows drown tight in concentration. With the whistle, Teo sped into action. His thighs bulged with the explosiveness of his push off, his arms pumping as he sprinted forward into position to receive the ball. A perfect kick that tapped him in the side of his cleat in neat timing with his long stride. Teo wove around one defender, brought his head up and passed to his teammate on the left side. Murkowski feinted right before taking the ball up the left sideline. As three defenders collapsed in on his position, Murkowski kicked the ball back into the middle of the field, which Teo caught on his chest and let roll down his long, lean body. With small dribble steps, Teo flashed around another defender.

He was within twenty feet of the goal. He dug in his left cleat and brought his right leg back. With a thud that left me breathless, Teo kicked the ball straight through the goalie's hands where it slammed into the back of the net.

I stood, cheering and jumping up and down. The man was a maestro of footwork. Even Brenna was up and hopping, clapping and cheering him on.

For the next hour, the Timber made eight more shots on goal—all misses, including one by Teo. The Dallas Flames missed twelve, much to their captain's mounting frustration.

"The Timber defense keeps collapsing." I squeezed my hands together between my bouncing knees, struggling to breathe through the last fifteen minutes of regulation play.

Harris, a strong Timber midfielder, managed to catch some space between two Flames players. He sprinted forward, his legs laboring to stay in front of the defensemen. He kicked the ball up field to Teo, who, with a quick swivel of his head, slammed a crossbody kick to Murkowski. Teo's kick soared high, in a straight, hard line drive toward the left side of the goal. Murkowski leaped and headed the ball toward the right crossbeam and into the side net.

The crowd went wild, many unable to believe the shot they'd just witnessed.

Teo dropped his hands to his knees, chest heaving, sweat dripping from his hair and nose. The back of his jersey clung to his back as he struggled to regain control of his breathing.

Shock, awe, and passion swirled through me. Teo was a superstar. One of the best players I'd ever had the privilege to watch. He raised his head and winked right at me.

I had to catch my breath. Oh, I wanted him in that moment with a burning need that nearly consumed me. No matter what Oren tried to do, no matter how scared I was about my possible future with Teo…there was no way—no way—I could give up Matteo Cruz.

"Hello?" I said, fumbling my phone as I tried to get the narrow sheath of plastic and glass between my ear and my shoulder.

I glanced at my watch. I might be late to practice at the symphony but then Teo and I would have the night to spend together. He'd had to travel for his first away series since we'd begun dating nearly two weeks ago, and he was due home within an hour of my rehearsal ending. Four nights was too many to be away from him.

Brenna hadn't said anything and neither had I—I assumed she was aware I planned to spend the night with Teo, much as I did every night he was in town.

The silence dragged on and I started to pull the phone away when I heard Oren's deep voice. "I told you I don't share."

I paused, swallowing hard. A light sweat broke out across my entire body.

"Oren."

Brenna stopped eating her cereal, her spoon halfway to her mouth. *Get your phone*, I mouthed at her. She shot off her chair and pounded down the hall, back in less than twenty seconds, the recording app already up on her screen.

"You don't get to be famous, Preslee. I don't want you to be famous. I don't want other men looking at those trim thighs I used to sink between."

"I'm not yours." My voice wasn't as strong as it should be. My body shook, trying to expel both his voice and the memories he brought forth.

The fear Oren instilled in me was visceral, ugly, and unwelcome. I pulled my phone back and pressed the speaker button, shocked by how steady my hands were.

"Oh, but I do get to decide. I'm the one who chose to give you up, but I never said you were free to do as you pleased."

"I am not your possession. You need to stay away from me."

"I could have grabbed you that night you were with him. On your first date. If I wanted to." My stomach dropped and my throat closed. Teo had been right. Oren had been following me, and I hadn't known. Danger remained imminent, constant, and, all this time, I'd stayed blissfully unprepared. I squeezed my hands into fists. No, I wouldn't let Oren take my safety or my sanity.

"I thought about it. How easy it would have been. You may be tall, but you're light. Fragile. I can break you again, if I wanted to."

My knees buckled and I caught the edge of the counter. "That's a threat. I plan to add it to my restraining order."

"Like that will keep me from what's mine."

Oren cut off the call.

I slid to the floor, placing my forehead to my knees. I took a deep breath, then another. And another.

Brenna's hand rested on the back of my head. "Hey. You okay?"

"Not really. He—he scares me."

Brenna crouched down in front of me and clasped my chilled hands in hers. "He scares me, too. But you know what? We have evidence that proves he has followed you and that he's threatened you. We'll go right now and take it to the police department. I won't leave your side until we sort this whole thing out. Okay?"

I nod, my eyes never leaving hers. "You sure you can do that?"

She smiled, brushing my hair out of my damp eyelashes. "Pres, this is what I'm here for. To help you." She helped me stand. "I'll always help you."

CHAPTER NINETEEN
Teo

I fed off the cheering crowd, pushing myself harder than I should have. Who didn't love adulation? Thousands of people screaming my name—major high. Scoring the only goal in the last minute of that first game?—another adrenaline dump.

Now we were in our last game of the three-game road trip. I missed Preslee with a fierceness that shocked me.

The head coach of Milan called me that first night after my winning goal, and we talked for an hour. He asked multiple pointed questions about my hamstring, which I answered with more candor than even I expected—much to my agent's fear and annoyance. I mean, who in their right mind would jeopardize a trade to one of the world's best *fútbol* teams?

Needing advice, I picked up the phone multiple times to call my father, mainly because I could not speak of my issues with anyone within the Timber organization—not even Jorge—for fear of what would get back to management. But I always set the phone back down without dialing. My father might love the female form, but I'd concluded as a teen he'd never loved any of his mistresses. His advice would be to do what was best for my career, never mind my growing need to see Preslee's smile each morning and to kiss her soft lips each night. And, *Dios mio*, to listen to her sing.

The first time she sang in my shower, I dropped the clothes I'd just grabbed from my closet and ran toward the bathroom door, listening to her with my eyes closed. *Santa Maria*, her pitch remained perfect, deep with resonance. Like Adele or someone of that caliber. Listening to her sing quickly became my second favorite pastime.

My first favorite was making love to her, because our sex blew me away. Preslee held my full attention and my dreams at night. I awoke from a dead sleep, aching with the need to touch and love her again. Then again.

The team set back to our line and I pushed thoughts of Preslee from my mind. The San Diego midfielder missed his pass, and the crowd groaned in frustration when my midfielder picked it up, driving forward, his eye flicking up to mine.

A defender blocked the pass so I moved forward, trying for a better angle. The defender, John Klein, dropped his shoulder and shoved me. The guy had a chip the size of California on his shoulder, unhappy because he hadn't made the American national team. Or so Id' been told. That didn't have much to do with me, but I was frustrated by his physicality. So was Jorge, our acting coach. He screamed at the referee, who turned to glare at John.

Hopefully, message received.

The ball moved back down toward the Timber goalie, Tim Varner. After another few minutes of play, Varner scooped up the ball and punted it back down the pitch.

My midfielder collected the pass and caught sight of me. He dribbled past one defender and kicked it to me.

I smiled, loving what I did. My lungs screamed as my legs pumped. I pushed forward. Klein shoved me out of the way, making me miss my stride and tumble to the grass. I rose, angry words on my lips, when the whistle sounded. Yellow card for Klein.

Not enough, but at least the *pendejo* was on notice. One more yellow and he was out of the game.

During my tumble to the ground, the San Diego defender sent the ball back to his midfielders. Play continued. My hamstring ached more than usual, but I managed to keep my head in the game and my body limber.

We paused for a water break. Thirty more minutes. I squirted more water into my mouth.

"What's up with Klein?" Jorge asked.

I shrugged. "Seems like he wants to play tackle."

"I'm going to pull you."

I shook my head. "I've never quit because a player got too physical with me before."

Jorge's dark eyes met mine. "You've also never just recovered from a hamstring injury before. He wants to take you down. Maybe out."

I crossed my arms over my chest. "I disagree. He simply wants to shake me up. I won't let him."

The rest of the team watched Jorge and I spar, their chests still heaving from the exertion. A few shot more water into their mouths.

I bowed my head. "Sorry. I was out of line. Do what you think is best, Coach."

He called out to Greg Pinson, our youngest player and a good striker. Solid mechanics, great technique, but so damn green behind his ears. "Warm up. You're going in to relieve Teo in five."

Greg's grin was broad, his eyes alight. "Thanks, Coach."

I smiled, too, but it felt sour. I hated being pulled from the game for any reason. Jorge knew this, which is why he clapped me on the back. "Make these count."

I did. My teammates understood I was our best offense, so

they fed me the ball. The first time, Klein managed to get his foot between me and the ball, thanks to a sharp shoulder to the chest. My chest ached, but my blood pounded in my veins.

No way would he get away with that again.

The next time I was ready for him. I feinted left before bringing the ball back right, shooting around him. The San Diego crowd understood good soccer and gasped at the speed of my move. I grinned, loving the open pitch and the feel of the ball knocking off my cleat just so. I lined up where I wanted to be and slammed off one hell of a kick.

I had just enough time to see it sail over the goalie's head and kiss the back of the net before Klein's cleat ripped into the side of my shin guard, up high, near my knee.

"Cabron!" I yelled as I fell forward, my weight too sudden and too much for my hamstring. A searing pain shot up from my knee, through my thigh and straight to my hip and even my chest.

I fell hard on my hands. Whistles blew. The stadium fell silent, eerily so. All I could hear was the blood in my ears.

A moment later came a smattering of boos that grew louder. I cradled my leg as I panted through the next wave of agony, not the least concerned by the sudden wetness on my neck.

"You don't fucking spit on my player!" Varner. He shoved Klein, hard. Another San Diego player ran up, and I gritted my teeth, trying to stand, trying to take care of Varner. My hamstring screamed in protest and my leg buckled.

The second San Diego player pulled Klein back. "Cheap shot, man!" he yelled, shoving Klein with enough force that Klein fell to the ground. "He was running circles around you because you aren't the player he is. I'm talking to coach. You're gone."

Klein didn't say anything, just lay there and glared at me. The second San Diego player came toward me. Menson. The captain. His words made more sense now. Menson put his left arm around my waist and lifted my right arm over his shoulder.

"Bad?" he asked me in a quiet voice.

"Pretty sure I just lost my deal with Milan." I gasped as I tried to put weight on my leg. "*Mierda*. Definitely lost that deal."

Menson cursed a string but helped me hobble forward with a surprising amount of restraint. The fans stood as the techs ran the stretcher out. They clapped when Menson helped me onto the board. Jorge jogged over, his eyes wide.

"You were right," I said in Spanish.

He nodded, his eyes darkening with displeasure.

"I'll talk to your coach once I know how bad this is," Jorge said to Menson, who nodded.

"I've been after Coach to drop Klein for weeks. I'll be sure to tell him what I saw." Menson patted my shoulder. "Sorry about the leg, man."

I lay back on the stretcher, forearm over my eyes, uncaring what the cameras made of this. Because I was angry, sick with the pain and unfairness, that Klein took the choice from me.

The call from my agent came within minutes of me getting situated into a private room at the hospital.

"Over?" I asked, trying to get comfortable in the hospital bed.

"Yes."

I squeezed my eyes shut, in too much pain and too tired to even rustle up the energy to curse.

"I'm sorry, Teo."

An orderly touched my arm. "We're going to take you back for the MRI now," he said. I nodded.

"Me, too." I clicked "End" and dropped my phone on top of my Timber uniform, its collar and chest still a darker shade of green that faded in gradual increments as the sweat dried from the shiny material.

CHAPTER TWENTY
Preslee

Brenna stayed true to her word and held my hand throughout the entire ordeal, from my initial phone call to the trip to the police department and my meeting with the officer, who took my information and slow-peck-typed up the report. Three hours later—transcribing my conversation with Oren took forever—I headed to the symphony where the conductor lashed out, telling me I'd put my own interests before that of the group. After fifteen minutes of his cheeks darkening to a shade near eggplant, I played the recording Brenna sent to me for him, too.

At least he quieted down, and we worked through the last few hours of rehearsal. Keyed up from Oren's call and the subsequent tongue-lashing from my conductor, I wanted nothing more than a hot bath and to lay my head on Teo's shoulder. To have him put his arms around me.

But he wasn't back yet from his trip to San Diego.

My car service pinged, letting me know it would be another few minutes, so I shuffled back inside the building, mindful of Oren's threat. I nodded at the security guard standing nearby, who nodded back with a smile. Setting my viola case at my feet, I scrolled through my phone, frowning.

Seventeen alerts and a bunch more texts and voice messages. What was going on?

Clicking through, my anger faded and horror built in my stomach. "Oh, Teo." His hamstring, his career in question. I scrolled through my contacts until I found Noah's name.

"Where is he? What hospital?" I asked.

"He's been released from the UCSD hospital. Jorge stayed back and is flying with him. They're on American. Um, where did I put the flight number?"

"Give it to me. I want to meet him at the gate."

"You think that's smart, Pres? I've been frantic to call you since I heard your voice mail this morning, but I've been fielding media all afternoon. If Oren's bugging you, then maybe you should just go home. Lay low. I mean, with Oren's call today."

"I've dealt with a career-ending injury, Noah. I know how hard it is to realize he might not recover. Do not screw with me about something as trivial as Oren at a time like this." My voice ended in a near-shout, and my face burned when the people in the lobby turned to stare at me, gawping at my outburst. I breathed hard through my nose.

"I read he couldn't walk off the field. He's hurt and he's angry and he's mourning. I need to be there for him, as soon as I can be."

"You felt that way?" Noah's voice rose, maybe in surprise.

We'd never talked about it. In fact, until this moment, I hadn't talked to anyone about what went through my head in those days and weeks following my trip to the hospital, the media frenzy as I was released from Northern's soccer program and then from the concerts I'd agreed to and finally, the voice program.

"Yes," I rasped. Clearing my throat, I said, "The feeling...it's awful because you have no control. Teo's always in control, needs it, is a better player because of it."

"Like you."

I narrowed my eyes before I dipped my head in an acquiescence. "Yeah. He's going to need time to get through this, but he's also going to need someone to rage at and maybe, when he's

173

ready, mourn with."

"I don't want him raging at you, Pres."

"You do it all the time."

"I do not." He sounded taken aback.

I smiled. "Give me the flight number. I'll catch a ride over to Sea-Tac now."

Noah sighed into the phone. "I'll do you one better. I'll send you a car."

"Fine. Meet us at the gate. I'm heading over now."

"Pres, you really shouldn't be alone now that Oren's threatened you."

I set my jaw, my expression hardening into what Noah called my pugnacious face. "Teo needs me."

We'd only been together twenty days. No way I could say I loved him. But I wasn't going to let him be alone in his time of need. Not if I could help him.

———————

I cursed the airport's rules and restrictions that wouldn't let me walk up to the gate to greet Teo off the plane and settled for a text: *At baggage claim.*

I didn't know what else to say, so I kept it short, to the point. He didn't reply. Twenty minutes later, Jorge strolled through the doors, a scowl darkening his face as he took in the crowd. Teo hobbled behind him, his leg stiff, and the crutches awkward despite his broad shoulders and thick arm muscles. I popped out of the chair and hurried forward, stopping just short of throwing myself against him.

Teo balanced on his good leg and beckoned me forward with his right hand. I slid in tight against his front, already tilting my face upward to receive the kiss I'd missed for too many days. My fingers sank into his Timbers sweatshirt as I lost myself in the feel of his mouth on mine.

"I missed you," I murmured against his lips. "And I'm so upset about your leg." I pulled back, my hands moving up and down his chest. "I didn't know until after rehearsal. Noah sent over a car. What can I do?"

"Take a breath." Teo pressed his lips to mine again in a short, perfunctory kiss that caused me to growl with need. "I am fine. Well"—he scowled down at his leg—"mostly fine."

I cupped his cheek and brought his gaze back up to mine. "A late hit. Klein's already been suspended."

Teo shrugged. "Doesn't fix my leg."

"Or your trade to Milan," I said, dropping my hand. We hadn't talked about it much, so I wasn't sure I had the right to bring it up now.

"Let's get to the car," Jorge said in his lightly accented English. "Away from the press who seem to have found you."

Teo gestured for me to go first, so I stepped in front of him, planning to grab one of his bags. Jorge waved me off. I sighed, clutching the strap of my purse as I led the way toward the exit, doing my best to ignore the journalists and fans snapping pictures.

Oren's words echoed in my ears, the threats causing me to shiver. But, if I wanted to be with Teo, this was my life now. I kept pace beside Teo, biting my tongue and pushing down my desire to take his arm and help him.

That wouldn't help his resentment just as my brother or even

Teo coddling me through Oren's threats wouldn't help. If the media was focused on me, then Oren wouldn't get to close. I hoped.

I'd—no, we'd—be okay. As long as I made damn sure Oren stayed away.

CHAPTER TWENTY-ONE
Teo

Getting to our building took nearly two hours, thanks to rush-hour traffic and my insistence we drop Jorge off at his house, not the Timber offices.

Preslee remained subdued throughout the ride—even more so than usual, which caused a chill to build along the back of my neck. I intuited she didn't want to talk in front of the driver, but her strange stillness gnawed at me even as she held my hand, her eyes dropping to my left leg.

"What's wrong?" I asked as soon as we entered my condo, rounding on her with a quick flick of my crutches.

"I'm worried about you," she said, dropping her purse into the usual spot on the chair I'd set there for her weeks ago. She removed her trench coat and hung it in the closet. My chest warmed, enjoying the routine—the hominess of the moment.

"I appreciate that. And for the record, I have a tear in the muscle. It's not that major an issue."

She grasped my shoulders and pulled me close. "Oh, Teo, that's great news!"

I buried my nose in her hair, wishing I could tug her closer. Close enough to wrap her legs around my waist and kiss her into the same drugged state I always fell into when we were together. But my leg would not allow for that.

"Something is bothering you." I pressed a kiss to her brow and pulled away. I managed to settle onto the couch, grunting at the effort to get my leg into a comfortable position.

Preslee twisted her fingers as she settled on the edge of the cushion next to me. "Oren called."

"*Mierda*. What did he want?"

"To—to threaten me. Tell me I still belonged to him." She raised those beautiful eyes to mine, hers muddied with worry and fear.

"You do not, you never did." I cupped her cheek in my palm, alarmed by the coolness of her skin. "You belong to yourself, Preslee."

She wrapped her free hand around my wrist. She huffed out a breath, forced her eyes back to mine. "He's the one who followed us that night."

I bit the inside of my lip to keep from cursing. Not that I was surprised—I wasn't. But the idea of anything happening to Preslee…that scared me. Deeply.

"Did you contact the police?"

She nodded. "Brenna went with me."

I wrapped my arm around her waist, pulling her tighter to my side. "I'm glad she was there with you. For you."

We sat there, quiet, absorbing each other's presence and warmth. Angry as I was about my leg—and I was livid—this moment brought peace.

My phone rang. Preslee leaned forward and snagged it off the coffee table, handing it to me.

"Mariana. You got my message?" I asked in English so that Preslee could understand the conversation.

"Yes," she replied, also in English. "I'm so sorry you've reinjured your leg."

"I didn't reinjure it. John Klein came in for a late tackle, trying to take out my knee."

Preslee shuddered, burying her face into my chest. She understood. That…that injury, with a ripped ACL or meniscus, a broken patella, might mean I couldn't walk well again, let alone play professionally.

"Can you come up here and treat me again?"

"I'm booked solid for the next five weeks."

"What if I bought out those appointments?"

"That's not fair to my patients."

I sighed, frustrated she was right. "Our team masseur doesn't have the quality of hands you do."

Preslee sat next to me and raised one eyebrow practically up to her hairline.

"You'll find someone. Talk to Mark Kepplenger at the university. I'll send him an e-mail now so he expects your call. Why don't you ask your girlfriend to help? She might not have a degree in kinesiology but she's played soccer, and I bet she likes to put her hands on you."

Preslee smirked, making it obvious she'd heard those last words at least.

"What if it's worse than the doctors think?" I asked.

"Then you'll never play at the same level again. But there's nothing I can do to help with that. Rest up. Do your physio. I'll call you to see how you're doing in a couple of days."

I thanked her and clicked off my phone. Preslee pressed tighter against my side, running her fingertips up my thigh. Even with an aching leg, the touch sent fire straight to my crotch.

"I'd be happy to put my hands all over you."

I eased down on the couch and put my hands behind my head. "Be my guest."

Preslee smiled as she darted into the bathroom to grab the bottle of oil Mariana had left there. She stepped back into the living room, her nude body my favorite masterpiece.

When Preslee was finished with me, my thigh—and the rest of me—was more relaxed than it had been since I left on the trip. Part of that was her soft skin pressed against mine. There'd been an article recently about the importance to women of daily cuddling. Maybe there was something to that for men as well. Naked cuddling that ended in orgasm, that was.

I pressed a kiss to her brow as Preslee snuggled tighter into my lap. My leg ached in a dull, annoying thrum, but I wouldn't change it—any of the last few weeks—if I couldn't hold Preslee in my arms now.

She mattered. More than I'd expected.

I didn't know what to do with that.

I spent the next ten days at home, spending most of my time rehabbing my leg. Thankfully, this injury was minor compared to my last one, because I'd spent all those weeks working with Mariana to strengthen the other muscles around my hamstring.

Noah called me on Tuesday to let me know John Klein was suspended for the rest of the year. "And even his own teammates don't want him back on the roster."

"It was a cheap shot," I said.

Noah grunted. "It's more than that. He's got a rep for being an asshole."

I scowled as I tried to stand, a deep ache flashing through my thigh as I settled onto my crutches. "Doesn't help my leg."

"No. But you do have Preslee there to nurse you back to health."

I smiled, thinking about my morning massage. And what that led to.

"I can feel your satisfaction through the phone. That's my sister, dude."

"I didn't say anything."

"See that you don't." Noah hung up.

Even now, weeks into dating, Preslee brought out emotions I never knew existed—contentment, pleasure, and maybe... probably... love. At least that's what I assumed this unexplainable feeling—almost electric, filling every part of me—was. With each passing day, my interest in Preslee deepened, along with my growing resentment of my imminent return to the Timber and the need to travel with them.

This morning, like many others, I puttered into my kitchen, smiling, as Preslee sang in the shower. I was off the crutches, *gracias a Dios*, and enjoying the limited mobility that had returned with being able to use both legs.

Her voice, her nearness, made my chest warm.

My phone rang. Picking it up, I hit the Accept button and said hello to my father, wincing before he began to speak.

"My son. The first call since your injury."

I frowned, irritated. I hadn't called in the last week and a half. I'd expected this level of frustration. "I've been busy."

181

"With healing or with your girlfriend?" he asked.

I frowned, displeased with his tone. "Both. More rehab, as you know."

"You have not played these last three games."

"Because Klein tried to destroy my hamstring," I snapped.

"I understood the sports therapist was helping."

"You've spoken to Jorge."

"Yes. Because *you* haven't called me to explain your injury."

"Then Jorge told you our trainer believes there is a tear in the muscle." Jorge had settled into the role as acting head coach, but he didn't love the position. He hoped the Timber found someone they wanted to hire for the long term.

"What of the Milan trade?"

I looked longingly down the hall, wishing I'd slipped into the shower with Preslee. Then I wouldn't be having this conversation. I'd be kissing her, kneading her luscious breasts, parting those soft thighs.

"Matteo? What of Milan?"

Right. My father.

"It's over. No deal."

The shower cut off. *Mierda.* I missed the opportunity. And she'd be at the symphony all day today.

"You not calling makes more sense now."

Preslee walked out of the bedroom in my robe, and I mourned her covered, damp skin.

I heard my mother's voice through the phone, but I couldn't understand the words. My muscles tensed further, my head to beginning to throb. "You're having this conversation in front of her?"

"She's the one worried about you, son. Your mother feels your young woman is keeping your head full of too many thoughts that are not soccer and this is why you haven't been able to play."

I clenched my teeth together hard enough for them to squeak. "And I asked you for privacy on this matter," I shot back.

Preslee wrapped her arms around my middle and laid her cheek against my tensed back. Within a moment, she pulled back, her eyes finding mine, filled with concern.

"Matteo, that is your mother you're speaking of." Papa's voice turned ominous. "You should treat her with the dignity of her position."

Much as I wanted to tell him that I didn't owe her respect or anything else, I chose not to cause any more tension with my father. I loved the man, and he deserved my respect. "I have to go to my physio. I'll call you soon."

My father sighed with a heaviness I'd never heard before, then offered to talk to me about my upcoming road trip. The one I didn't want to go on because the idea of leaving Preslee alone terrified me now that the closed-circuit security cameras in the area proved Oren was the man in black following us after dinner that first night we spent together. Of course, that information came in after the little *cabron* threatened her. But it also gave us a stronger case against him. One I had a lawyer following up on because Oren would never—*never*—frighten or hurt Preslee again.

I tossed my phone onto the counter and leaned forward, letting my head drop down to my chest. Preslee's hands massaged the aching muscles in my neck, I groaned. After a few moments, I spun around, sweeping her up into my arms.

"Are you okay?" She rested her head against me.

"If I am with you, *dulzura*, I'm okay." I sealed my lips over hers as I laid her back on the just-made bed. Forget breakfast, my injury, my father, my mother's intentions or Oren's. I stripped the robe off Preslee and blazed a trail down her throat to her shoulder, sucking gently in that spot she loved where the two met before easing down farther across her breasts and belly.

"Teo," her voice rose as I nipped at her hip bones. "Your physical therapy."

"Not yet," I whispered against her silky skin. No. First, and most important, I must lose myself in Preslee's body. In her passion for me. And maybe, just maybe, I could delude myself for more weeks that the situation with my parents—my mother—would improve.

CHAPTER TWENTY-TWO
Preslee

"You'll be back on tomorrow?" I asked as I walked down the symphony's front hallway. I waved to Peter, the night security guard, who nodded back. I'd been here too long, but I'd needed to pass the hours while Teo traveled with the team. Five days was the longest he'd been away from me, and I'd hated going to sleep alone each night. Funny how quickly I'd become addicted to sleeping not just in Teo's condo, but in his bed.

"*Si*. Well, more like the middle of tonight. I miss you, *dulzura*."

I smiled, enjoying the pout in Teo's voice. "Me, too, but your team needs you."

He snorted. "I do not see how. I cannot play, especially since the tear isn't improving as we'd hoped. I'm sure the coaching staff will discuss my move to the permanent injured list."

"I hope that doesn't happen, but if it does, you can heal completely and play better next year."

Teo remained silent. He must hate the idea of no longer playing at the elite level.

"I talked with management and Jorge. About me moving to the coaching side of the organization. It would save the team player salary."

My mouth popped open. "Is that…you want to do that?" I asked.

"I want to be near you. I'm thirty-three. No longer in my prime no matter how much I wish to be."

"But your career." That's all I could squeeze out. Shock didn't cover my current feeling. I wanted to ask Teo if he was doing this for me—for us—but I feared the answer. Teo was known for his focus and dedication to the sport. If a European team wanted him, he'd be a fool not to join that organization.

"None of that," he said, his voice crisp. "I can coach. It isn't the same as playing…" His voice trailed off. "But I get to stay in the sport I love."

My heart ached. "I wish I could hold you. At least your hand. I hate that we're having this conversation on the phone."

"Will you stay at my place tonight?" Teo asked. "I want to kiss you awake when I get there."

I stepped out onto the sidewalk, craning my neck as I looked for Brenna's brown hair in the sea of evening revelers looking to enjoy their evening at Pike Place Market or The Showbox. Some businesspeople hustled between the tourists and concertgoers, their briefcases and bags tucked close to their tailored slacks.

"Sure, I can do that. Can't wait to see you, Mr. Sexy Soccer Coach."

"You know, when you put it that way…" Teo chuckled.

Brenna waved at me from across the street, her hand popping up over the shoulder of one of the women in a business suit. Brenna's smile brightened—I'd texted her about an hour ago, asking if she'd like to go to dinner and a movie. I'd spent all my free time with Teo after his injury, which increased Brenna's hostility.

"Oh! I see Brenna. I'll see you in a few hours."

"Can't wait."

I smiled, about to wave back at Brenna as she walked toward me, but her happy face was obliterated by Oren's angry one. He slapped my phone from my hand, his mouth contorting into an ugly sneer.

Instinctively, I stumbled back, away from Oren's thick, clenched fists. Stupid, stupid mistake. It put me closer to the street, and Oren used my momentum to push me into the crowd.

"Preslee!" Brenna's voice rose as it filled with fear.

"Let me go!" I shouted. Oren ignored me, his jaw clenching as he stared straight ahead.

I tried to dig my feet into to the pavement, but my ballet flats couldn't get purchase thanks to their nonexistent grip.

"I'm not going anywhere with you," I yelled, flailed my arms. God, why didn't someone help me?

"Shut up. Just shut up. You'll do as I tell you."

"Let. Me. Go." My throat already hurt from shouting. It'd be worth it if I could get away. The look in Oren's eye...I shuddered.

"Is there a problem?" A man in a suit asked. Oren lifted his free arm—his left arm—and punched the businessman. I watched, lungs compressing with horror, as the man slid to the ground, blood gushing from his nose.

A woman screamed, another man shouted. Oren ducked his shoulder, which slammed into my empty lungs. Black dots floated and danced in front of me, blocking my vision.

He planned to take me somewhere. To hurt me. Again.

No.

I kicked and clawed. I inhaled and screamed. Oren grunted as my nails shredded the skin on his neck, dropping me. I managed to land on my feet, though I tumbled forward onto my palms. Staggering, I pushed forward into a sprint, cursing my ballet flats.

Oren's fingers closed around my forearm, and he yanked me back toward him. I lashed out with my foot, screaming again. Vaguely, I was aware of Brenna's tear-filled voice and the general milieu of the small but growing crowd. My attention remained on my tormentor—the man who I'd given control of nearly a decade of my life. His eyes narrowed and his big, beefy arm raised. I ducked, jerking my arm, trying to break his hold.

He yanked me toward him, and I cried out as pain seared up into my shoulder, but I refused to give up. Last time, Oren beat me and I was too afraid to react. This time, I couldn't allow him that chance. I had to fight.

With my free arm, I brought my bag up, aiming at his head, but he blocked my clumsy effort with ease, his fist catching me near my ear. He threw me against the side of a car.

Just like that, I slid down the slick metal, ears screaming against the pain blossoming in my head.

His big hand gripped the short hairs on my crown, yanking my head back as he plowed his fist into my stomach. Bile rose, fast, and I vomited, my stomach a roiling mass.

"Stupid, stupid whore. I told you I wasn't done with you yet."

I couldn't breathe. My entire body hurt. I collapsed into my own sick and curled into a ball, waiting for the next blow. It hurt, as did the next. I tensed, preparing for the indescribable pain sure to follow.

It didn't happen.

Raised voices drifted in and out of focus around me, but I hurt too much to lift my head. My stomach, my head, they swam in a weird gray haze. I put my hands down, trying to push myself up. A hand clamped on my shoulder, and I flinched away, slamming my shoulder into the car behind me.

"It's okay, ma'am. You're okay now. We're waiting for the ambulance." Not Oren. I lifted my head, my eyes unwilling to focus.

Blue. Uniform.

"Police?" I asked, my voice raspy, barely more than a whisper.

"Yes, ma'am. I'll stay with you."

"He hit me. Oren."

"We know. We saw."

"He's hurt me before. I filed a new restraining order."

"That explains a lot. He fought us, too."

"Will he go to jail?"

"He won't hurt you again, ma'am. He's in the police car."

"She's my friend!" Brenna cried. "Let me…I just need to…he attacked her."

I closed my eyes and curled back up into a ball, everything aching.

———◆———

The blow to the head resulted in a concussion—my second from Oren. Once the pain medication kicked in, the body aches eased to bearable. My left arm was abraded and my skin bloomed with bruises, but those aches faded, too.

Until the nurse came in and changed out my fluid bag. "Is there something wrong?" My concern spiked, pushing aside some of the pain.

"We needed to change your pain medication. Don't worry, this one's safe for pregnancy."

"She's pregnant?" My brother, Noah, shouted from the doorway. His open-mouthed expression must have mirrored my own.

The nurse, an older woman with dark gray curls, frowned at Noah. "Who are you?"

"My younger brother," I muttered.

"You're pregnant?" he managed to choke out.

My chin wobbled, but I held my composure long enough to ask a more important question. "Am I still? Oren hit me in the stomach." Tears pooled in my eyes.

Pregnant. And my brother knew before Teo. This wasn't right. Any of it.

My brow furled as I considered the possibility. We'd been careful. Teo used condoms. I took birth control—except when I felt sick after our initial and failed hookup. I hadn't been able to keep anything down that one day, including my pill.

One month into the best relationship of my life, and we weren't ready for a child.

Were we ready for a child?

My hand curled protectively over my stomach. Cosmic or otherwise, I now held a piece of Teo within my body that no one could take away.

"No bleeding. That's a great sign. I can bring in a sonogram and we'll double check."

I settled back against the pillow, my lips pulling upward into a huge grin. "Yes, please."

"I guess you're happy about this," Noah muttered.

I turned my head on the pillow. "Don't say anything. I need to talk to Teo."

"Too late," Noah sighed. Moving aside, he gestured back to Abbi, Mom, Brenna, and Nate in the hallway. I scowled, annoyed my family knew before my baby's father.

"Why isn't he here?" Nate asked. "This awesome guy I've yet to meet."

190

"Because he's traveling with the team," I replied. "I was on the phone with him when Oren grabbed me. Oh, God! He has to be so worried."

"I texted him," Noah said. "He knows. He responded about twenty minutes ago to say he planned to catch an immediate flight back."

Brenna stood quietly at the back of the crowd, arms crossed tight under her breasts.

"What's wrong, Bren?" I asked.

She swiped at her eyes. "I was so scared." Her voice cracked. "I never thought Oren would…" She mashed her lips together and shook her head.

"I don't know how he knew I'd be at the symphony. I shouldn't have been. Practice ended more than three hours before I left."

"Why were you?" Nate asked.

"I was working on the electric piece Asher sent over. The acoustics there are better than in the practice facility I'd have to use otherwise."

Noah frowned. "Teo said he'd called a lawyer about Oren. He wanted to assign a bodyguard to you. I shouldn't have told him no."

"Bodyguard?" I wrinkled my nose, but then considered it. If someone was there today to help me, someone who knew what he was doing, maybe Oren wouldn't have grabbed me. "How's the guy who tried to step in?"

"Getting a lawyer." Abbi set her lips in a grim line. "I hope he sues the pants off Oren."

Brenna twisted her hands together, her agitation distracting me. "I'm glad the cops were able to get to you so quickly," she said. "Thank goodness a patrol car was on the same block."

Noah shook his head. "I don't like that it came down to luck. *I* should have gotten you a bodyguard."

"The police officer told us Oren is all scratched up. He said you did a number on him." Nate sat on the edge of my bed, pulling my attention back to him. "I'm proud of you, sis."

"Not as much as he deserves," Noah muttered, sitting on the other side and taking my other hand.

Big—as in tall and broad—brothers crowded me. They had since birth, being all hardwired to protect me.

"Probably not, but I'm not sorry I marked him." My nails were ragged. "I'm a mess."

"You smell worse," Nate said.

"I threw up when he hit me in the stomach."

Noah stood up and walked to the window, tension clear in his shoulders, the tilt of his chin.

"Maybe you should quit dating Teo. You're in the news again." "Why?" I asked.

Abbi pulled a paper from under her arm. "Front page."

"Timber Striker's Girlfriend Attacked by Jealous Ex."

I dropped the paper, my ears buzzing. "They pulled it all back up?" I whispered.

My mom sat in the seat Noah had vacated. She smoothed my hair from my forehead. "Not yet. But it's a matter of time, I think. Then they'll delve into your dad's death."

My throat convulsed. My mom's eyes were red-rimmed, tired. She looked old now. For the first time in ages, she looked every one of her sixty-three years. "I'm sorry, Mom. I…"

"You will *not* apologize for that. He loved you. Just as we loved him." Mom stood and joined Noah at the window. He wrapped his arm around her. My brothers were here as much for my mom as for me.

The wound left by my dad's sudden death ripped open, bleeding fresh, as it did every time I thought of him driving down to Portland one year after Oren's attack to make sure I was okay. I squeezed my eyes tight, wishing tears would ease the pain. They never did, which was why I'd quit crying.

Even without opening my eyes, I knew it was Brenna who'd just taken my hand. "This story is juicy. Briar will tell you that. Maybe Noah's right and now's the time to step back. Give yourself a break."

"Not helpful," Abbi snapped. "You and Teo are good together. Mom and Aunt Briar said to tell you they're thinking about you. They were in LA for some music thing with Asher and Hayden, but they're driving back now."

I found Abbi's concerned gaze over Brenna's shoulder. "They didn't have to do that."

Abbi rolled her eyes. "Like I could stop them."

My mom's face paled when she came back into my line of sight. Lia could barely stand to be in the same room with her. Briar told me both Lia and her dad's commanding officer called my mom to notify her of David's death. My mom didn't collect her older girls for weeks, and Lia had to cobble together meals and ways for the girls to get to and from school and their activities, all while dealing with her father's death. That was more than most adults could handle, and Lia was fourteen at the time.

Lia had every right to be angry with our mom. *I* hated our

mother's treatment of her older daughters, mainly because I couldn't understand how my loving mother could show such coldness to her children.

What type of mother would I be? I was going to have a baby. I wasn't ready. Yet I couldn't wait to hold this beautiful child. I smiled, drifting in the daydream of a perfect miniversion of Teo running around with a soccer ball.

"If you're feeling up to it, I'll help you shower," Mom said, startling me. I yelped as my muscles contracted, then I lay back, biting back a moan. "Then Nate can take me home."

Getting up sounded painful. The drugs were working their way through my system, making me sleepy.

Brenna noticed my sagging eyes. "I'll stay here with Pres. You go home. When she wakes up, I'll help her get cleaned up and get her discharged."

"I need new clothes," I sighed, wrinkling my nose at the thought of my outfit. The nursing staff had cut off my already-ripped top and my skirt, but my bra and panties were saturated with my vomit. More, Oren had touched me, violated my personal space and my safety. No way I'd ever wear any of those items again.

"Done and done." Abbi propped a shopping bag from an elite boutique on the small table next to the bed. "I was in there when I got the call. Everything's your size."

My smile turned watery but it felt so good. "Thanks, Abbi."

"For you, auntie? Just about anything." She leaned in and bussed my good cheek.

My family said goodbye; I think I responded. As I slipped into a deep, dreamless sleep I pictured a beautiful brown-eyed child I would hold in just nine months.

———◆———

The soft woosh of the door opening woke me. Brenna lay curled up in the chair, magazine open in her lap, snoring softly, and Teo stood in the doorway, his tall, broad-shouldered body outlined by the florescent hall lights.

He strode into the room, dropping a bag on the floor at the foot of the bed. He wore a badly rumpled suit, the tie long gone, sleeves rolled up and top three buttons undone, showing the gray T-shirt underneath.

His eyes zeroed in on me and some of the tension drained from his face.

"Preslee?" he asked, his voice hesitant.

"Here."

His hand sought mine, wrapping around my cool fingers, bringing warmth and safety with him. He leaned closer and his scent tickled my nose. Warmth spread through my chest. He came here straight here from the airport, straight from his soccer match. Fatigue and fear still pulled at his features, but his beautiful brown eyes lit up with relief as they skimmed my features.

"Dulzura."

His pet name. I smiled against the sleepiness tugging at me. Teo was here.

Everything would be okay.

CHAPTER TWENTY-THREE
Teo

"Why are you awake?"

"Because you opened the door."

I edged in closer, wrapping my other hand around hers as I sat on the edge of the bed near her hip. My lips compressed into a thin, angry line as my eyes traced the large knot on her forehead.

For the first time in my life, I'd chartered a private jet. I plowed past my coach, ignoring Jorge's comments and the questions from the sports media outside the locker room, phone pressed to my ear as I made hasty plans. Getting to Preslee mattered more than a possible fine, suspension, media nightmare.

Oren beat Preslee years before: she told me of the broken ribs, fractured face. How bad would she be this time?

My chest loosened enough for me to take a full breath—my first since Noah texted me: *She's stable. Awake. Worried you'll be upset. Don't know what happened to her phone.*

Then a little later: *In room 412. Private, like you asked. She's sleeping.*

"Oren grabbed you as you were walking out of the symphony hall?"

"Yes. When I wouldn't stop fighting and yelling, he picked me up. I'm assuming he planned to take me somewhere."

Her voice cracked on the last word as a tremor built and slid through her. Her pupils dilated—from the pain or fear—and her breath grew choppy. I should have pushed harder for the bodyguard. I should have pushed the lawyer harder.

I'd failed Preslee, failed to keep my woman safe.

Emotions rippled through me but I managed to keep my fingers as steady as my voice. Preslee needed my strength now, until she regained her own. In this, I could not fail her. I bowed my head, not wanting her to see the anger and fear building there.

I almost lost her.

Brenna sat up in her chair, rubbing her hand over her eyes. "Teo. Did he wake you, Pres?"

"No. He didn't." She gripped my hand harder, perhaps sensing my need to stand, to pace, to push out the adrenaline coursing through my system. When I met her gaze, her eyes were a soft, pale green. "I'm glad you're here."

"I shouldn't have left." I knew it then, but I ignored the jittery, unsettling feeling that still fluttered just under my skin. Even now, as I gazed into Preslee's eyes, I kept thinking about what could've happened.

As soon as we finished the game—one I orchestrated from the sideline to a win of two-nil, thank you very much—I pulled out my phone and ignored the press, my duties to the team, and called Preslee. I couldn't wait to hear her voice. And that's when my night went to hell. I could still hear her cry when Oren grabbed her.

Seeing her now brought all my emotions forward: the unrelenting fear I wouldn't see her again topped the list. I leaned in pressing a soft kiss to her forehead. I wanted to ask her—right now—to move in with me, but she'd never mentioned our long-term future.

Doubt crept into my mind, but I reminded myself that she needed time—time to trust me.

"I'm so sorry I wasn't here for you."

"Soccer's what you do, Teo. You travel a lot for your season. I knew that when we started dating."

I cupped her chin, my eyes directly over hers. "I want to keep you safe. Make you happy."

She gripped my wrists. "You do. I am."

"Since we're up, you ready for that shower, Pres?" Brenna yawned as she stood. "You smell gross."

"I'll help her." I flashed Brenna an annoyed look, unwilling to put up with her jealousy tonight. "It's about midnight. I'll call someone to take you home."

"You must be exhausted," Preslee said, her angel brows pulling down toward her nose. I couldn't resist the urge to kiss the tip.

"Not like I'll sleep at home, worried about you," Brenna snapped.

Preslee turned back to me. "I'm glad you're here, but I'm sorry I'm so disgusting."

I raised my fingers to her lips. "If you want to shower, I'll help you. Then you should rest."

"I told Pres I'd help her." Brenna's lower lip thrust out. "It's not going to be sexcapades tonight. She's been through major trauma."

I had to drop Preslee's hand, afraid I'd squeeze her fingers too hard, as I waited for Pres to make her decision. She sighed, her gazed flicking back and forth between us. My frustration morphed into agitation. Preslee didn't need a fight now. She needed calm, a chance to heal.

"Thanks, Bren, but I need to talk to Teo. Maybe you could get us some coffee?"

Her scowl turned more petulant as she stalked from the room.

"She really doesn't like me."

"It's the newness of me dating anyone after so long." Pres didn't look any more convinced than I was by the argument.

She struggled to sit up, and I leaned forward to help her. Her skin glowed milky white—ethereal. But even with the scrapes on her cheek and the lump at her temple, her porcelain skin glowed, her cheeks blooming with color.

"I didn't want you to see me like this." She plucked at the blanket over her knees.

"I like seeing you. You're beautiful. And you're safe." I paused. The word "love" hovered on my lips. I rubbed my thumb along the smooth, unblemished skin of her cheek and settled for, "I missed you. This trip was even harder than the last."

"I missed you, too, but I wanted to be clean when you showed up. Before the…the attack, I planned to be at the airport to greet you."

"Sounds delightful." I smiled because she seemed to need it. "Next time. But I'm just thankful you're okay."

"I am." Her face filled with a radiance that stole my breath. I leaned in, needing to be closer to my siren. The abrasions on her cheek glowed angry and bright against the pearlescent wonder of her skin. She clasped my hands in hers, and I squeezed back. I craved her touch, the connection to know she was safe.

"I'm better than fine." Her eyes shone bottle-green bright in the dim light. "There were so many witnesses, there's no way Oren won't go to jail."

"That's positive. My lawyer's helping build a case to ensure Oren stays in jail for many years." Confusion filled me. Why did she look so happy?

Relief I understood but not this beautiful, fierce joy. I cupped her cheek, needing to be part of that happiness.

"There's more. My nurse brought me news." She paused for a moment. "Good news, I think."

I waited, my heart pulsing in my chest.

"I'm pregnant."

I sat back, shock rocketing through me, a dozen mini explosions starting in my toes and drifting upward, cutting off my ability to think.

Preslee. Pregnant.

"Pregnant?" I asked.

"Y-yes." Her voice faltered.

"How? Are you sure?"

Preslee's fierce joy faded along with the brightness of her eyes. "That's what the nurse said."

"And the baby…this is our child?" I asked, trying to keep my expression and voice calm. Neutral.

"Of course." Her confusion twisted and became something else—not yet anger but definitely not pleasure.

My stomach twisted. I closed my eyes and inhaled sharply through my nose.

"I've been taking my pill, same as always, but the nurse said it's so early there shouldn't be any problems. Thankfully, Oren's punch didn't dislodge the baby even though my stomach's pretty sore."

"He hit you in the stomach?" I asked. That was my voice? No, not that garbled, husky tone.

Preslee settled back, her eyes widening. "Yes. The doctor said I was lucky. Just bruising. Nothing permanent."

"Good. That's great. How many times did he hit you?"

She touched the knot on her forehead. "A few. Are you...are you angry?"

That beautiful bloom in her cheeks had dissipated completely. I wanted it back, but she slid away, her face in shadows in the poorly lit room. I struggled to find an appropriate response, my father's words circling my head: *Even knowing she might trap you as your mother sought to trap me?"* chased by Preslee's: *I'm pregnant.*

"No, I'm not angry. I'm surprised." Disappointed, too, because I'd wanted Preslee to be different—to love me for *me* and not what I could give her in material terms. She'd said my money didn't matter.

I'd trusted her.

I never trusted women. I couldn't—I'd seen my father go through too many, grasping at his wealth and power. Like my mother.

"You just wish Oren had punched our baby out of me."

I blinked at her, trying to follow her thoughts. Did I? "No, Preslee. God, no."

"You do," she breathed. "You don't want a baby with me."

She pulled her legs up, grimacing from the blows her slender body withstood. She scrambled from the bed. Her gait was uneven, but she managed to slam the bathroom door as I dodged machines and scampered around the bed.

"Preslee. Let's talk about this."

Nothing. I knocked again. Louder. Not caring if I woke up the whole damn hospital.

"Preslee. I want to help you."

"We've been here before, Teo. Just go."

"And you wonder why I don't like you," Brenna said. She stood in the doorway, arms crossed over her chest, eyes narrowed. "You're a self-absorbed asshole."

"This is between Preslee and me," I gritted. I slid my hands through my hair. Pregnant. Blow to the stomach. She could have lost the baby before we ever knew about it. I wanted the baby I made with Preslee. *Of course I did.*

I knew this is what I wanted as soon as I met her beautiful eyes when I walked into her hospital room, love for our child shining through her, making her glow. Yes, I wanted this. I wanted to share in Preslee's happiness. I loved her. I loved our child already.

"Get out of here, Teo. You've done nothing but make her cry."

I turned, biting back an angry retort.

"That's my lover in there. I plan to talk with her about *my* child."

"Fuck that," Brenna snapped. "You don't want a kid. You don't even want her, not now that you knocked her up." She looked me up and down, a sneer building. "You are such a selfish asshole."

Sleep had proved elusive since I left Seattle three nights ago, and now, I'd been up for more than twenty-four hours, my adrenaline crash hitting me so hard I could barely stand. Hearing Preslee cry out, too far away to do anything about it…I'd nearly gone crazy.

And on top of those raw emotions came this: a baby. *She'll try to trap you* my mother had insisted, nearly yelling each time I spoke to my father this week. I'd scoffed then. Now…now, my mind pitched and rolled, unable to cling to much except that I loved Preslee.

I loved her.

But could I trust her? With my heart? With my child?

I didn't know. We'd never said the words, never come close to saying them.

My father married my mother because of me. Would I do the same? Did I want to?

My plans, my carefully crafted plans—I gave up my dream to play in Milan, not fighting again with Roberto said they pulled out. I'd been angry but also relieved because I could woo Preslee slowly, build a life with her. Now, all that lay in rubble at my feet.

"Go home, Teo. You've done enough damage in less than five minutes than Oren did with his fists. At least *he* only broke her body."

Brenna squirmed around me. Her hatred, flashed from deep in her eyes, virulent and ugly. "Get out of here. You're making the situation worse." She snarled, and I stumbled back.

Brenna leaned against the doorframe. "Pres. It's me. I'll help you wash your hair."

The door cracked open. I wanted to shove it open and pull Preslee out and into my arms, as I wanted to, one look at her expression stopped me.

Preslee appeared fragile. All color leached from her face. Her eyes were dull, her face streaked with tears. She'd remained dry-eyed when she thought I might be cheating on Mariana that night I carried her home from the bar, but this time, tears streamed down her cheeks.

Brenna slipped through the door. The snick of the lock reverberated through my mind.

"Preslee," I whispered again, flattening my palm against the door. The sound of running water drowned out my apology.

I slid down to the floor, planning to wait them out.

"What are you doing here?"

I turned to see an older woman in scrubs.

I leaned my head back against the wall. "I'm waiting for my girlfriend to come out of the shower," I said.

"She's in there by herself?" the nurse yelped.

"No. Her friend's with her."

"Oh. Then you need to leave."

"I'm not leaving," I said, indignant. I was her lover, the father of her child. I *wasn't* leaving her.

"If you don't, I'll call security. It's after visiting hours."

"The nurses had no trouble letting me in here fifteen minutes ago," I gritted.

She narrowed her eyes and crossed her arms under her ample bosom. "That young lady said you might make trouble." She pressed a button on the side of the bed. "I need security."

I ran my hands through my hair over and over, staring at the door, willing Preslee to come out. Each moment of this evening fell apart further. "I can't leave her. Not now."

A blue-uniformed guard stepped into the room. The nurse's eyes softened a little. "Look, if you want your girlfriend to heal, the best thing you can do is give her the opportunity to do so."

I gritted my teeth. Much as I wanted to cause a huge scene, the guard's wary expression, the Timbers' probable response, all those reasons stopped me. I left the room.

CHAPTER TWENTY-FOUR
Preslee

Being clean should have made me feel better. It didn't. Nor did the comfort of my new silky soft pants and sleek, embroidered tee. Brenna helped me into the socks Abbi bought me, along with the motorcycle boots I'd lusted after for months. Leave it to Abbi to try to cheer me up with awesome footwear. Didn't work.

Brenna fumed as she helped me dress, finally bursting out with, "You're so much better off without him."

I doubted that. Sure, I knew we weren't ready for a child. We still needed to learn each other's idiosyncrasies. Like Teo only slept on the right side of the bed. And I liked tea before I went to sleep. Little things, maybe, but important details of sharing time together. I'd hoped for more.

And, yeah, I expected something from him. If not excitement at least… No, I wanted him to *want* a child with me. Sure, he traveled a lot, but his job with the soccer club required it. I would never ask him to stop.

Had he paused, the concern flicking over his face, because he thought I wanted him to stop playing soccer?

Maybe Brenna was right. I clearly didn't have the instincts to find a quality relationship like my sisters' and Abbi's.

But…maybe the baby shocked Teo.

Maybe he thought I'd gotten pregnant on purpose.

Oh, no. Oh, no, no, no! He was *rich*. Babies with clingy girlfriends happened to rich men. And then I remembered, one of our first nights together, him telling me about his father and mother. That his mother had gotten pregnant to make sure his father stayed with her. *Fuck*. What if Teo thought I was doing the same thing?

I put my head in my hands. I never considered that idea—how it would look to the outside world. It's not like I wanted Teo for his money. His smokin' hot body, definitely. For his focus, his passion, his innate goodness.

He must have thought I'd lied to him that day we went to the barbecue—that I'd wanted nothing more than to force a forever-connection between us. While he'd never said so, I'd picked up on the fact he didn't want a relationship like his parents'. From his comments, I got the sense the distance between them, his mother's use of Teo as a bargaining tool, ate at his belief in love—in it *lasting*.

I would've curled up tighter, but my stomach hurt too much from Oren's blow. I cradled my belly, wishing I handled telling the conversation with Teo differently. Wishing he stroked my hair as he whispered Spanish endearments in my ear as he did every night as we lay together in his bed.

"Better he did that now than after the baby comes. Then the media attention would be unbearable. God, imagine if you had to deal with all that rejection at once."

"Stop," I whispered.

"I mean, you think this media churn is bad, what happens when you birth the heir to that massive fortune?"

"Brenna. Not now."

"Whether he wants to be responsible for your affair, you have rights, and he's going to pay up." Brenna's chin jutted and her eyes narrowed.

"I don't need his money."

As stupid as it sounded, his money intimidated me—that kind of immense wealth brought scrutiny. The media crucified me when Oren attacked me all those years ago, and since then I shied far away from any form attention. I gave up my budding music career, thankful to back away from the limelight and its constant questions, the way the media picked at my every misstep and bad hair day. Same with soccer—for a while, not having to give interviews and see myself on some sports blog was a relief.

I never told anyone, not Abbi or even Brenna, I'd been offered a lucrative two-album contract while I'd been living in Portland. By then, I fixated—and hated—the new hellish low of my life. The idea of jumping back into anything near that level of degradation made me physically ill.

If I hated the faint glare of local scrutiny, the inability to get a latte without people commenting on my hair, nail color, or sunglasses, how would I feel about the international attention that came with a relationship with Teo? Why was I just realizing the importance of these thoughts?

Because I'd been so wrapped up in him, in loving him, I hadn't considered enough of the consequences of my actions. Once again, I failed myself by letting my emotions rule me.

The pounding in my head grew to an unbearable thump.

I refused to get back into the hospital bed. It stank of my sick. Instead, I curled up into the hard chair near the door. Brenna perched on the edge of the bed, her face concerned as she watched me struggle with my emotions. I shut my eyes and considered my past.

I missed making music I loved. While I liked the intricacies of classical music and the symphony, I preferred the sharp one-four-fives of modern music.

I had tucked away my love of performing outside the haven of the symphony forever, but recording the song with Asher, then the performance at the Timbers game… it unlocked that desire to entertain. Now that I'd done it again, I had to admit I'd missed it more than I expected.

"Doesn't matter if you want it. We'll make sure you get it."

I needed Brenna to leave me alone. "I need some coffee."

"You can't drink caffeine while you're pregnant."

"That's inhumane," I exclaimed. "And how do you know that?"

Brenna shrugged. "I read it somewhere. I'll get you a decaf mocha. Decaf should be fine."

"Perfect. Thanks."

As soon as Brenna left, I called the nurse. "I need to check out."

"Not without a ride home, dear. You're still in observation period for your concussion."

"My boyfriend went to get the car," I lied, looking her straight in the eye. I wanted to go home, now.

"Are you sure you want to go home with him?"

"Why wouldn't I?" Had Teo said something?

She didn't look convinced so I played another card. "We're expecting some media since he's a soccer player. I'm hoping to get out before they see me. It's…well, it's embarrassing." I dropped my eyes, hoping I'd played her sympathy.

She sighed, the capitulation I needed. "I'll get the paperwork. Your boyfriend's going to watch you?"

"Of course. He'll bring me to my doctor if there are any symptoms."

He wouldn't, but someone who loved me would ensure my continued health.

I followed her to the nurses' desk and signed the appropriate papers there. I glanced around, scowling, as I looked for Brenna's long brown hair. I sighed with relief, thankful for these quiet moments. I couldn't deal with any more from her right now.

I started in surprise when Brenna said, "And just what are you doing here, missy?"

I glared up at her, acutely aware of the nurses bustling around us. "I'm checking out."

"You need to stay for observation," Brenna stuttered.

"No, I need to go home." I handed the nurse back her paperwork and walked toward the elevator.

"Miss Jennings! We need to wheel you to your car."

"I decline." I entered the elevator.

Brenna slid in next to me just before the door closed.

"You're acting…I don't know…kinda crazy."

I took the mocha she handed me.

"I want to leave before the media shows up. If they find out Teo's back and not with me…" I swallowed, a convulsive effort to regain control of my emotions. I'd cried once. I needed to get over it.

Brenna slid her hand in mine. "Smart thinking. Wait inside the doors in the lobby. I'll let you know when the ride's here."

"Thanks, Bren."

We made it home without incident, Brenna uncharacteristically quiet. Teo wasn't there. He hadn't left a note, nothing. I went straight to my room, locking my door. Brenna knocked.

"Need any help? Want to talk?"

"No. I'm going to crash. The pain meds made me sleepy." I kept the door closed, refusing to look at Brenna as I lied. My face and stomach hurt more now. I crawled into my bed. I wanted to call Teo but I didn't know where my phone was.

After all I'd been through, I remained so naïve. I believed Teo when he told me he cared about me. Maybe he did. But I don't think he ever considered a future with me. That's what hurt.

CHAPTER TWENTY-FIVE
Teo

The truth slammed into me as I sat in the back of the pristine Subaru that picked me up from the hospital: I just walked out on my pregnant girlfriend. *Santa Maria*. She must be furious with me. The hurt blurred her eyes, but now…she would be angry, and rightfully so. I'd head back to the hospital, sit in the waiting room. I stared out the window of the car, irritated by the paparazzi nearby.

More would be at the hospital now. Fatigue blinded me even before the flashes sent me staggering as I walked toward the cab I'd asked to wait for me.

"Teo! How do you feel about Preslee being in the hospital?"

"Her ex-fiancée attacked her?"

"Is it true he smashed her voice box, and she'll never speak, let alone sing, again?"

"Didn't you want to see your girlfriend? Did you break up before you left on your last trip?"

I turned around, refusing to let them print more rubbish about my relationship with Preslee. "She's resting. I'm going back to see her as soon as I can."

As I walked to the elevator, I dropped my palm to the back of my neck, trying to ease some of the tension there. Brenna wanted me out of Preslee's life. I knew that and I *still* did exactly what she suggested.

I trudged up to my condo and fell into my bed, hugging Preslee's pillow to my chest.

My phone's sharp ring dragged me out of a restless sleep.

"Bueno?" I blinked back the grit in my eyes. My clock read 5:47 a.m. I bolted upright, my heart tripping faster than it did when I sprinted the length of the soccer pitch. My first concern was Preslee.

"*What* were you thinking?" Noah growled. "Why did Preslee leave the hospital last night *without you?*"

"She left the hospital? How? When?"

The breakup question that reporter flung at me made more sense.

Noah's sigh filled the phone. "I don't know. She didn't tell me. I hoped she'd talked to you—you know, her boyfriend." He paused as I tried to wrap my head around all the information flying at me. "Please tell me this is all a misunderstanding."

"How did she leave? Is she okay?" That seemed like the most important detail.

"With Brenna, of course. Goddammit, Teo. She was beaten yesterday. Oren punched her multiple times. Why aren't you with her?"

"Because Brenna and a nurse teamed up and kicked me out of the room," I bit off, fatigue and anger mixing into a toxic stew boiling over in my belly. Nothing had gone right in the past few days. I hated sleeping without Pres in my bed. We'd lost two of three our games and my hamstring refused to loosen up enough for me to benefit the team as a player. But the look on Preslee's face when she thought I didn't care. I swallowed hard. Why hadn't I handled her news better? Why hadn't I kissed her like I wanted?

"Look, you're clearly exhausted. Get some rest. But you

should talk to her. Soon. This looks bad."

"It does. Because it is. When she told me…I didn't handle some news well."

"Please tell me you didn't walk out after Preslee told you she was pregnant," Noah's voice filled with concern.

"No! I wanted to stay, but Brenna and then the nurse…" I let the words slide into silence.

"Pres wanted you to know first. I've never seen her so happy. Did you yell at her?"

"I would never yell at her."

"Well then, why did Brenna kick you out?"

"See, Preslee was upset that I wasn't more excited. But it was a shock, you know?" I sounded defensive.

"What do you think is going to happen when you're sexing it up with my sister?"

"Well, I didn't expect her to get pregnant the first month she was with me," I bit back.

"You think she planned this? What…for your money?" Noah's growl caused the hairs on the back of my neck to rise. "You think my sister's a mercenary? Have you talked to her *at all*? She's one of the best people I've ever met. I told Nate you made her happy, you fucking prick!"

"I *do* make her happy."

"No wonder Brenna kicked you out. You know what? Just stay away from her. Jesus, I can't believe you."

The call ended.

I pressed the phone against my head and groaned. The only other person in Preslee's family that I could maybe count on as an ally, and I'd pissed him off, too.

I called Preslee, just needing to hear her voice. My call didn't even go to voicemail.

Cold sweat slicked my skin. She'd blocked my number. *Mierda*, this didn't bode well.

I scrolled through my phone, trying to figure out who I could call. Abbi might listen to my side. If I knew her number—or could retrieve it somehow. Not likely now. Brenna wouldn't give it to me, neither would Noah.

I squeezed my eyes shut, trying to come up with a solution.

It never came.

Instead, I relived the pain creeping into Preslee's eyes when I didn't react with joy to her pronouncement. With both Noah and Brenna telling her I was a lowlife scumbag, Preslee might never forgive me.

CHAPTER TWENTY-SIX
Preslee

"Want something to eat, honey?" Brenna asked.

I stumbled to the couch with a curt no. Curling up hurt too much, so I lay there, stiff and sore. Brenna handed me my phone—the one I'd dropped yesterday—and I inspected the dented case. The phone itself was surprisingly unscathed—and fully charged—so I called Lia, Briar, Abbi, my mom and both my brothers. Noah stopped by an hour later, just before eight o'clock, knocking hard.

As soon as Brenna opened it, Noah barreled in, hazel eyes flashing, his brown hair disheveled.

"You stay the fuck away from him, Pres. *Away*. I'm getting him traded somewhere he won't bother you again. To Argentina. Yeah, back home so he's thousands of miles away."

"Good." Brenna handed me a cup of water and my pills.

"But he's your best player." I sipped the water and took the pills grudgingly. I didn't want to do anything to hurt my baby.

"Correction. He *was*. His injury's made him a liability. A media one as well as a physical one. Martin agrees his lack of honesty with the coaching staff about the continued problems with his hamstring is the final straw."

"You talked the GM into this?" I folded my arms across my chest. I winced as I touched a bruise.

"Who cares? He's leaving." Brenna said. "Now you can focus on getting well and getting over him."

"Yeah." Noah sat on my dainty coffee table and grasped my hands in his. He rubbed the back of my hands with his thumbs, the gentle motion making me sniffle. "I'm so sorry he left you last night, Pres."

I glared at Brenna. "You called Noah and told him that?"

Brenna crossed her arms over her chest and scowled. "He left you. Of course I told your family that."

"The whole family is behind you. I talked to Lia and Asher. If it comes down to a legal fight for custody, we have the resources to win."

"What are you talking about?" I asked.

Noah leaned forward and pressed a kiss to the smooth part of my forehead. "Don't worry about it now."

"When does he leave?" Brenna asked.

"Soon." Noah stood. "I want him gone before the next game."

"But that's in two days!" My heart stuttered, my righteous anger—built upon his desertion and the realization he thought I'd trap him into marriage—dissipated. I might never see him again.

"I wish it was today," Noah growled. "You're not dealing with someone who thinks you'd try to trap him for money."

I dropped my eyes, not wanting Noah to see the tears gathering there. I blinked in rapid succession, forcing them back. So Teo did think my pregnancy was a plot to dig into his pile of money.

He thought the child was a tool, not made from love. I bit my lip, thankful I'd never said the words to him. If I had, would he have considered them a ruse, too?

Noah took my bowed head as capitulation. "I'll take care of this for you. Don't worry about anything but healing." He kissed my cheek.

After Noah left, the media harassed me. I refused to answer, and Brenna called the symphony's marketing department. The director, Samson, agreed to put out a statement saying I was recovering and thanking everyone for their concern.

Brenna left an hour later to pick up the last of my prescriptions, a prenatal vitamin with extra iron.

Teo knocked on my door less than ten minutes later.

"I must talk to you." He looked worse than me, and Oren's blows left me stiff, the areas purple and puffy. "Your brother's trying to trade me, but I don't want to go."

"You walked out on me last night." My chin wobbled.

"I wouldn't have left the hospital if Brenna's shouting hadn't brought in the nurse."

Wait. What?

Teo barreled on, before I fully processed that statement.

"I know you don't like hearing this, but Brenna does not want us together."

My confusion mounted. She didn't trust Teo—I understood that, but his take on the situation seemed excessive.

"You know I lo…I care for you, Preslee."

I waited, silently begging him to say he loved me. I'd thought he might. But he waited, his eyes shadowed.

"Tell me one thing." My voice broke. "Do you think I got pregnant on purpose?"

He hesitated, and my chest ached worse than any blow Oren delivered.

"I know I want to be with you." His voice was careful, more clipped than usual.

I mourned the lack of accent and musicality. I loved Teo's voice, the slight lilt to his baritone. More, I mourned his belief that I would treat him as his mother had his father. I closed my

217

eyes, hating what I had to do—for both of us, but, most importantly, for our baby so he or she was never in the same position Teo found himself in as a child.

"You were supposed to be different. To care about me."

"Do not lump me in with the filth from your past." He gripped my shoulders and I knew he wanted to shake me. Looking at the bruise on my forehead he dropped his arms then scrubbed his face.

"You're hurting me more than Oren hurt me yesterday. I trusted you." I bit my knuckles, hard—the last barrier against deep, ugly sobs.

"Look, I get that I messed up. I should've handled you telling me about the baby better. But you must know you matter to me. The child matters to me."

Screw it. I'd pinch my skin if I needed to. It was my body, my messed-up life. I dug my nails into my forearm, wincing at the pain, focusing on it.

"Stop it." Teo's eyes filled with sadness. Or was it secrets? I didn't know, and I didn't care. I pressed harder until I drew blood. At least the tears disappeared. I wasn't crying over him, over a failed month of my life. I got a beautiful baby out of it— total win for me. Focus on the pain. Breathe. Focus on the child. Exhale. My baby. Mine.

"You no longer have any right to tell me what to do!" I shrieked.

Teo stepped nearer. He didn't touch me, and I told myself I couldn't have handled that. At the same time, I wanted him to pull me into his chest, to tell me the past few hours were all a misunderstanding.

"Don't do this to us, Preslee. I'll fight for you. I'll fight the trade, but only if you'll move in with me."

Disgust coated my tongue as I glared at him. "Figured out ditching the preggers girlfriend makes you look bad, huh? Well, there is no us, not if you think I got pregnant to trap you. The accusation lit up your face. Noah confirmed you said as much to him, too." I swallowed. All my plans… I swallowed again, barely able to speak past the emotional shrapnel clogging my throat.

"You surprised me! We've taken all the precautions. I just…I just wasn't expecting it. This." He stepped in again, brought my chin up to meet his gaze. "But I want you, Pres. I want our baby."

I wanted to believe him. I did. But those were my emotions cheering me on. I must remember he left once. He'd do it again.

"You said I had to be the one to end this. I'm ending it."

His gaze was strong, his features stoic. "Does it matter that I'm in love with you?"

My heart stuttered with the pain. I forced my eyes to stay firmly on his. I shook my head. "You had a chance to tell me that before—before you thought I'd act like your mother. Or want to hold on to you only for your money."

I didn't bother to ask him to leave. I went into my bedroom, shut and locked the door.

Once again, we were right where we'd started. I never learned from my mistakes.

———◆———

I refused to come out of my room, even after Brenna ordered Teo to leave.

"You need to take your meds, Pres. Come on. Open the door."

I did with reluctance. My lip trembled and the words tumbled out. "I love him. I don't want him to go. I just want to be with him."

Her cheeks slackened and her eyes rounded. She pulled me into her bony chest, causing me to gasp from the contact against my sensitive flesh. "Oh, honey," her voice cracked as she sniffled into my hair.

"He might have only considered me a fling, but I can't stand the idea of him being with anyone else. I can't stand that."

Brenna blinked, her brows pulling low. "You—you really love him?"

I nodded, unable to speak passed the lump in my throat.

"It's too soon. It's just infatuation," Brenna muttered. Brightening, she said, "Come on, you can't be this sad. You have the baby to consider. If he loves you, truly loves you as you deserve, he'll want to stick around. Nothing will keep him away from you." This time her voice filled with absolute certainty.

"It's over." I made sure of it.

"Let's go shopping. Even if it's just online."

I pulled out of my best friend's embrace to glare at her. She sighed.

"Prada might make you feel better." She smiled as she pushed my bangs back. "It'd make me feel better for you."

"Some way you'll survive my breakup," I said, my voice dry. I lay down on the couch and pulled up the blanket Brenna put there. I took the pills she handed me and drank the glass of water.

"If you won't shop with me, how about a movie?"

I shrugged. I didn't care about any of that. I just wanted Teo. His arms around me, the feel of his naked chest against my cheek. I rubbed my fingers against the hem of his T-shirt I'd changed into after I told him we were over.

Pathetic, I know but I needed to feel safe. Teo made me feel safe. Or had. I huddled there, my eyes and throat aching, the emotions too big and fresh for any release.

Sometimes the hurt lodged too deep for tears.

"Get up. C'mon, sweetie."

I opened my eyes and glared at Brenna.

"You picked my lock?"

"Well, yeah. It's for a good cause. You've holed up in here for two days. You need to eat. Not just for you but for the baby. Abbi called, but I took care of that. Got you out of everything but that gig with Asher on Friday. The whole rest of your crazy family has called. Many times. They need to chill."

I snorted. Like she could talk.

"Go away."

"No. You've moped. It's time to get up and do something."

I waved in the general vicinity of my window. "I can't go outside without being mobbed. The reporters called me like a hundred times to see how I feel about Teo's trade."

Brenna sat on the edge of my bed. "I'm worried about you, Pres. This is the lowest I've ever seen you." She grabbed one of my arms, pulled it out to trace her fingers over the red and bruised skin. "The baby, Pres. Start thinking about our baby girl."

"*We* aren't having a baby," I snapped, irritated by her coddling. By her constant presence. That's why I'd locked my door in the first place—to get away from Brenna's forced cheerfulness. "*I* am."

"I'm going to help you. You're not alone. I made you waffles. Some good-for-mama waffles. Eat a few bites. I'll bring them to you here."

"Fine," I sighed. "I'm going to pee and brush my teeth."

I was out of toilet paper; I walked out to snatch some from our half bath just in time to see Brenna throwing away a huge bouquet. I stopped, staring at the beautiful hot pink gerbera daisies. My favorites. I'd mentioned them to Teo one night when he asked me how to romance me.

"Not with roses." I'd wrinkled my nose.

"You don't like roses?"

"I do."

"But?"

"Roses say you're just going through the motions. They lack originality."

"What would be a romantic gift?" He'd raised his eyebrows.

"For you or for me?"

"Either."

"Well, if you insisted on sending flowers, my favorites are daisies. The bright pink gerbera ones. Otherwise, maybe viola strings." I shrugged.

"Strings aren't romantic."

"But I always need them. Like bow rosin."

"Try again."

"That's the point," I said with a smile. "You should come up with something for me."

"Like pink daisies?" At my nod, he asked, "What would you get me?"

I'd bit the tip of my thumb and considered him. "Concert tickets to the South American band that's coming into town. Or that beer you liked at dinner last night. Some Serrano ham because you like it in your omelets, which I'd make for you." I'd lowered my voice and swayed in closer. "A new tie to wrap around your neck while you were otherwise naked."

Teo's pupils had dilated. "That's a good gift," he'd said, his voice raspier than usual. His accent had become more pronounced, too. I'd smiled, liking the power I wielded.

"I'd pull you by it to your bedroom before I shoved you into your chair."

Teo's Adam's apple had bobbed. "I want this tie." Then he'd pulled me close and kissed me, his hands shaking a little as he'd cupped my cheek.

"What are those?" I asked.

"Just some flowers," Brenna said with false cheer.

"Would you get me some toilet paper?" I asked. "It hurts to bend over."

"Sure, sweetie. Are the bruises getting better?"

"Ah, a little." I forced my eyes not to dart toward the trash bin. "I need to pee." I tried to look pitiful.

Brenna trotted off, and I dug frantically through the bin, looking for the card. If the flowers were from Teo he would've sent a card. I darted back to the edge of the kitchen as Brenna approached, my mission unsuccessful.

She took in my compressed lips. "I'll bring you breakfast in bed."

I nodded. "'Kay. Just give me a few."

Brenna brought me a tray a few minutes later. I smiled at her even though the idea of food caused my stomach to roll. She made a point of including one of the flowers she must've salvaged from the garbage on the tray. Probably because she remembered they were my favorite.

I nibbled through the waffle. "Teo sent the flowers, didn't he?"

Brenna shrugged.

"I want the card, Bren."

"But it'll just upset you. You shouldn't get upset now. It's not healthy for you or the baby."

I shoved the tray away. "The card, Brenna." I kept my gaze steady, palm up, waiting. "It's mine."

She grimaced as she pulled it from her back pocket. She sighed, a long, drawn out affair, as she handed it over. She grabbed the tray and stalked from my room.

Once she was gone, I opened the envelope. I recognized Teo's handwriting because I'd become even more obsessed with the man now that we weren't seeing each other. I knew the press labeled his last soccer match yesterday the worst in his career—not because he played—he didn't. But neither was he the cool and collected player they were used to seeing. He yelled at the referees and his teammates from the bench until finally Jorge had him escorted to the locker room. According to one blogger, Teo trashed part of the locker room, too.

Everyone focused on our alleged split because we were no longer photographed together, and my excuse of needing to rest and heal grew thinner by the day. The media attention was insane now that Oren had been refused bail—the only positive to come from all this. Three other women had stepped forward to testify against his abuse. Between that and my public beating and thwarted kidnapping, Oren was going to prison. I didn't delude myself into thinking it would be forever, but I knew it would be for many years.

I'm sorry. I handled the situation poorly, but I love you. Please, talk to me. M

I couldn't. No way. I'd cave.

I buried the note in my sock drawer because my underwear drawer felt too personal.

But I was unable to part with his words.

I texted Abbi. *Can I come up and see you?*

Course. Mom's here. Would you rather we came to you?

Not with Brenna's near-constant barbs against Teo. Since I told her I loved him, Brenna pointed out all his worst qualities. Problem was, he didn't have many. He'd been a model boyfriend.

I missed him. Terribly.

No. I'll come up. Need out of my place. It'll be a few.

Over the past couple years—since my dad's death—Briar, Abbi and I grew closer. Lia remained more reserved, but I knew she cared about me.

I wished my mom had been a better mother to her, but she hadn't, and my brothers and I were part of the reason for that. I couldn't imagine having to grow up at fourteen, as Lia was forced to. She'd become so successful, then married a wonderful man. I didn't remember her first husband Doug well, but Asher Smith doted on Lia. Part of me envied Lia her relationship with the rock star. At twenty-seven, I still failed at finding love—mutual love, anyway.

"Pres!" Abbi bounded up and wrapped me in a hug that just didn't quit. I hugged my niece back hard, glad to be here. Abbi was only seven years younger than me—closer to my age than her mother, Lia, though not by much.

"I hope you don't mind that I called Aunt Bri," Abbi said, pulling back. "We all want to know how you're feeling."

I shrugged, but my stoic expression cracked.

Abbi's eyes narrowed and a look passed between her and Briar. "Let's get you some tea, and you can tell us what's been going on." A sheen of worry sat atop her smile.

"What do you want to know?" I asked. "Besides the fact I'm pregnant and Teo's been traded."

Lia sat next to me. Each year, Lia grew more beautiful. Her dark red hair glowed, and her gray eyes focused on me with an intensity that kept me speared to the couch.

Lia nodded, her teeth sinking into the corner of her top lip. "I take it this was unplanned."

"Yeah. All of it."

"We'll get to the trade. Let's talk about the baby. You cared about him enough to have sex," Briar, the pragmatist, said.

I glanced down at my fisted hands. "I thought we'd be together forever." The silence grew, waiting. "I love him."

"You're not in this alone, even though I know you feel that way right now," Lia said, shooting Briar a withering look.

I swallowed back the thick plug of emotion filling my throat. "I know it's different. I'm twenty-seven and have a great job…" My chin trembled. I tilted my head back and blinked hard, not wanting to waste any more tears. "I wanted him to want me."

Lia sighed. She picked up my hand. "What you're feeling

now is so jumbled. I remember when I was sure Asher didn't love me." She looked away. "My emotions spiked and fell, and I wasn't dealing with the added hormone dump from pregnancy, too." She smiled with rueful delight. "My advice, for what it's worth, is to focus on what *you* want to do. But I think you owe it to Teo to give him a chance. He's involved whether he wants to be or not. And if you both decide he's going to give up rights, it's easier to handle that now." Lia cocked her head, gave it a little shake. "That's if you want the baby."

"I'm keeping the baby. I already love her. Him." I frowned as I slid my hand over my flat stomach. Pathetic maybe, but I loved that I'd always have a piece of Teo. I would never fall in love again. Teo was my last, my only. If I could be sure he wanted me because he loved me, not to fix the media mess, I'd run upstairs to him right now.

Lia's smile warmed her gray eyes so they sparkled. "As hard as it seems now, you won't regret motherhood."

"Especially if I'm lucky enough to have a child like Abbi. She's pretty amazing."

"Yes, I am. Like my mom and aunts." Abbi winked.

"I'm proud of you, Preslee," Lia said. "You've dealt with a lot and keep coming out fighting."

I threw my arms around Lia's shoulders. She hugged me back, just as hard.

"Oooh, group hug," Abbi squealed, her arms circling us. Then another body smooshed into my back.

"I refuse to cry. You know I hate to cry." Briar mumbled. "Think positive. I'm going to be an auntie. I love being an auntie!"

Lia laughed and brushed the bangs from my eyes. "Let Preslee breathe. She's got a lot to process."

"Thanks," I smiled.

Briar sat in the chair across from me while Abbi plopped next to me. "So, spill."

"Have you talked to him?" Lia asked.

I shook my head. "Not since I kicked him out the other day. I read he's back in Buenos Aires."

"So why do we hate him again?" Abbi asked. "I mean, he considers your feelings. From what Brenna said, you two spent all your time together. She was so despondent the one time I came down to borrow sugar. Like she lost her favorite plaything."

"He left me in the hospital after I told him I was pregnant," I whispered.

Lia's lips mashed into a thin, angry line. "Hate the bastard."

Tears pricked the back of my eyes. "Wish I did. He said...he said the nurse kicked him out."

Abbi patted my hand. "Did you ask Brenna about that? She would know, right?"

Briar settled back in her chair and mentally ticked through what she knew about Teo—intelligence pulsed in her eyes.

Abbi got up and went to the kitchen. She came back with sparkling water for all of us. "Drink. Water's important for you."

Briar tuned us out, which made me even tenser. I gulped my glass while Abbi played with her bottle.

"How did Oren find you?" Briar asked.

I shrugged. "The newspaper. Or a blog. I don't know. But he'd called the week before so he was obviously keeping tabs on me."

"But you left practice late that day. Hours after the rest of the musicians—after seven p.m., right? And you came out the front, not the back entrance the musicians normally use."

"He followed Teo and me home that night after the soccer match. Maybe he watched me and got lucky," I said.

"How did the media know you were leaving the hospital in the middle of the night? There were quite a few pictures showing you without Teo. That's what set Noah off, made him push for the trade."

I shrugged. "Maybe one of the nurses tipped off the paparazzi. I don't know. Noah's refused to talk to him and he hasn't called me." Which, now that I thought about it, seemed weird. But he hadn't left even one message—not on my phone, my social media accounts. Nothing.

Briar pulled out her phone.

"What are you doing?" I asked.

"Texting Noah," Briar said.

"No!" The word exploded from me. My sisters and Abbi stared at me. "No," I said again. "Please don't. I don't want to know."

"But, Pres—"

"No!" I stood, my legs shaking. "He wants the sex without the commitment, and I can't do that."

And I walked out of Abbi's condo, back to the cold darkness of my room.

CHAPTER TWENTY-SEVEN
Teo

I slipped into the room, staying to the back, trying to remain unobtrusive. I hadn't been in The Vera Project before and the space was bigger, cleaner than I expected. The large, curved stage sat at the front of the room. Hundreds of people clumped together on the concrete floors, dancing and raising their drinks over their heads as the beat seemed to overpower their better judgment.

Yep. A full glass of something cascaded down onto a teased head. I shook my head as I chuckled, thankful for the break in tension. Abbi turned around and met my gaze, her eyes widening. I tipped my chin toward her, but before I could make my way through the crowd, the next song began and Preslee walked out on stage.

Her voice filled the large, spacious room, wrapping around me as it did the hundreds of other patrons, soothing my aching muscles and ragged heart. A throaty, rich sound I couldn't help but fall in love with all over again.

The smile tugged the corner of my lips as she harmonized with Asher, hitting the notes with crystal sharpness. Asher smiled at her, his excitement at working with such talent evident in the way he bounced on his heels before turning back to the crowd and singing the hell out of the next line, bending his knees and touching the hands of the people in front of him.

She looked beautiful. She wore a short, black skirt and a loose, red blouse in some semi-see-through material. I'd never seen it before but it set off her pale skin and dark hair to perfection. She looked soft, fragile but with an inner glow that must come from the pregnancy.

I shouldn't be here, at this Seattle club, but I didn't have to report for work at River Salado until Monday. I ticked through my options: Did I want to buy out the rest of my contract to pursue Preslee here? I asked for another meeting with the Timber management, this time without Noah's knowledge. Jorge would be there at my side, just as he'd always been. I knew he'd put in a good word for me with the owner.

In any organization I played for, I ensured a healthy working relationship with the coaching staff—this time Jorge and I already had a great working relationship. He wanted me to stay on as a coach. Preferably, the head one. Jorge's expertise made him a wonderful offensive coordinator, but he lacked the English vocabulary and the charisma for the head coach interviews.

My phone buzzed, but I ignored it. It'd be more of the same from the Timber PR specialist: *Your terse statement regarding your relationship with Preslee Jennings did not stem speculation. We have a serious media issue we must address.* The ones from my mother were much less expected though just as annoying. *Come home, Matteo. Your father's heart broke with your latest media disaster.*

I scrubbed my hands over my eyes and into my hair. Since I boarded that airplane for New York, for those games over a week ago, my life spun out of control.

Pres deserved tonight's adulation, especially now that she didn't need to continue to fear Oren. I rubbed my chest, wishing I could touch her now as she lit up the room with her presence.

She stamped her foot and lifted her chin as she hit a long note. She seared the space, holding the rapt audience captive, her love of singing apparent.

"Why are you here?" Brenna snapped. Preslee, bobbing to the beat, glanced over as she lowered the microphone to her waist. Her eyes widened. I dipped my head and her expression softened a little.

She smiled at the crowd and raised her arm. The crowd roared with approval as she lifted her mic and sang the high notes, trilling in perfect balance to Asher's deepening base. No wonder Asher wanted her on his next album.

"I bought a ticket." I couldn't tear my eyes from Preslee. Her skirt ended mid-thigh, giving the men here an eyeful of her toned, pale perfection.

"She doesn't want you here. You're the one who walked out on her."

I took a sip of the Scotch my waitress handed me, refusing to let this little woman become an even bigger thorn in my side.

Brenna sidled in closer, her body plastered to mine. My muscles contracted hard, refusing the contact. "You're going to upset her again."

"Preslee's life is *hers*. If you let her live it, she would be much happier."

Brenna reared back as though I'd slapped her. I might be many things, but I'd been bred from birth to treat women with gallant politeness. Unfortunately, that cost me the only woman I wanted. No, loved. But Brenna didn't deserve the courtesy she never once showed me.

Preslee segued into a song I remembered hearing her sing in my shower once—a heart-wrenching lament of her lost lover. Each time Pres sang, "Wishing I didn't know," my heart sped up, trying to preserve my insides.

My phone buzzed, then immediately again. I pulled it out of my pocket and read the message. I closed my eyes against the message.

"Bad news?" A cruel smile curved Brenna's lips.

I hated the woman almost as much as I hated the words flashed up on my small screen.

"My father's taken ill. He's been hospitalized. That terrible enough for you? I'd ask you to tell Pres why I had to leave, but I know you won't. Abbi saw me when I came in. She'll let Pres know."

Walking out of the venue nearly killed me. I stood in the same room as her for the first time in days, and my body ached with the need to touch her, to run my fingers along the soft skin of her cheek and into the silk of her hair. But once again, my life conspired against me.

CHAPTER TWENTY-EIGHT
Preslee

The high from signing—from the screams and adulation—buoyed me, causing me to walk as if on air.

"You were fantastic!" Brenna cried, clasping her hands under her chin.

Singing tonight proved how much I wanted to do it again. But this time, I'd do it for me. For the love of a melody or a specific message. Being in control of my career was as great a high as hitting a crisp B or sinking into a series of triplets, both of which I'd done tonight. Done well.

My smile fell when the dark head I'd been searching for didn't appear. "Where did Teo go?"

Brenna folded her lips in. "He didn't say. Exactly."

"I saw you talking to him, Brenna."

"He had to leave," Brenna snapped. "He probably only came for the press. So he doesn't look like an uncaring ass."

"The soccer club released a picture of him in at their offices in Buenos Aires yesterday. Why would he show up tonight and leave immediately?"

Abbi bounded over, her hand clutched in Clay's. I hadn't seen Abbi's boyfriend since the barbecue at Lia's almost two months ago. His band spent most of the past few months touring up and down the West Coast as they prepped for a larger, country-wide tour.

"Where's Teo?" she asked.

"Let's get you home and fed. You're a growing girl." Brenna suggested, pulling on my arm.

"I'm talking to my family, Bren. Chill." I turned back to Abbi, who eyed Brenna with something close to concern. Brenna had become even more mother-hen since she found out I was pregnant.

"Why don't you get me another water?" I suggested, smiling at Brenna to reassure her of my good humor even as, inside, I fumed over her continued hovering.

"What's her deal?" Clay asked.

"I don't know. She's gotten so much worse. She spoke to Teo, and then he disappeared." I bit on my thumbnail.

Abbi's expression darkened. "I don't like that he left. What did she say to him?"

The high of finishing my set so well, of seeing Teo's proud smile in the audience, faded, leaving behind a dull pounding in my head.

"Seems like a long way to come for a show," Clay offered. "I mean, the flight from Buenos Aires is, what, twelve, fourteen hours or something?"

I nodded, a frown building between my brows.

Brenna came back, handing me my water, and stopping the flow of conversation.

Clay and Abbi hugged me. "I love hearing you sing," Abbi said. "You should do it more often."

I uncapped my water and gulped most of it down. "I think I might."

"Cool," Clay exclaimed. "Talk to me about that. We'd love you to sing and play on our album."

"And Hayden's been drooling about the idea of a whole record of duets." Briar hugged me, too. Hayden snuck around my other side and kissed my cheek.

"Don't talk to anyone else, love. I've had dreams of your voice and my piano."

Briar wrinkled her nose. "That sounds gross."

"Crikey! Not like that. I just think we'd make a magical duet," Hayden reiterated, stepping back. "But only for songs."

"He's cute flustered," I said.

Briar nodded. "He is. But what the hell, Hayden? That's my sister. My preggo sister."

"I know that, Bri." He ran his hand up and down the back of his neck, his cheeks darkening. "Fair dinkum. I didn't mean anything by it, Pres. You know I think of you as a sister."

"I know you love Briar heaps."

Hayden smiled, his sun-kissed head bowing low over Briar's as he kissed her forehead. "That I do. And we'll make an Aussie out of you yet."

I laughed but then grimaced at the pain in my side. The bruises faded but weren't completely gone. My bruised abdomen challenged my ability to sing at full capacity, but the performance turned out fun, exciting even.

I stifled a yawn and saw Abbi do the same. She snuggled in tighter to Clay's chest.

"We're out," Clay said. "Great performance, Preslee. You stole the show."

He pulled Abbi toward the door. She turned to wave before they disappeared.

"We're heading out, too," Briar said. Hayden leaned down and whispered something in her ear, making her grin as she glanced at him from under her lashes. "I'll call you tomorrow."

"Yeah. Sorry I haven't been good about answering it. It's just…" I shrugged. "I'm still getting tons of media calls. I've blocked probably twenty numbers now."

"I understand that all too well," Briar hugged me and whispered in my ear. "He came to see you."

I nodded, my throat tightening. I missed him. More than I should.

Brenna brushed my bangs out of my eyes. Just like Teo used to do. I lowered my eyes, not wanting to deal with her reaction to the tears I couldn't hide.

"How about a bite? My treat."

"I'm not very hungry. But thanks."

"You can't lose any more weight, Pres. You've always been thin, but now you're barely visible straight-on. I swear, I'm going to castrate that man and shove his balls down his throat for hurting you." Her eyes narrowed as the unholy glint of malice lit up her face. "He'll rue the day."

I gripped my stomach as it gurgled, unhappy with the image. "No violence. You know how I feel about that. Who says 'rue' anyway? What's happened to you? Spinster and rue."

"I signed up for the daily vocabulary word. There are tons of great ones we don't use regularly."

"Because they're not part of a normal person's vocabulary."

"Pres…"

"I need to take a shower. I'm sweaty and want to wash the club stuff off me."

"It's just that I miss spending time with you."

I sighed. We walked in silence for almost two full blocks. "If you want us to be close, then there are some things you need to do."

I stopped and faced her. Her brows were pinched but she

nodded.

"First off, you need to stop taking shots at Teo. He's the father of my baby."

Her lips tightened. "He hurt you."

I shrugged. "I hurt myself more by not listening to him."

She glared, but I held up my hand.

"I'm serious, Brenna. Lay off. Not just on Teo but on trying to run my life. It's *mine*. You don't have to like my decisions, but, as a friend, you should respect them."

She fumbled until she gripped my hand. "I don't want to see you upset. I want you to be happy."

"Then trust me."

She gazed at my face for a long moment before she dipped her head in acknowledgment. "I'll do my best."

"Thank you. Now tell me what he said."

Brenna dropped my hand and scooted back. When I didn't back down or speak, she sighed. "Fine. His father's going into the hospital."

I clutched my elbows. "Oh, poor Teo."

"See! This is why I didn't tell you."

"I need to call him."

"You didn't bring your phone."

I hadn't because my phone wasn't in its charger on the kitchen counter—where I was sure I'd left it earlier that evening. Unfortunately, I'd spent too long on my makeup to look further.

Brenna slid her arm around my waist. "Being upset hurts the baby."

Instead of answering, I glared, saving my breath.

Brenna shook her head. "You've been so moody since you

found out you're pregnant."

No point in answering—she didn't care to hear my response anyway.

"I'm starving. If you won't let me take you out, let's go up so I can order some Lo Mein."

"Isn't work slow?" I asked.

She smiled. "I got a one-off job a couple of weeks ago. It paid well. So, c'mon. It'll be fun. Like old times. My treat."

My shoulders slumped. A couple of weeks ago, Teo and I laughed and loved together. I sighed as Brenna ushered me into a café.

"What do you want? Remember, you're eating for two."

"I don't know," I sighed. "You pick. I'm going to the bathroom."

I chose to ignore Brenna's crestfallen expression.

———◆———

The warm water both stung and relaxed my body, making me shiver and moan. I knew I should've showered last night. But exhaustion slammed into me as we rode home—one of the strange changes I'd noticed in the last week. There were days I simply couldn't keep my eyes open.

I woke, worry over Teo's father's condition weighing on my mind. I considered flying down to be with Teo, but I kept my mouth shut, unwilling to share my thoughts with Brenna.

I didn't know when our relationship shifted—maybe while I dated Teo—his words came back to me. Brenna did hate him. She was happier now that we'd split.

Maybe that's why I no longer considered Brenna my closest confidant.

"Want to eat something?" she asked as soon as I walked out of my room.

"Later."

"Pres, you have to think about the—"

"Later." My voice rose as I glared. "Where's my phone?"

"You said yesterday you left it on the counter," Brenna said.

It wasn't there. I continued to look, my agitation increasing. Brenna stood and brought me a plate of toast.

"Eat."

I picked up the dry bread and nibbled. I swallowed the bite down with a sip of water.

"I think we should move," Brenna said.

My mouth dropped open. "What? Why?"

"I think the change would be good for us."

"For *you*. You want out of Seattle. You said there were too many programmers here, making it hard to find full-time work."

"Fine. I want to move. But getting away from these memories is smart. Keep our baby healthy."

"*My* baby, Bren. This is *my* child, my responsibility. No one else's. Ever."

Hurt clouded Brenna's eyes but she nodded. "You're right. Your baby."

"Mine and Teo's. Who I will talk to about our child. As soon as I find my phone." Gah! Why couldn't I remember where I'd put it? "I'm not moving. This is where my family is."

"You want to be near your sisters. I know how much they mean to you. Fine. We'll stay here and I'll help at night with the changing and feeding. We'll get through this together."

I crumbled the bits of toast between my fingers. Why wouldn't she see what I was telling her? "That's not fair to you," I said, striving to remain diplomatic though irritation caused my voice to rasp. "You deserve to go after your dreams."

"I'm helping. So just get used to it." She grabbed my plate and took it to the kitchen. "I'm off to work. Why don't you meet me for lunch? It'll be fun! We haven't done a lunch date in forever. Since, you know, you met *him*."

Frustration boiled over, and I slapped my hand against the counter. "Why do you hate Teo so much? I just don't get it. From the very beginning, you were dead-set against him."

Her shoulders were stiff and she kept her back to me.

"What aren't you telling me? *You* haven't dated anyone in months. Maybe if you found someone…"

"I don't want to date right now! I just—" She turned back toward me, her eyes blazing. "Men hurt you. They want to fuck you, then they're gone. You're pregnant and alone because of a *guy*. He wasn't enough for you. He walked out of that hospital room—and that was the *best* thing that's happened. You finally realized you deserve more."

Brenna picked up her purse. She swiped up her keys from the rack by the door and slammed out of the condo.

———◆———

I sat there, stunned by her fury. Not just at Teo, but at me, too. Because I deserved more.

He walked out—and that was the best *thing that's happened.*

Brenna shutting Teo out of my hospital room after telling him to leave, Brenna throwing away his flowers, not wanting to give me the note. My missing phone.

"You've done nothing but push him away from me."

I scrubbed my hands over my face. The coincidences added up, but, then, I wanted Brenna to be the scapegoat for my broken life. "And I let you do it. Oh. Oh. *I let you.*"

Then Briar's words came back to me: *How did the media know you were leaving the hospital in the middle of the night?* My stomach roiled as I pondered the answer.

I wanted to be wrong; my legs shook as I walked to Brenna's room. Starting in her closet, I opened every shoebox, her favorite place to stash her important papers. An old boot container held a stash of pictures. All pictures of the two of us, from our first day of first grade up through college graduation. Our arms were wound around each other and we were laughing. The later ones, from high school, showed a different look on Brenna's face. The look my sisters and Abbi wore when they were in the same space as their men with a need that would never be satiated.

I love you, Pres. How many times had Brenna said that to me? My teeth sank into my lip. Dread ate at my gut.

I opened each of her drawers, threw everything on the floor. I yanked back her sheets, emptied her pillows and eventually dumped the mattress off the bed. *Let me be wrong.* Because I always hung out with Brenna. My best friend—the one with whom Teo originally thought I was having an affair.

I yanked too hard on her nightstand drawer, and my phone clattered to the floor. She *had* taken my phone. I clicked it on as I sank to the floor. I clicked on Teo's number, only to see a notification saying that number was blocked.

Frantic now, I opened my social media accounts. She blocked him there, too. From all my accounts. He had no way to get in touch with me. How long? Was there a way from me to tell how long ago she'd taken away his ability to contact me?

Was that why he came down to see me that night after the hospital? I'd been so hurt he hadn't called me, texted me—something—but I'd never bothered to think why he hadn't done so.

My stomach roiled, and I pressed a hand there. I kicked my way out of Brenna's room, uncaring of the mess I'd made.

Back in the living room, I grabbed my laptop, biting my thumbnail. I changed my password for my laptop and all my social media accounts, making sure to use random combinations I wrote into the note app in my phone—I'd never remember them all—and then changed my phone pass code, my stomach aching with these measures. Next, I reopened all lines of communication with Teo once I was sure Brenna couldn't sabotage me again. I was about to type out an e-mail when a notification popped up. Brenna was on her social media account now—while she was supposed to be at work.

I sucked in a breath as I laid my fingers over the keys. I knew the actions I was about to take were wrong. Unethical. I took a deep breath and fired up her e-mail account, no longer caring about her privacy. Not if I was right. Not if...

I scrolled through her messages. She'd said two weeks ago, she had a one-off job. One that paid well. But she'd been *here* two weeks ago, tending to me after my breakup.

There. The name caught my eye as a noise of despair spewed from my mouth. Nausea flashed up my throat. *Lucia Romero de*

Cruz. Teo's mom. The woman who didn't like me. The woman who threw the big party when Teo returned home a few days ago.

Brenna corresponded with Teo's mom. Multiple times within that five-day period before we broke up. Before I could change my mind, I typed out a message.

To: Lucia Romero de Cruz

From: Brenna Lansing

Re: Urgent! Preslee knows

She knows we wanted to break up Teo and her. She also thinks I'm the one who leaked the information about his hamstring.

I left it unsigned. I wouldn't break Brenna's trust—my ethics—more than I already had. Now the waiting began. I walked into the kitchen and poured a cup of the expensive decaf Brenna brought home last week. I drank it out of a mug she'd given me ten years ago when I first started drinking coffee.

I placed my hand against the large picture window in our kitchen, tracing the small raindrops that slithered across the glass, the ache in my chest expanding with each breath.

I picked up my laptop and sucked in a breath. After releasing it slowly, I opened the lid. Brenna's e-mail program was still open...with a new message from Lucia.

My fingers shook, but I managed to open the message.

You'd better keep her quiet about the brat. If not, I stop all further payments.

The front door opened.

"Since you didn't seem like you wanted to meet me for lunch, we could..." She caught a look at my face. "What's wrong? Did something happen to the baby?"

I dropped my laptop into her hands. She read the message

before closing it. The click of the laptop snapping shut made me flinch.

Brenna heaved a deep sigh. Her breath shuddered then broke as she collapsed back into the same chair she sat in earlier. "I wanted this to end so differently. But I should have known better."

"You knew I loved him. I *told* you that."

Brenna picked at her linen skirt. "I know you do, but Lucia was dead set on keeping you two apart. I figured, all things considered, it was better to go along with what she wanted. You'd get over Teo and come back to me."

"Don't lie to me." My voice stayed low, but I used that dead-serious tone my brothers—and Brenna—feared. My temper might be slow to build, but I held a grudge like no one else.

"He's a *man*. He would've hurt you eventually. He—he already did!" She flapped her arms, her face more animated by the moment. "He walked out on you at the hospital."

"Because you practically forced him out! Yeah, he told me that. You and that fucking nurse teamed up and made him leave," I yelled. Oh, it felt amazing to yell. I picked up one of the throw pillows and threw it as hard as I could. It landed on the bar, sending my coffee mug crashing to the floor. The dark liquid mixed with shards of ceramic bits, splattering the fridge and white cabinets.

"Did you press the call button to get her to come in? You did after you—what?—bribed her in the hall. Didn't you?"

I turned back toward Brenna, my chest heaving. I picked up another pillow and threw it, too.

"Calm down," Brenna pleaded. "It's not healthy for the baby, Pres. He broke your heart."

"Wrong!" I screamed. "He struggled to come to terms with the fact I was pregnant, something I totally understood because I felt the same way. But *you* took the decision from him. From me."

"Only because I want you to be happy, Preslee." She crept nearer. I backed up, glaring. "He can't make you happy."

"That's *my* decision to make—*my* life. I broke up with a man who loved me because you colluded with his mother! You knew I'd be upset. You, of all people, knew I'd think it was Oren all over again because I shared how much his cheating, his attack hurt me."

"Don't be angry, Preslee. I protected you."

"From *what*?"

"From another messed up relationship." Brenna leaned forward, her voice sincere. "Look, Lucia already dug into your past and found out about Oren and the beating at Northern. I didn't want you to relive that time with Oren, so I told her I'd take care of your relationship if she didn't hurt you by dredging that back up."

I inhaled deeply, trying to untangle the emotions barreling through me. Anger, frustration, fatigue, and betrayal warred through me.

"Well, it came out anyway," I snapped.

"I didn't know Oren would come after you. I swear I didn't."

I stepped back. These revelations kept getting worse. "You told Oren I'd be at the symphony." The words came out breathy, barely audible as the ache in my throat increased.

"It's not what you think," she said, tripping over her words.

"You told Oren where I'd be that night. The man who took away all my dreams. You told him. *After you heard him threaten me.*" I breathed the words, unable to get enough air in my lungs to do more.

"He wasn't supposed to go crazy, just frighten you. You always come back to me when you're scared or hurt, so you would've left Teo, and we could be the family we're supposed to be."

I stared at her, too shocked for even the anger to break through. Finally, the ringing in my ears calmed. I swallowed, trying to moisten my dry mouth.

"I almost lost my baby because of his attack. Did you think about that, Brenna?"

"Contacting Oren was a mistake. I see that now. But, Pres, I did it out of love." Her eyes were beseeching.

I sank into one of the chairs just before my knees gave out. No way this was real.

"Look…I love you enough for both of us." Brenna's eyes were adamant. She came forward, slid onto her knees in front of me. She clutched one of my hands, the other resting on my belly. I froze, too shocked to move.

"I want to be your everything, Pres. I'll take care of you and the baby. We'll make this work. We'll be a family."

"Get off," I breathed, recoiling as my body went taut. "Stop touching me."

Brenna stood, her eyes defiant. "What about when you're fat from pregnancy or you haven't slept in a week and are covered in baby shit and stale breast milk? Who'd want you after you've been sick with the flu for a week, after watching you try to puke up a lung? He won't want to see that. It's not sexy."

I stood, too, needing to feel on even footing with Brenna.

"That's what love is," I said. "And I had that with him. I would *still* if you stayed out of my life. He cared about me; it wasn't just about the sex."

"I've loved you for *years*. I'm the one who's held your hand, from Corey when he lied about having sex with you at prom, to Oren, and even your breakup with Teo. I'm the one who got you through all those relationships. I see *you*, Preslee, and I love the woman you are. I don't want to change anything about you. I just want to be with you."

The words were heartfelt, romantic even, but each one filled me with deeper dread. She'd twisted everything we were for years into an unhealthy relationship.

"Just give me a chance." Her voice carried urgency, her eyes bright with need. The way she looked just as she awoke. I shuddered, wondering if she'd been dreaming about me some of those times. "I'll make this up to you."

"You can't. Ever." I swallowed down bile, but just barely. "Our friendship meant something to me, and you dirtied it." I took a deep breath and severed our shared secrets, hugs, tears, and every critical moment for the last twenty years. "You need to leave."

Her mouth gaped wide, her eyes bugged.

"You can't mean that. I'm the one who got you through the morning sickness for fuck's sake."

"And you're the one who set me up with Oren originally. Did you know he beat up on women? Is that why you suggested we hang out at that party? Then…then you said we should move in together. It'd be fun."

"We had fun," she choked.

"I've spent the last six years miserable. What you're talking about—that isn't love, Brenna. You're selfish and cruel, and I'm not sure I'll ever forgive you for it."

She looked like a fish taking its last breath. Something inside me twisted and died with her in that moment, but I didn't break eye contact. Finally, she firmed her lips, set her shoulders and slunk into her bedroom.

CHAPTER TWENTY-NINE
Teo

"Matteo!" My father kissed both of my cheeks before pulling me into a bear hug. His skin shone with its normal sun-kissed bronze.

"I thought you were in the hospital. I planned to go there after I changed."

"Come sit. Eat. You traveled all night again?"

I nodded, feeling numb. I ran out of Preslee's show, expecting my father to be intubated, sickly. Close to death.

I ran my thumbs over my dry eyes. "Mother texted me you were unwell. That your physician admitted you to the hospital."

My dad's brows drew down. "Clearly not true. I'm healthy as an ox. You, however, look older than I." His eyes mirrored my reflection, but I was even more broken than the unshaven, rumpled man in them.

"It's been a rough couple of weeks," I sighed. I tilted my face up to the sun, needing the warmth. My father's hand clamped on my shoulder, giving it a little squeeze.

"Your mother will join us shortly. We'll talk to her about this misunderstanding."

"It wasn't a misunderstanding. She knew I went back to Seattle. She came into your study while I was making the travel plans."

"Why were you there?"

"To meet with the Timber owner and talk to Jorge."

"But you planned to come back to River Salado."

I shook my head. "I want to stay in Seattle. I want to be near Preslee. She's pregnant."

A smile tugged at the corners of my lips. That, at least, was a positive from our relationship. If I could just get Preslee out from under Brenna's orbit, I knew I could talk some sense into her. Talk her into moving in with me. Where she belonged.

"Pregnant?" My dad rocked back on his heels. "That's unexpected."

I nodded. "For all of us."

He grunted, his eyes narrowed. "But you're happy about this?"

My grin grew. "Oh, yeah. She's the only woman I could want to mother my children."

I must talk to Noah again, try to get him to see reason. I planned to stay in Seattle, against his wishes. But we shared family now, if only through my connection to Preslee. My forever connection.

"When will I meet this young lady who's stolen your heart?"

"Never. She's no longer Matteo's girlfriend," my mother's clipped voice came from the edge of the patio. Her red lips curved up in a knowing smile. "They broke up. And now your son is home, where he belongs."

I met her eyes, saw the same flat triumph in them that I saw in Brenna's just last night. "What did you do?"

My mother's linen-clad shoulder raised in a negligent shrug.

My father came to my side. "You involved yourself in our son's relationship?" My dad's ruddy complexion turned darker, his nostrils flaring.

"She's just trying to get our money, Raul. That's why she fell pregnant. I wouldn't have said anything, but she knows I worked with that other American, her friend."

"What?" My father demanded.

"You destroyed her faith in me—you and Brenna." Several pieces of the puzzle clicked into place. But one piece remained missing: my mother's motive. "For what? To ensure my continued unhappiness? What am I being punished for this time, Mother? Talking to Dad about my love life instead of you? Wanting to be happy?"

My father's eyes narrowed as he looked at my mother. "I will deal with you later."

"Raul, really, there's no reason to chastise me like a naughty child."

"Then quit acting like one," Dad snapped.

I settled into a wrought-iron chair; my spinning head clamped tight between my two hands.

"Matteo? You look unwell."

"I fucked up, Dad. Big time."

"No more so than I. I worried about this young woman and how tangled into her you were. I should never have spoken of her, of my concern, to your mother. If Preslee is what you want, the woman you love, I'll do what I can to help fix my part in this. For you. And my grandchild."

His smile wavered, but his eyes filled with happiness. He began pushing for me to find someone to love, to marry, for the past few years. The idea of a grandchild appealed to him as much as having a baby with Preslee appealed to me.

My mother stormed off, slamming the door behind her so hard one of the glass panes fell to the patio, shattering.

"That's the mother I know."

"She's this bad with you?"

"Always? No. But she was never happy."

My father rubbed his fingers along his jaw. "Because of my…

indiscretions?"

I met his gaze, holding it for a long moment. "Losing my nanny was pretty hard on me."

Papa pressed his lips together in a firm line, dipping his head in acknowledgment. "She loved me once."

"Honestly?" I said, turning back to stare at the broken door. "I think she always has."

"That doesn't excuse her behavior toward you."

"No, it doesn't." I dropped my head to my thumbs, rocking back and forth a little. "I need to get back to Pres. I left to come here because I was worried about you. But she hasn't answered any of my messages. Leaving last night destroyed her already fragile trust in me. As did my leaving her in the hospital when she told me she was pregnant."

"And she is angry?"

"Worse. I hurt her, and I don't know if I can fix it."

My dad's blunt fingers wrapped around my wrist. I lifted my head, uncaring all my emotions were there, swirling for my dad to see.

"Tell me, son. Between us, we will find a way."

CHAPTER THIRTY
Preslee

After snatching my keys and phone from the counter, I ran into the hall, my focus on one thought.

"Slow down there, champ." Clay steadied me as I bounced off his chest.

"Whoa! What's wrong, Pres?" Abbi grabbed my hands.

"I have to find Teo." His name came out in a wail.

Clay glanced between the shut door of my condo and my wild eyes. He rubbed his palms up and down my arms, trying to calm my shuddering.

"Let's go in your place and talk," Abbi said, sounding all calm.

My back bowed straight. "No! I'm not going back in there while Brenna's there. She lied to me," I gasped. "She lied to him. I need to go...I need..."

"We'll go up to our place." Clay wrapped an arm around me as we walked down the hall. The farther we walked from Brenna, from her lies, the more my mind whirred with all the ways I'd let Brenna manipulate me.

Once in the elevator, I lunged across the space and pulled Abbi into a hug as my breath caught on a sob. "I'm so glad you're here!"

"Are all pregnant women this emotional?" Abbi asked. "I don't know if I can go through this ever, if I'm going to cry each time someone brings me a mocha."

"You brought me a mocha?"

Abbi shoved it into my hands. "Decaf, skim milk, extra chocolate. Just the way you like it." I took a sip, let the sweetness slide across my tongue, the heat calming my raging nerves. I smiled at her as I knuckled tears from the corner of my eyes.

"I would do dangerous things for a mocha, but that's not why I'm glad to see you."

Abbi's face scrunched down into a scowl as she took my hand. "What's going on, Pres?"

I sucked in a breath. I pulled my phone from my purse and clutched it and my mocha like they were lifelines to a sane world.

"You're scaring me, Pres," Abbi whispered.

I turned to meet Abbi's shadowed eyes. "Brenna plotted with Teo's mom to break us up."

Abbi's mouth popped open, and her eyes narrowed to slits. Clay cursed loudly, and I nodded in agreement.

"Holy hell. Brenna?" Abbi squeal-sighed. She fiddled with the hem of her shirt. "That's—well, that's horrible."

I logged into Brenna's e-mail application from my phone. Pulling up the message, I handed my phone to Abbi.

After reading, she handed the phone to Clay and grabbed my hand. Clay read the message, running his finger over his top lip.

"That bitch," Abbi growled, sounding exactly like Lia as she marched down the hall. She opened her door with a slam before whirling back toward Clay and me. "She's not ruining your life."

"She already did."

"Want me to stay?" Clay sounded nervous.

Abbi hugged him, laying her head against his chest. Their intimacy made my chin wobble. My face crumpled when Abbi whispered something in Clay's ear. He kissed her temple and headed back out the door, relief flooding his features as he escaped my presence.

"When's the next flight to Buenos Aires?" I asked, stomping

around their living room.

"On it." Abbi slid her butt onto a bar stool. She turned back, caught my quivering chin and stood again, ready to wrap me in a much-needed hug. "Ah, honey, I'm so sorry."

"She said she broke us up because she loved me." I stepped out of her arms and gulped my mocha, needing something to mask the bitterness from my mouth.

"We'll deal with Brenna later. You haven't talked to Teo since he left?"

I shook my head. "Brenna blocked him from my phone, all my social media accounts. And I found my phone in Brenna's nightstand." I scrubbed my palms over my cheeks. "I planned to call Teo last night, but I fell asleep on the ride home." I glanced up at Abbi. "That's definitely hormones."

Abbi's mouth dropped again. "Unbelievable. Teo was at the show last night," Abbi said. "Maybe he's still in Seattle."

I shook my head. "I finally forced it out of Brenna. He left the show early because his dad's ill. It must have been serious for him to leave so quickly."

Abbi rubbed her hand up my arm. "At least you know why he didn't say hi."

Even amid the heartache, pleasure flushed through my system. This is what I always wanted—this closeness with my family. "I need a new place to live."

"Why don't we kick Brenna out?" Abbi's voice turned biting. "She's not living in the same building as me. Clay pulled some strings to get us this condo. The bonus of living near you has been fantastic. I'm not moving just because Brenna's a horrible person. I already did that runaway thing once. Doesn't solve any problems."

I squeezed her hand. She gripped mine back.

"You found Clay," I whispered.

"You own that place," Abbi said. "Not Brenna. There's no way that woman is staying in this building now that we know she's a backstabbing bitch."

I snorted out a laugh that turned into a hiccup.

"Why aren't you angrier?" Abbi asked.

I considered her question. "I am. I'm also devastated. Brenna's been my best friend since elementary school."

"But?"

"I know Teo got played and used just as much as I did. I keep thinking about how right we were together when we were alone—just us. He told me he loved me."

Abbi tilted her head, those blue eyes sparkling in anticipation. "Aw. He did? I'm not sure I can miss your reunion now." She blew out a breath. "Yeah, I know. It's between you and Teo."

"You have a lot of your mom's romanticism in you."

Abbi rolled her eyes. "Yeah. Not news. Here's the plan: Clay and I boot Brenna from your condo while you fly to Buenos Aires. If Brenna won't leave because I tell her to, I'll call in the big guns."

"Noah and Nate?" I asked.

Abbi laughed. "My mom and Aunt Bri."

I nodded. "That'll do it."

"We'll get the locks changed on your condo."

"Wait! I should call Teo. To make sure he'll even hear me out." I sucked in a deep breath. "I'm scared."

"Of course, you are," Abbi said. "Here, give me your phone." She grabbed it from my hand and punched a series of buttons.

"What are you doing?" I squealed.

She shooed me back as I made a desperate grab for my phone.

"Teo? This is Abbi." She ducked my leaping attempt. "No, Preslee's okay. Physically, anyway. I'm hoping you're asking means you've decided you want your kid."

"Abbi!" I yelled. "Give me the phone. Now."

"Yep, that's Pres. She's so loud for a skinny mini. She needs to talk to you." Abbi tossed the phone toward me, smart enough to realize she better not get too close herself.

"Teo," I murmured into the phone.

"You're okay? The—the baby?" he asked, anxiety spiking through the words.

"Yes. We're both good. I need…I need to talk to you. I'm so sorry for the way I behaved the other day. I was scared you wanted to leave me and I thought I was being smart, but then I just found out Brenna's been talking to your mom, strategizing to keep us apart."

"Breathe, *dulzura*."

My nose stung when I heard the endearment. Maybe…maybe he'd hear me out. "Brenna called Oren to let him know I'd be at the symphony. She or your mom leaked the information about your hamstring."

"I learned much of this myself earlier today. That's why I'm flying back, private jet and all, to see you. I'd hoped you'd listen."

"I will. I'm so sorry, Teo. So sorry."

The line crackled.

"We've hit turbulence and the copilot wants me off the phone."

"Okay. When can I see you? I need…I have more to say to you."

"I get into Sea-Tac in about six hours."

"Okay." I stood. "I'll grab my car and pick you up."

"No way!" Teo snapped. "We won't get to talk about anything if the media finds out I've come back to talk to you. My flight attendant is grabbing at my phone. I'll come to you as soon as I can. I have much to say to you, too."

Those words crept across my skin, ominous little spiders of doubt.

"What did he say?" Abbi said.

"That we need to talk."

Abbi crossed her arms. "Duh."

"I need to be at the airport. I need to talk to tell him I love him…" I stopped. Would it work? "I'm meeting Teo at his gate. Doesn't matter he said no."

"Not sure you'll be able to get access, Pres."

"The jet goes to a private hangar?" I asked.

Abbi shrugged. "Probably. Want me to find out?"

I nodded. "Yeah. I've got an idea." I smiled, which turned into a grin. Then I laughed. "Will you find out, please?"

"Sure. I like this sparkle in your eyes."

"I need to go shopping," I decided. "Will you help me?"

She hopped off her bar stool. "This is gonna be epic."

CHAPTER THIRTY-ONE
Teo

Preslee's call had woken me from a bone-deep sleep. I stood, stretched. I went to the bathroom and washed my face. My eyes were still bloodshot, and my muscles jerked, fritzing over the time zone changes.

Preslee's words flowed through my head: she planned to come to me. I sighed out an aching breath of relief. Though I was glad to know Pres was no longer under Brenna's control, my first thought was to comfort her. She'd been betrayed by her best friend, after all.

I couldn't wait to hold her soft cheeks between my palms and kiss her soft, sweet lips. But my body craved hers—desperate to make love to her—and I wouldn't pay attention to much else if I took her lips or considered the pale luster of her skin or the shadowy dip between her hip bones and stomach. One of my favorite spots. I shifted, trying to take my mind off loving her up before I even saw her.

Would her body have changed already? Soon, I would see the signs of my child growing inside her.

I pressed my forehead to my linked hands, wishing I could go back to the night in the hospital. Tell her I loved her then. Tell her how excited I was to be a father to our child.

My passion—from my formative years to now—was soccer. Paparazzi were the price I paid for the rush of bending a ball into a net in front of ten thousand or more screaming fans.

I didn't want to give that up, but I'd known even then my injury meant a shift—I would no longer hold the spotlight or score the gaming-winning goal.

Per Timber management, I didn't have to give up my dream out of hand. As I'd told Preslee that night she'd been attacked, my goal evolved. Coaching brought me a different kind of satisfaction, one I thought, with Jorge's help, I could build into something more exhilarating than scoring a goal. Maybe. But first, before I signed or tore up anything, I must talk to Preslee.

We taxied then stopped.

"Señor Cruz, there's a guest at your hangar. Do you wish us to drop you here instead?"

"Do you know who it is?"

I didn't want to get lambasted by the media. I didn't have answers. I was too tired to be civil.

"Señorita Jennings, I'm told."

"Get me there." Fatigue slid off my shoulders as the buzz of anticipation built around my thrumming heart.

My eyes roved over her. She wore a skin-tight, beige catsuit. I exhaled sharply as did the pilot and copilot exiting the plane behind me.

"She's mine," I growled.

"Lucky bastard," one of them muttered. I didn't bother to answer because Preslee raised the microphone to her lips.

I stopped on the bottom step, ignoring the pilots who bumped into me. Preslee sang. To me. Like I asked to her all those weeks before. I stepped forward, just one step, but she held up her hand, her eyes, those pale green irises brimming with emotion, as her voice dipped lower.

Spanish. She sang to me in Spanish. She didn't speak Spanish. She must have memorized the lyrics.

I wasn't familiar with the song. But I figured it out as she hit the chorus the second time. *"Mi Ancla."*

My Anchor.

What this woman did to me.

I strode toward her as she began the third verse. I cupped her chin, nudging the microphone out of the way, and pressed my lips to hers. God, I'd missed her. Her eyes, her smell, her short hair. But mostly the way her body fitted to mine. Her smell enveloped me, and I moaned.

My lips were on hers. For the first time since my trip to New York, everything settled into place. Her soft skin was between my palms, her warm body pressed, pliant, against mine.

My own version of heaven.

"Preslee," I moaned against her eager mouth. I gathered her closer. *"Dulzura."*

"I owed you a serenade," she whispered.

I touched my forehead to hers. "Promise me something?"

She nodded.

"You never wear this outfit again." I all but growled the words and my hands gripped firmly into the flare of her hips.

Those black angel brows swooped low. "You don't like it?"

I slid my hands from her face down to her throat over her breast. Her breath broke as I continued to trail my fingers lower.

"I love it. So did my pilot and co-pilot. Both of whom might be out of a job." I pressed a kiss to the corner of her mouth. Then another to her jaw just below her ear. A third to the soft, fragrant skin where her neck met her shoulder. "What I want to do to you."

Her fingers tangled in my hair. "Teo," she gasped. "Please. Oh. I've missed you."

"Have you? Upset you broke up with me then?" I touched the tip of my tongue to her rapid pulse.

"God. Yes."

"Not enough. We'll get there. First, I want to take you home. This need for you…it's great. Maybe more than the first time."

"Yes." She pulled back and met my gaze. She took a little breath. "I love you. I'll always love you."

I smiled as I pressed my lips to her. I kept my eyes open to take in each of her features, mesmerized by her black brows and lashes against the creamy perfection of her skin.

Her lids fluttered up. Her eyes were celadon from desire.

"I love you, too."

She hiccupped a sob. "God, I needed to hear that."

"Come. Let's get in the car." I tugged her forward. "Did you come just wearing that?"

She shook her head, her cheeks blooming crimson. "I brought a hoody." She cleared her throat. "It's yours."

I appraised her. "This I like. Let me see."

She grabbed my gray Timber sweatshirt, tugging it up her arms. It fell to her knees. I followed the line of her leg down to her high-heeled nude boots.

"Mmm, nice. I know what's beneath, but the rest of the men who wish to see are left wondering."

I tugged her forward out of the hangar. A sleek black SUV waited.

"Car service?"

I nodded. "I didn't know you were meeting me. How did you get here?"

"Abbi drove me. She said she and Clay would come back and

pick up the microphone and amp."

"Text her that's unnecessary. The hangar is locked after final maintenance checks. I'll get you a new one."

"I borrowed it from Clay."

"I'll buy Clay a new one." I helped her into the car, clambering in after her. "Send your text, *dulzura*."

I slipped my hand over her knee, resting it possessively on her thigh. She inhaled sharply but did as I asked.

After dropping her phone back into her purse, she rested her head against my shoulder. I leaned down, pressing my nose into her soft, short hair.

"I missed you," she whispered. "I hate the mess I made of everything."

"Preslee, love." I caught her lips in another long, stirring kiss that heated my blood past sanity. I drew in several long lungsful of air before I managed to exit the vehicle. Preslee took longer. I ducked back into the car to see her scrawling her name on the back of a napkin.

I sighed, knowing I must master these pangs of jealousy. Preslee was beautiful. Men were always going to stare at her, perhaps covet her, no matter my feelings on the matter. And I didn't like it.

Preslee turned back, a soft pink tinge creeping up her cheeks. She handed the driver his napkin and stood next to the car, gazing at me as uncertainty built between us.

With a mental *fuck it*, I grabbed her hand, thankful when she exhaled in a quick puff of air. We must talk through our concerns and fears—no doubt about that. But I didn't want the paparazzi's camera's continuous flashes or shouted questions.

"Did you and Preslee get back together?"

"Is it true she's pregnant?"

"Are you getting married?"

"Is she moving in with you?"

"Did you quit soccer to move in with her?"

She nibbled at her lip.

"The only comment I have for you," I began, "is that Preslee Jennings is the love of my life."

A slew of raised voices pursued us into the building, but I ignored them all.

"Thank you for that," Pres said, her voice low.

"I meant it."

Her dark lashes rose as we stepped into the elevator. "Thank you for that even more."

Her low-heeled boot caught in a crack between the elevator and the lobby and she stumbled. I dropped her hand and scooped her up against my chest.

Her feet dangled off the ground as I plastered her to my body. Lust flared hot in her eyes.

"Always falling into my arms." I nuzzled my nose into her hair, needing this. Her breasts felt fuller as I crushed them to my chest, her waist narrower. Her hipbones were prominent, even through her catsuit and hoodie. "You're thinner than the last time."

"That's because," she stopped, swallowed. "Morning sickness."

We'd already given the pap quite an eyeful. "I don't want this all over the news, Pres. Inside."

The elevator doors slid closed. My finger hovered over the button.

"Your place or mine."

She shuddered. "Yours. I'm not ready to go back to mine yet."

After pressing the button, I cupped the back of her neck and pulled her closer. "I'm so pissed at you for believing Brenna over me."

"Oh," she squeaked, eyes wide and bright green in her pale, china doll face. "Yes, you should be."

I forced my feet back and bent to pick up her fallen purse. As I slid it into her palm, my brain and heart thudded with possibilities. Preslee looked tired, rumpled, and all-together delicious.

She chewed on her lip, her eyes latched on to my face. The longing in her gaze reached deep into me and unlocked all the feelings I tried to shove down. I had to look away.

As she'd said before, *I can't be second place.* I shoved my hands into my pockets.

Her hand tightened around her purse's slim strap. "I need to tell you things," she stuttered, eyes wide, uncertain.

"We will."

"Teo, I—"

The elevator dinged, and I pressed my hand against the door, making a sweeping motion for her to go through.

When we reached my door, I asked, "Ready?"

"No."

I stopped and stared at her, confusion and annoyance spiraling up through my chest. "You came to the airport. You wanted to talk to me?"

"I—I do," she stuttered. She licked her lips, her face flushing bright red. "But I'm scared, and I need to think."

I picked up her hand, slid my palm over hers. Tingles slid up my arm. I'd missed intimacy with her. Her smell, her touch.

Just knowing she was near. "Your bangs grew. They stay behind your ear."

She patted her soft black hair, sending static through it. "Yours is shorter. I like it."

She dropped her hand to her stomach. She looked more fragile than ever. But at the same time, she glowed, like a light illuminated her from the inside.

She seemed more grounded.

Silence swirled around us as I let her into my condo, uncomfortable but not unpleasant. She dropped her purse on the chair and still held my hand. She bit deep into her lip again, the silence eating at her.

Whatever she wanted to say, she struggled to get the words out.

"I made you promises, Preslee You didn't believe me."

"You left me," she whispered. She shoved her hands under the hoodie's arm holes. Her eyes were wild, her face too pale. Her chin wobbled. "I never would've walked away if I knew how much I'd miss you. Finding out I was pregnant...I worried you'd think I tried to trap you into a relationship you didn't want." She huffed out a breath.

"I did think that," I was compelled to admit.

"I don't want the relationship my parents had," she said. "My dad cared for my mom, but he didn't love her. He did his duty. I—I couldn't be that, act like that. Disregard your future happiness."

"Stop projecting your parents' relationship on us."

I wanted to touch her but I knew I wouldn't stop. Her smell surrounded me. Her eyes called to me. I wasn't going to be able to resist her for very long.

Her eyes were filled with sadness. "It's what I know."

"My parents are a mess, too. My mom helped orchestrate the news about my hamstring. She and Brenna are a pair."

"I know. They talked. I don't know who set it up. But I found your mom's e-mails in Brenna's account."

Mierda. No more. I tugged her until she settled onto the couch and then I dropped my head into her lap. "My mother decided you weren't the right woman for me." Her thighs stiffened under my cheek. "But you are. You're the only woman I've ever loved. Ever."

"Teo," her fingers were in my hair, smoothing the strands. "Did you have to quit soccer?"

"No. But I'm not sure what I'll do next year. My dream's been changing since we started dating. Maybe from my first injury. I'm not ready to quit being involved in the game. I hope to stay here, in Seattle, maybe move into that coaching role Jorge suggested. Noah brought it up originally, before you and I imploded."

Her hand stilled in my hair and she lifted my face so I met her eyes. "I wanted you to want *me*."

"I do." God, did I.

"I—I want you for you, too." Her lips trembled, and her eyes begged me to believe her.

"You're tired. Come, I'll put you to bed."

A small smile slid across her lips, but I could see the pain in her eyes. "You like doing that."

"I do. Because I get to undress you."

I picked her up, and she wrapped her arms around my neck. The joy of her nearness settled me.

"What are we doing?" Preslee asked, her voice quiet.

"Getting ready for bed." I kissed the tip of her nose.

"I mean us. How are we going to make it work? Did the Timber management say you could stay here? Weren't you traded?"

"I don't know yet. I think they'll let me stay. I refused to sign the paperwork, so the trade isn't official. River Salado will be angry, of course, but I love you, Preslee Jennings. And I'm not giving up this chance with you."

She rested her head on my shoulder, drawing a line from my throat to the collar of my dress shirt. "I love you, too. So much... these feelings hurt."

I slid my hand out from under her knees. Desire flamed fast and hard. "Excellent."

Her face slackened with shock.

I leaned in close so I could see each faint freckle on her cheeks. "Then you might want me almost as much as I want you."

She smiled, and I fought the urge to grip her even tighter to me. "Arms down."

I slid the silky material from her shoulders. I sucked in a deep, aching breath at the sight of her smooth stomach between the two stalwart pillars of her hip bones.

"Pres, that's our baby." My hands palmed the smooth skin, covering it completely. I leaned forward again and pressed my lips to her belly button. She cupped my cheeks and bent down to find my lips with hers. The kiss stayed sweet, unrushed. I asked if she wanted *me*, not just my body and the release I could give her. Her mouth, its gentle pressure, told me I was loved, wanted, needed. I sighed into her, my eyes sliding closed.

I broke the kiss, stood and swept her back into my arms. She didn't open her eyes.

———

I rubbed her belly in long strokes. Her lashes fluttered, and my chest tightened with anticipation. That first blink, and I stared into pale green eyes. Her black angel-wing brows pulled over her nose in consternation.

"What time is it?" Her voice was scratchy from sleep. Sexy as hell.

"About ten."

"In the morning?"

"Yes, you slept all night."

"I did." She noted my changed clothes. "Do you need to go somewhere?"

"Yes. I set up a meeting with the Timber owner and executives at three thirty."

"What do you want from that?" she asked.

"To stay here. To be with you and our child."

I settled deeper into the mattress, pulling her tighter against me, my arm trailing over her cool skin. She shivered and I pulled the covers over us, tucking the top of her head under my chin.

I scooted closer, my hands back on her stomach. For the love of...I couldn't take it. She was so soft, warm. So right.

"God, I want you, *dulzura*," I muttered into her hair.

"You think the Timber management will make this hard for you?"

"I don't know. But we'll come up with a plan after my meeting. Something where I can hold you every night."

"I don't want to give up my career. I told you before that I want to be your partner, not just your lover."

"Will you consider us a partnership if I ask you to marry me?"

She gaped.

"I'm serious, Pres. I'm so in love with you. You're part of me whether you're with me or not. I hated being away from you. Not seeing you every day, it was like a physical wound."

"You're serious," she whispered, awed.

"Of course."

"You've got a soccer season and—"

"We can make this work. I've got the resources to make it work."

"But—"

"Preslee Jennings. I want to give our baby *my* name. I want to wake up in the middle of the night with you when you're tired and maybe even grouchy from lack of sleep." I raised my eyebrows, and she blushed. Preslee loved to sleep. "And know this is the life we made together. I want this. I want us. Plus, now I have family in Seattle, too."

She wound her arms around my neck. "You meant it? Wanting to marry me?"

I startled, my hands coming up to cup her hips. "Of course."

"Then I accept."

I pulled the ring from my pocket and picked up her left hand. I slid a large square-cut diamond solitaire onto her ring finger, and pressed a kiss there. Satisfaction warmed my chest, spreading out into a deep contentment. The only other time I'd felt something similar was when my invitation came to join the Argentine national team.

"A perfect fit. I'm glad." I narrowed my eyes and growled,

"You're mine." I smacked her bottom before caressing her hip.

"Where'd this come from?"

"From New York." My lips drifted over her shoulder.

"Oh," she whispered, her voice catching. "Oh."

"As soon as the symphony and soccer seasons are over, we're holing up in the Bahamas or St. Bart's. I'm holding you hostage there for weeks."

"What if I want a big wedding?"

"We'll have one later. I'm sure your sisters and mom will like that. So will my dad." I pressed another kiss to her lips.

She kissed me back and my body warmed.

"I love you, too, Teo Cruz."

I pulled back a little. "It's actually Romero de Cruz."

She rolled her eyes. "That goes even better with Preslee."

"Fits you like a glove."

"Only with you can I laugh and kiss at the same time." She chuckled as her lips pressed to mine with more fervor.

EPILOGUE
Preslee

"You're doing great, *dulzura*. Just great."

"I'm in labor, Teo. It's not great. It hurts." I moaned the last word before I gritted my teeth and tried to breathe through the contraction.

Teo kissed my sweaty forehead. "You're tough, Pres. I'm proud of you."

"Then you push the baby out," I screamed.

The doctor's chuckle floated up from between my splayed thighs.

I sat up and bore down, in part because I had to and in part because glaring at my OB-GYN proved impossible from a prone position. Teo caught my angry gaze and turned his chuckle into a cough.

"She's a bit busy to see your death glare," he whispered.

"Felt it, though. One more push at the next contraction, Preslee. You're doing great."

My belly tightened and I growled, sitting forward to bear down. The baby slid from my body and the unbearable pressure eased. I fell back, exhausted.

Teo's hand slipped against my palm, his thumb stroking my skin.

"He's perfect."

Teo turned to grin at me, and I answered him.

"Want to cut the cord?" Dr. Hughes asked.

Teo nodded. He squeezed my fingers before stepping back.

A moment later, the doctor laid the baby on my chest. Instinctively, I cupped the back of his head, snuggling his tiny body against my breast.

Teo leaned his hip onto the side of the mattress, his eyes full of awe, his larger hand cradling both mine and the baby's small head. A pulse thrummed at the top and I leaned in to kiss it. "He's gorgeous. Oh, my gracious. Can you believe how perfect he is?"

Teo wrinkled his nose a little. "He will be once he has a bath." The doctor, nurses, and I laughed.

"Thank you for my son," he whispered against my temple.

I snuggled the baby tighter to my chest. "Thank you for loving me. And marrying me."

"Always." He kissed me, soft and full of love. "Let me send a text to the family. I'm sure they'll be bursting through the doors soon."

"Your dad leading the way," I teased.

I reached up one hand and gripped his fingers. Raul and I hit it off. Lucia and I...not so much. Raul arrived in Seattle days after Teo and I were engaged and immediately bought a house for himself and another for us, not too far from Lia's place. I balked at the generous gift, but he shrugged off my concern, saying with Teo's position as interim coach for the rest of the year and our desire to stay in the Seattle area, he needed something nearby. And we needed a house with a yard for his grandchild.

When Raul informed us he and Lucia were in the process of divorcing, Teo took the news well, telling his father he supported his decision. Later, Teo told me, as we lay in our bed in our new house, he felt relief. We both hoped Raul could find someone—

just one someone, Teo said too seriously—to love Raul the way he deserved.

"You're my world, Matteo Cruz."

"So not too upset with the way we worked out?"

He straightened my rings on my finger, pressed a kiss there, as he did every day. I loved the ritual nearly as much as I loved the man.

"If you're happy coaching, I'm happy. I got you, didn't I?"

"Sure did. But I got the better end of the deal." Teo winked. "I get my lullaby every night."

ACKNOWLEDGMENTS

As always, thank you, Chris. Your unwavering support and love shine through in all you do for the kids and me. I couldn't ask for a better man, and I'm thrilled to wake up with you each day.

To my family, thank you for your patience with my dream—and letting me hang out in my head WAY too often.

LERA ladies and gentlemen, thank you for being so supportive, for making me love writing again and for sharing your knowledge so freely. You are the best-est.

To my AuthorLab writing pals: You keep me on task and keep me motivated. I love your commitment and passion. I love reading your posts and stories. And I love how diverse our group is.

To Deb, thank you for seeing the big picture—and making sure I see it, too.

To Nicole, thank you for the advice on Seattle.

To Jan, I loved working with you. Thanks for the thoughtful comments. Looking forward to next time.

To my Divas, especially Jane—you kicked ass with the eARC's and I can never thank you enough.

To Clarissa, once again the cover is gorgeous. I love working with you.

And to my readers and reviewers, thank you for your time. It's precious and I'm so, so glad you spent some of it with me.

ABOUT THE AUTHOR

With a degree in international marketing and a varied career path that includes content management for a web firm, marketing direction for a high-profile sports agency, and a two-year stint with a renowned literary agency, Alexa Padgett has returned to her first love: writing fiction.

Alexa spent a good part of her youth traveling. From Budapest to Belize, Calgary to Coober Pedy, she soaked in the myriad smells, sounds, and feels of these gorgeous places, wishing she could live in them all—at least for a while. And she does in her books.

She lives in New Mexico with her husband, children, and ginormous, piano-hating Anatolian Shepherd, Mozart. When not writing, schlepping, or volunteering, she can be found in her tiny kitchen, channeling her inner Barefoot Contessa.

ALSO BY ALEXA PADGETT

SWEET SOLACE (Book One of the Seattle Sound Series)

She Knew Him When

When they first met, she was far too young—seventeen, and already in love with the man who would break her heart. Asher Smith was an up-and-coming songwriter, but he knew better than to show his fascination. He wrote a song for Dahlia. And then he moved on. His whiskey-rough voice made him a star, even as fame extracted its price.

He Never Forgot Her

When she sees Asher next, Dahlia Dorsey is the widowed mother of a teenager, a reclusive writer. She's given up on happy endings—she can't even script them for her characters. But a moonlit beach and the touch of an old friend turn loose her pain and her desires, whether she's ready or not.

They're Risking It All

Dahlia's career is on the rocks. Asher's family is falling apart. Neither can chase a passing attraction. But for two souls wounded worse than they can admit, the connection between them is a balm too precious to refuse—and a thrill too exhilarating to resist . . .

BETWEEN BREATHS (Book Two of the Seattle Sound Series)

Grief brought them together

A hospice center is no place to fall in lust. But with his world cracking during his estranged mother's last days, Hayden Crewe needs something sweet to focus on. It doesn't matter that he's the backbone of Australia's hottest international rock group—here, watching his mother die, he's more alone than ever. So when he meets long-legged, clear-minded Briar Moore, he suddenly knows exactly what will fill the hole inside.

Fortune will drag them apart

Briar has just escaped a job and relationship that nearly crushed her. Crawling out of the wreckage of her previous life, she's done playing it safe. Sexy, vibrant Hayden is what she wants, and Briar is going to take him. For as long as she can…

Out of heartbreak comes hope

With their time short and the ghosts of their pasts haunting every moment, Briar and Hayden know they've fallen too deep. While those few, intense days changed them both forever, everyone knows a connection this intense should burn out as fast as it ignited…

HOLD YOU CLOSE (Book Three of the Seattle Sound Series)

Searching for peace

Mila Trask's trying to forget happiness. Her much-wanted pregnancy ended in a crunch of steel and pain. Her career has been derailed and her body scarred by a stalker no one else believes in. And Murphy Etsam, the man she thought would love her forever, has shot into international rock stardom on the pure fury of the song he wrote when they broke up. But Mila has to talk to him one last time…

Running from the truth

One glimpse of her in the crowd and Murphy knows a year

of drowning his sorrows in booze, fame, and other women hasn't erased a molecule of his passion for lovely, maddening Mila. Too bad Mila's stalker picks that moment to attack.

Too close to doubt...

With both their lives in danger, the ex-lovers are forced into hiding, to face the trauma and misunderstanding that wrenched them apart—and to battle the chemistry that still urges them together. There's no going back to what they had before. But the future is theirs to claim...

MANY SOUNDS OF SILENCE (Book Four of the Seattle Sound Series)

An Awful Night

Maybe she should have sensed the envy when her friends told her how smart, beautiful, and confident she was. But once her mother married a rock star, college freshman Abbi Dorsey suddenly had *too* many things going for her. One night she can't remember produced a brutal set of photos the media—and the student body—won't let her forget. No matter what she does, she can't escape the fallout... or the threat of more to come.

A Great Lie

Green-eyed senior Clay Rippey has a famous father of his own, and he knows the sting of betrayal. From the moment he sees Abbi, he can't stop thinking about her. He's not the relationship type. But he can play one for the press...

A Dangerous Hope

There's nothing made up about the desire sizzling between Abbi and Clay. But a bond built on fear and faking it doesn't lead to happy endings. Too bad sticking to the safe route is all but impossible...

FROM THE FIRST (Book Five of the Seattle Sound Series)

Sudden Impacts

The car that slammed into Evangeline Mercer knocked her life apart. Her body will recover, but when she looks at the orphaned girl from the other car, she's lost in memories of her own awful time in the foster system. Evie won't let little Paige go through that nightmare, and she finds an unlikely ally in Kai Luchia, Paige's newest friend and champion...

Hidden Fears

At 22, Kai is the lead singer in a chart-climbing band. He's got frontman good looks and cash to burn. But fame and fortune don't quiet the demons of his past. Or maybe it's just that shy, sultry Evie has given him something better to desire...

Hurried Hope

When Paige's case comes to a crisis, Kai and Evie have one reckless shot to take her future into their hands: get married, and fast. They'll keep her safe. They'll sate the lust that taunts them. And they'll have each other, without any messy feelings to sort out. Unless racing away from the truth just leads to a bigger crash...

MOONSHINE EYES (A Seattle Sound Series Novella)

Sometimes, one glimpse is all it takes to fall in love...
Seth didn't come to Barcelona for a girl. All he wants is a genuine

connection with a rock star father who took off a decade prior. But when he catches the eye of a stunning girl across *Avenida Diagonal*, his plans for a boring, normal life go straight out the window...

After a family secret sent Ramona's engagement crashing to the ground, she fled Milan in a hurry. Her heartache finds a cure the moment she spots Seth. Soon enough, she feels more alive than she ever had with her fiancé.

Even though Seth makes her happy, Ramona can't help but feel the pull of her family back to Milan. She must ultimately make a choice: retreat to the safety of the life she once knew or take a terrifying leap into love.